Witch Hunter

WILLOW SEARS

mischief

Mischief
An imprint of HarperCollins*Publishers*
77–85 Fulham Palace Road,
Hammersmith, London W6 8JB

www.mischiefbooks.com

A Paperback Original 2013

First published in Great Britain in ebook format by
HarperCollins*Publishers* 2012

A catalogue record for this book is
available from the British Library

ISBN-13: 9780007553488

CONTENTS

Contents

Prologue

The mist was trying to cling to the valley floor but away from the trees the vapour had all but burned off. On such bright spring mornings the sun will always win. The horses still snorted tiny clouds from their nostrils but hers was the only one breaking the stillness, whinnying as it shook its head and chewed on its uncomfortable bit. She leaned forward to issue a terse command into the ear of her mount, and it too fell silent. As always for initiations she wore her *bassaris*, her long cloak of fox skins. It symbolised new life and the sacrifice that was about to be made for it.

Beneath the cloak was a simple white cotton gown, but below the swell of her breasts a pentagram had been drawn in blood-red, inverted to represent the goat of lust, its horns pointing upwards at the heavens in defiance. Her hair flowed down her back, darker red than her cloak, with raven streaks running through it. She glared at her prey, her fiery eyes heavily lined in black and further accentuated by a narrow band of crimson painted across them from ear to ear. Her teeth were bared and showed bright against the scarlet of her wide lips.

'You understand why you are here and the nature of your punishment?' she snarled.

The prey looked through her fringe with forlorn eyes, unable to stop the tremble in her voice that was due to the morning chill and the panic gushing through her young body.

'Yes, Miss Morgana,' she managed to whisper.

'Then run,' Morgana said.

The condemned girl let loose a sob and looked back at the long slope running away from her, down to the scattering of hedges in the valley bottom that would offer her so little refuge. There was only a gentle climb on the far side, stretching up to the cover of the wood nearly a mile away. Those trees offered the only real chance of escape. She would never make it. She turned to face her tormentors one last time, searching for any signs of clemency, but the mounted Priestess angrily gathered a wad of saliva and spat it at her. And so she ran.

She had rarely needed to break into anything more than a jog since her schooldays and immediately felt the judder of her belly and heavy breasts. She cursed the extra weight that had caused this sentence to be passed upon her. She had been dragged to this place straight from her bed, and her attire proved only a hindrance.

Her slippers flew off immediately to leave her barefoot on the dewy grass. Her short nightgown rode up to flash her chubby bare behind, pale in the morning brightness, though nowhere near as white as the skin of the hunter girls behind her, whose whoops and jeers chased her down the hill.

Morgana watched her fleeing quarry with rising excitement and turned to her girls with proud delight. They were formed into a line on foot, their seething fuck-hunger palpable. Although they had to await her command they were at the very limits of their obedience. They had to hold each other back with raised elbows, gripping handfuls of each other's flesh as their desire threatened to boil over, grasping each other's hair to prevent any breaking of the line before the order was given. Despite their nearly uncontrollable lust any such disobedience would be ruthlessly punished, so they restrained one another out of necessity.

Their faces were lit with anticipation, none more so than the one gaining her first taste of the hunt. That girl wore the smooth red dildo at her groin, strapped in place over her deerskin leggings. The red of the dildo showed that she was to be blooded that day. All the girls wore the same: tight hide leggings constraining their ample thighs, and loose white smocks, many of which would be ripped off and discarded as they closed in, so that they fell upon their quarry with their chests bare. Their

3

harnessed dildos were allocated by the Priestess herself, all smooth and hard but in varying sizes to signify seniority or current favour.

They wore ivy wreaths and painted faces, a few with pentagrams charcoaled onto their foreheads, one with a third eye drawn and coloured there, a couple with sanguineous tears painted on their cheeks, falling from eyes smudged with heavy black makeup. They all carried their staff – their *thyrsus*, to give it its proper name, though most of them privately referred to it as their fuck-stick. It was a rod some four feet in length, topped with a large pine cone. The shaft was wrapped in ivy and the end dressed with foliage, most of the girls opting for nettle leaves. It was their symbol, the staff carried by the legendary *bacchantes*.

In ancient mythology they used the *thyrsus* to strike rocks and trees to elicit water or honey, or plunged it into rivers to turn the flowing water into wine, their lifeblood. Or they used it against the hunted, employing what was in truth a symbol of fertility to trip their victim and beat them into submission, before tearing them to pieces and even gorging on the still-warm flesh. Her girls had not quite descended to such barbarity, but the Priestess still sometimes felt she should reach the scene of the 'kill' in good time, just to be on the safe side.

Morgana turned her head from them and sought the gaze of the Master. He was flanked by two male escorts.

They were all tall in their saddles, though he of course was the largest. His frame seemed even bulkier when swathed in his cape. Everything about him was black: the shirt beneath the heavy outer covering; the britches, stretched taut by the wide girth of the charger beneath him; his long boots in the stirrups; his gloved hands, one holding the silver claret goblet and raising it to his thin, pale lips. His eyes could scarcely be seen under the wide brim of his hat, but she saw his nod towards her, his acknowledgement that proceedings should begin. She felt the jump of adrenalin inside and turned again to her baying pack of hunter girls.

'Get her,' was all Morgana needed to say.

They were off in an instant, pushing away from each other to try and gain the lead, shrieking in their excitement. None of them was slight of build. All had thick thighs and paunches, big bottoms if not big breasts. But they were relatively fit and used to such exertion. Their prey was already flagging as they whooped after her. She was looking desperately back over her shoulder, having not yet even reached the first cover of the bushes. She would do as all other victims did. She would drag herself panting into the hedgerow, see the long climb up to the woods and know that it was impossible to get there. She would scramble around to find somewhere to hide, realising above her panic that it was a fruitless exercise. Then, with her heart banging in her chest and her lungs defeated, she would crouch amongst the scant cover of the bushes and await her inevitable capture. By the time the pack found her they would be beside themselves with bubbling desire, and she would bear the full force of it.

Morgana knew she had to get there soon after her girls did. She watched them follow their quarry into the thicket, scattering this way and that to find her and dig her out. She heard the raised cry of triumph and saw them dashing through the bushes towards the sound, each intent on getting her hands on the newly unearthed prize before the others, since the most gratification was to be gained from being one of those to overpower the victim, being one of the first to force a way into her when her body was quaking and whilst she still had the strength to scream her frantic passion into your ears. The scramble to get to their prey would be frenzied, and would leave her ravaged.

The Priestess kicked her horse into action and trotted down the hill. When she got to the mêlée the girl was already stripped bare, her body smeared with mud, grazed from their raking nails and red from their slaps. Her nipples were inflamed and pointing skywards, the flesh of her breasts flecked with nettle rash. She was on her back, her arms pinned to her sides. Her hips had been raised from the ground and her thighs forced wide apart so that a huntress could get on her knees between them. Her buttocks were being harshly gripped to hold her steady while she was taken. Some of the girls stroked their prey's belly and chest with their nettles. Some bent over to pinch or bite her nipples. A couple of them concentrated not on their victim but on her lover, trying to pull her off by the hair so that they could take a turn of their own.

Morgana unhurriedly dismounted, smiling at the writhing mass before her. She went to her saddle bag and withdrew the huge silver penis. Its smooth surface gleamed in the sunlight. It was heavy to hold, solid metal. When it was on, it protruded a full eight inches from her body and was thick enough to fill her palm, so that her fingers could barely encompass its girth. There was a gentle upward curve to it and the head was formed into the distinct shape of a fat glans, tapering at its tip. It was the *queen*, as befitted her status.

She watched as the girls plundered their victim, moving her one way and then another, taking turns with their toys and fingers. Tears were streaking the face of the victim when Morgana stepped in and moved her onto all fours. She held her and delivered smack after smack to her poor wobbling bottom, turning the already scratched and welted flesh a deeper red. The girl cried out even louder but could only manage to thrust her battered posterior out into the hail of slaps. The puffy quim was visible between the large thighs, engorged by bliss and tingling nettle stings, treacherously glistening with the excitement that allowed her to be taken so deeply.

Morgana took off her cloak and spread it upon the ground alongside the girl. Then she lay upon it, with the gleaming silver spear phallus curving up towards the sky. The girl eyed it through her streaked hair, and then bit her lower lip to mask its trembling. The girl knew what she had to do, but still the Priestess ordered it.

'Impale yourself,' was the command.

The girl squatted over the silver penis and very slowly lowered herself, her tremors evident as soon as the tip spread her plump sex and disappeared inside her. She pushed down more, her eyes screwing shut as she slid herself down the cold length and took it deep. The surface of the toy was too smooth and her quim too slick to prevent it slipping all the way inside her, filling her completely. Her puss lips kissed the black leather harness as she rode the toy up and down, with Morgana's nails gripping her rump and helping her movements.

She was breathing hard and threatening to come, but even with help from the Priestess she was tiring quickly after her ordeal. Morgana pulled her down to arrest the movements, embracing her tightly whilst calling forth the girl who was the subject of this hunt initiation, the one still sporting her bright red dildo. Again, the protocol was known but the Priestess still felt obliged to spell it out.

'Fill her *c lus*,' she commanded.

The red-dildo girl hunkered down behind the quarry to study the little pink ring up for sacrifice. It was wet with spit and slightly open from the fingers that had invaded its tight confines, but the initiate took pity and reached for the battered vial that had been presented to her in the pre-hunt ceremony to be used for this very purpose, and that she now wore on a string around her neck. She removed the bung and dribbled the clear oily contents along the length of her dildo and onto the twitching bottom now at her mercy. She then took a firm grasp of the girl's hips, pressed her toy to the target and drove herself forward.

The victim's squeal almost broke into a scream but she bit her lip just in time and took the slide inside her, even pressing backwards to help its passage. She was given some respite but lust soon took over and she was taken, her soft cheeks splayed apart by the Priestess as the initiate slapped ruthlessly hard against her. Stuffed and filled and with her flesh quivering from the shock waves, she was brought to a rapid, hard climax. However, even when the dildo was finally removed, her ordeal was not yet over. All attention turned to the sound of slow clip-clopping hooves amongst them, which presaged what she must still endure.

Morgana looked up at the Master on his mount and grinned broadly, clutching the victim tight to her with the metal appendage still completely embedded in her body. He studied the scene for a while, taking stock of the girl's bottom and sex.

He dismounted, his eyes firmly on the girl's rear end as he made his slow approach. He opened his cloak and unfastened the front of his britches so that he could haul out his huge thick erection. The wretch looked around to see his fat meat bobbing up and down with the blood surging into it. He took a small bottle from his inside pocket, removed the cap, held her hair and thrust the bottle under her nose so that she was forced to take a deep breath of the emanating vapours. Her jaw dropped open.

'Oh, my God,' she whispered.

'Yes,' he said with a sneer, 'I am.'

He presented his great erection and pressed forward slowly, more so than the newcomer before him, since he was twice as thick as the toy she had sported. Very gradually he broke the girl's resistance and slid the full length inside her. It seemed an impossible quantity of turgid flesh to take. She howled but held still, the ecstasy spread all over her face. Once he was fully embedded he waited for her muscles to grip his girth and squeeze him. This pressure, plus the ache within his bladder, was enough to make his erection flag just a little. He exalted in his power over her. She would remember this act for ever, just as they all did. None of them would ever take a fatter cock than his, certainly not in their bottom. To be stretched open by him was bliss enough. They would dream of this experience in all their private moments and pray that he would come to them again one day to repeat it. Nothing else they did would ever match this moment. No one else would ever be more in their thoughts.

The girl sank down against her Priestess, the feeling all too much to take. He roared in triumph and proceeded to slide his cock in and out of her backside, taking it nearly all the way out and then driving it home to slap hard against her buttocks over and over. The girl was very nearly passing out but Morgana showed rare compassion, pressing her full lips to the girl's open mouth and kissing her lovingly, trying to give her the strength for one more climax before he finished.

He threw his head back and bellowed, slapping the wretch's defenceless bottom as he came inside her. He gritted his teeth as the tremors rocked him. As soon as they subsided, he slipped his softening prick from her, unceremoniously stuffed it back into his britches and remounted his horse. The wretch gingerly slipped off the metal toy and stood on shaking legs.

Currently there was a two-tier system for his girls: those on the periphery, sworn to secrecy and schooled in the rituals though not allowed to partake in them, except as victims if they broke any rules or conditions; and the bacchantes, his fully-fledged initiates, who lived and worshipped exactly by his code, who purified their skin and swore to do anything in his name, the more immoral and degenerate the better. The entire British Isles yielded few more than a dozen girls who had such dark hearts, such wanton souls that they would seek him out and embrace his vision of perverted nihilism. He needed more. He needed genuine victims to reward their loyalty.

He spurred on his horse and trotted out of the wood with his escort in tow. The orgy would continue in his absence, for the hunters were now crazed with desire after this show. Their reverence for him would be raging inside and they would want to demonstrate their homage through depravity. They would jostle for the chance to indulge themselves further with the initiate, and then they would fall upon each other, as if possessed.

The bushes would be alive with their gasps and cries, the sound of sex and slapping flesh. It would have been surreal and horrifying for anyone who chanced upon the scene, but this was impossible since all the lands around were privately owned, and no one would ever dare trespass. It was his secret dominion. Here he was God, and anyone who was either lured there or strayed onto these lands would feel the full force of his divinely demonic lusts. Indeed, they might never get to see the real world again, even after he was finished with them.

1

Mimi decided early that it was a perfect day for a picnic. She knew the perfect spot too, found just a few weeks ago when she had been out walking alone. She had been drawn off the beaten track after sighting a fox. She had tracked it through to a small clearing where she had stayed crouched behind the greying trunk of a fallen oak, watching it as it played around and pounced upon leaves and insects. It had been a magical few moments. She had felt a sudden surge of elation at this window on nature. She had seemed at one with the world, experiencing a mixture of freedom and security, cosseted as she was by the dense foliage surrounding her.

She had also felt a rather uncharacteristic urge to *frolic*. She had flashing images of herself stripping off right there, although such daring public naughtiness was hardly her forte. She might even have gone through with it if it hadn't been rather too chilly that morning for whipping your bits out, especially when brush-tailed wild animals might be watching. If she had been there with someone else, though, and that someone had taken it upon themselves to ravish her, maybe forcing her over that same fallen trunk and ripping her knickers away to leave her at his mercy, why, then there would have been little she could do about it. No one would have been around to come to her aid, there would be nothing she could do to resist being plundered, maybe even spanked ...

So a picnic it was, and lazy Dominic would have to play the loving boyfriend and drag his arse out of bed to accompany her, even though he had sounded so uninterested in the whole idea on the phone. He didn't even seem to care that he would be off back to college in a few days and this would be one of their last chances to be alone for a while. Fortunately that morning the Spinster had gone off to garner the latest village tittle-tattle, giving Mimi free rein of the kitchen to prepare a picnic for two without prying eyes and uncomfortable questions. Dominic was her secret and tongues would be ceaselessly wagging if anyone knew they were an item.

Getting out of her room and having the run of that gorgeous wisteria-covered cottage was a treat in itself, however brief such moments were. She loved the place. One day she hoped to have enough money to buy just such a property within the village, but for now renting a room was a more than acceptable alternative, despite having to share with the spinster landlady. It meant a time-consuming drive to reach work in Oxford, but the quiet leafy lanes could make your heart soar with optimism when the early sun lit the green, flint-strewn fields and the beech woods behind, and brought the hedgerows alive. It had been a different story in her first winter, when any snowfall or thick ice rendered the roads impassable and forced her to exist for days off pub food or remnants in the freezer. She didn't care though. Anything was worth it to live here. She had coveted a place in the village for as long as she could remember.

She had grown up in the nearby town where Dominic now lived. Her parents would bring the family out here for summer picnics in the glades or autumn walks amongst the copper-leaved trees. They provided many of her fondest childhood memories: colour-splashed meadows, swallows dipping and zipping over lush-cropped fields, dew-covered cobwebs amid frosty thickets, or pristine snow blankets and freezing breath. Sun or rain, it was always special. She tried to imbue her lethargic boyfriend with the same enthusiasm as they sauntered through those woods on the way to her Secret Location, but he had his standard couldn't-give-a-fuck face on. He seemed so one-dimensional sometimes that it wearied her. How their short relationship had continued was a mystery.

He was tall and nicely muscular, and good-looking in a posh-student way. Plus he had the most delectable of pricks: slim but very long and silky-smooth when erect, which was often. It seemed to have a mind of its own. It certainly had more go than the rest of him. A few times when she was making advances he had seemed to be crying off, only to be outvoted by his own member. And once unleashed it could certainly hammer home with the best of them, even if its owner was more than a little unimaginative when it came to dirty business.

The staying power and speedy recovery rate of his young erection ensured she was never left disappointed. That was not something she had always been able to claim in the past, so it was worth clinging on to, even if the man himself could barely raise the passion to hold her hand, better still delight in the promise of the secret place she was taking him to. He could gather even less zeal for the smells and the promise of the day that were firing her, or for the snatched views across the landscape of her childhood haunts.

The timelessly pretty villages and hamlets here were dotted around the countryside, some more easily reached across the fields than by the narrow roads. To her they all seemed like miniature empires in sleeping valleys, all unique despite their close proximity, all holding their own wonderful secrets that were jealously guarded from outsiders. In more recent times these outsiders had come to populate the villages. The steep rise in house prices forced the locals elsewhere as wealthy Oxford and London commuters took over. Affluence was pervasive, but nowhere lost its ancient, deep-set notion of serfdom, of the poor locals giving service to their richer land-owners. The old customs and folklore were maintained and even the new wealth could not diminish it. The newcomers simply had to absorb the traditions or suffer isolation.

Before Mimi had even moved into her room, some nine months ago, her gossip-happy landlady had shuffled her fat posterior from house to church to village hall telling anyone who wanted to know that a young journalist from the *Echo* was to be her new tenant. Fortunately, the Spinster also told everyone that she was a local girl, so Mimi found herself more immediately accepted than some of the London incomers would be, although she still noticed some reticence when being spoken to. She guessed she would have to live there a good many years before this wore off.

She also noticed that she became a hub for gossip. If certain blabbermouths wanted a scandal spread around they often 'accidentally' divulged their secret within her earshot, as if she had the power to splash it across the front pages. This didn't bother her. Hopefully one day the local scandal might well prove to be the roots of the very story she was desperate to break, the one that did indeed make headlines and get her noticed.

She would be the first to admit that in nearly five years at the *Echo* she hadn't made the impact she had intended. She was well-liked and appreciated but she suspected this was more for her prick-pleasing attributes than for her journalistic prowess. She had the kind of looks that many men seemingly found hard to ignore, although they tended to induce private thoughts of filthiness rather than outward declarations of love. She was blonde and by many accounts very pretty. She received plenty of compliments about her large blue eyes and her sunshine smile, but it was her body that brought out the lust in her admirers.

You could just see indications of extra weight under her chin but if she stayed hiding behind her desk you might never realise that she was quite a big girl. Her breasts were a nice handful and still perky and there was a paunch but by no means a roll. It was her bum and thighs that carried most of the excess. Her bottom stuck out from the pronounced dip at the small of her back, defining a round curve down to the heavy tuck. In loose skirts she thought she looked like she was wearing a small Victorian bustle, so she always stuck to tighter ones, even though it might look as if she was trying to show off her biggest asset.

Her thighs and calves were thick but firm and soft white under the stockings she habitually wore for work. As soon as she got home it was straight into clothes more suitable for country living, but when at the office or out seeking stories she always took to her high heels and hosiery and squeezed her fat bum into hip-hugging skirts, although her intention was always to look businesslike rather than plain sexy. She wasn't entirely happy with her body. If the glossy mags were to be believed, her figure should have been a turn-off for most. However, for so many it seemed one to lust after, to build your dirtiest fantasies around. One former beau had told her plainly: 'The thought of your bare arse bending over in front of him could send any sane man senseless. You are the kind of girl you want to touch, to kiss and squeeze, to bury yourself deep inside.'

She even found that drunken girls at office parties hugged her for longer than was considered appropriate, or snatched New Year kisses from her under the pretence of doing it to wind up the guys.

She was certainly no tease though. She wasn't quite ready to settle down but within her was the feeling that she should be looking for something more meaningful than a few dates and some quick, urgent sex before an inevitable petering out. All this made her question the wisdom of her more-off-than-on relationship with Dominic, who at barely nineteen was seven years her junior.

She had met him when following up a story about lads from the area disappearing 'without trace'. In the last few years five males from the locale in either their late teens or early twenties had abruptly departed, leaving friends and family behind without any warning. This would have been odd, were it not that such deathly quiet villages were a graveyard for youthful ambition and could not compete with the brighter lights of any town or city. As for 'without trace', this wasn't quite an accurate description of their disappearance, since all of them wrote home telling loved ones that they were fine and settled. These letters had continued to arrive at fairly regular intervals. True, in these days of mobile phones and texts, it was strange that they solely communicated by letter, but if you had escaped and didn't want to be found and dragged back home, it was the safest form of contact. All the boys shared one thing in common: they were bright, fit lads who were expected to do well in life. Maybe it was merely the weight of expectation that drove them away, and once one went others followed the example. One thing was for sure, there was certainly no front-page story in it.

Mimi now met Dominic less and less often, and not just because her work made her keep odd hours or he was busy with his college studies. Despite his obvious intelligence, the immaturity – or, to be fairer, the lack of life experience – was beginning to tell. It was nice to have an athlete in bed but Mimi was aware of his shallowness. He was also somehow detached when they had sex. He would slam into her from the back as avidly as any former lover, but she never felt his simmering lust before they got to bed or any closeness during the act.

It was hard enough finding time and privacy for them to do anything, which sometimes led to snatched shags down dark lanes, trying to get the job done before the chill air numbed the desire. Considering their lack of opportunity, he never seemed as desperate for her as an on-heat teenager should have been. He wasn't always grasping and fondling her or pulling her in for kisses. He waited until a chance presented itself and then without much preamble gave her a breathless seeing-to.

They just didn't quite connect. Maybe they would have done if they had ever opened up about what they each wanted. He had once crawled naked over her lap, jokily asking to be punished. She had given him a few light smacks but too light-heartedly for it to go anywhere. Inwardly she had squirmed with the embarrassment of it all. If it had been the other way round, if he had dragged her over his lap and dealt a series of stinging slaps to her big bum, she was sure, despite never having received such treatment before, that she would have simply loved it.

Once, when the Spinster had gone to her sister's for the night, they had actually had time to watch a bit of internet porn together before climbing into bed. They had looked at a few sites, jumping around a selection of video clips, their choices acting as unspoken demonstrations of what they each found appealing. She was surprised when he chose a short clip of a naked man bound with thick ropes and bent over, yelping as a corseted Mistress forced a strap-on into his rear end. Mimi had said something about how much of a fuss the man was making and if it had been the other way around the girl would have been expected to take it all without complaint.

'Well, having a big one up the bum can hurt, as I'm sure you know!' he had replied.

Actually, she didn't know. She probably wanted to find out but for some reason she never had, although everyone seemed to be doing it these days. Plenty of girls told a different story, that it was a scintillating experience not to be missed. By the way he was talking, it sounded like he hadn't missed it either. Another time, they had been indulging in some simultaneous oral with him on top, lapping at her bud whilst pressing a slender smooth vibrator into her puss. Only later, when she recalled how he had slightly wiggled his hips above her and pushed his behind back a little more, did she realise that he might actually have wanted the toy forced inside him. Basically, if both of them were displaying signs of submissiveness then it wasn't going to work, and if he was bi-curious or trying to figure out if indeed he was gay she did not want to be fumbled around with while he made up his mind.

Relocating the secret picnic spot proved harder than she thought and Dominic didn't help by getting exasperated. Eventually, when they did find it, he was typically underwhelmed. He seemed more distracted than usual, not really listening to anything she said. He hardly looked at her, more often glancing at his phone as if imploring it to receive some important message that would get him out of there. As ever he stuffed his food down as if he hadn't eaten in weeks, barely noticing the trouble she had gone to in preparing it.

She had made a point of only buttering the baguette, leaving the cut sections otherwise bare and wrapping the intended contents separately, since he was so fussy and was always changing his mind about what he did and didn't like. She didn't want to give him any excuse to moan. No matter how many hints she kept dropping about being alone and isolated he refused to pick up on them. When he started checking the time she knew he was planning to get out of there without giving her what she needed. As always she would be forced to initiate things, and that was irksome.

He was idly holding a piece of buttered baguette, silently aghast that there was no more ham to fill it, even though he had put half a sliced pig into his last one. She sidled over with a mischievous smile, curled her hand around the bread and ran it up and down the length in a wanking motion whilst telling him that the French stick reminded her of something. Having your penis compared to something crusty and yeasty is probably not every man's dream but her suggestive hand action was enough to do the trick. She spotted his ever-lively prick stirring in his jeans and seized her chance before he could back out.

'Looks like he wants some attention,' she said.

The evidence seemed indisputable so he could do nothing except mumble something ineffectual like 'not here' whilst she ignored him and unzipped his jeans. She fumbled inside and gave a little gasp as his hot member was suddenly in her palm and growing against her. It was a feeling she could never tire of. She loved to clutch a stiffening prick and feel it swell in her grip. Sometimes you could even sense the pulsing rush of blood and the rise in temperature. For just a few brief moments it was to feel the essence of sexual power, of uncontrolled desire, and to know that it was aimed at *you*.

There was surely no greater compliment a cock could give you than to fill up in your grasp. As his had been constrained beneath tight briefs she got it in all its expanding glory. For just a few wonderful moments it seemed like it might go on growing for ever. She would have loved to feel it swell inside her, stretching her open and surging into her hole.

'So, Dominic,' she said, 'what shall we do with this?'

She didn't like calling him Dominic. She would prefer to shorten it but he simply would not allow such things. 'Dom' would have been less of a mouthful and it would certainly be nice to think of him as a Dom even if it was so far from his real character. He didn't even have the gumption to tell her what he wanted done with his gripped prick. She teasingly stroked it up and down but he remained impassive, still clutching his section of buttered baguette as if eating more lunch was a far better option than doing anything sexual. Well, if he wanted some meat to fill his roll he would get it.

She prised the bread out of his hand and forced the split side of it around his shaft so that it nestled like a large sausage in a bun. He at least smiled at this. She was giggling saucily and grasping the bread, twisting it against his shaft and running it up and down, using it to gently masturbate him. She could see the smear of butter on his skin and she pictured him sliding into her tightest passage without warning, forcing her over the tree trunk and entering her and pushing relentlessly deep inside her. She could scream but no one would hear her, and he might just stuff her knickers into her mouth anyway. Even his slim cock would stretch and maybe even hurt her, but the butter would ensure his forward glide proved unstoppable …

He didn't move. He let her continue her gentle tease but she was feeling full of lust, too much to not make this situation dirtier. She reached for the tube of mustard and squirted a thick line of it down his length to complete the hot dog. He was panting harder and his cheeks were colouring but still he kept his passion contained and didn't force it upon her. She didn't *want* a mouthful of hot mustard but she would have sucked him to his balls if he had ordered her to. With the bread disintegrating and his cock a smeared mess there was nothing else to do but give up and give herself to him.

She was desperate for him to rip off her clothes and force her over the tree trunk but he didn't, so she had to do it herself. Her knickers came down with her pedal pushers and she kissed him breathlessly for just a few seconds before going forward over the trunk, to leave her chubby pale bottom sticking out for him. His former reluctance was gone because he was now in command. He held her hips and was inside her in no time, surprising them both with the sudden depth of his entry, helped both by the butter and her slickness.

He held her as he caught his breath and she felt an unfamiliar tingling warmth spread inside her. It gave her a rush in her belly and made her slightly panicky – just like a mouthful of hot curry can do – and then she realised it was the mustard singeing the delicate skin of her puss. She let out an 'oh!' at this unintentional S&M rudeness and wondered if his prick was burning too. As if in answer he gave her a sudden barrage of arse-slapping thrusts, grunting over and over as he bashed against her cheeky rump and had it dancing. He kept on going too, as if needing the rapid action to soothe his itch.

She was aware of the sun on her bare skin and the sound of birds chattering around them. She was used to outdoor sex but it still felt so *rude* to be doing it there in broad daylight. It seemed such a bestial act, surrounded by gentle nature. She tried to make herself squeal louder, to add to the risk of them being caught, but, even though she knew the chances were infinitesimal, she still couldn't bring herself to increase her volume. She wanted to talk like a slut in one of those porno clips they had watched. His quick-fire, bum-splatting thrusts deserved it. Imagine having the courage to yell out like they did, to beg him to do you any way he wanted. If she could only do that she would get it in the bum for sure. She could plead for it. She could say, 'Please stick that big cock in my ass!' just like those horny porno girls did.

Imagine having the courage to reach back and pull your cheeks apart while you said it, to actually display your most private place to him, to cry out that you were dying to have him in your bum. She trembled at her own thoughts but he couldn't read them. He continued to slam into her and it was just enough to take her over the edge before he juddered and came. She loved the hot hit of his ejaculation within her. She was so glad she was on the pill, even if it did compound her weight problem. The feel of him shooting inside her always heightened her own orgasm.

He slipped out and she stayed where she was, eyes closed, allowing the warmth of her climax to gently spread through her. While she was feeling so horny she didn't mind her bare bottom being so exposed. It might even encourage him to go again and finish what he'd started. Maybe he would even try something new, like giving her a good hard spanking before he sank inside her once more.

There were rustlings from behind her and she imagined him searching the undergrowth for thin sticks to use as canes upon her defenceless rump. She had no clue how much it would hurt her but just to be used in such a fashion would surely outweigh any pain. She would take any sexual indignity from him at these moments, do anything he commanded. She didn't care if he bit her arse, smacked her soft quim, covered her exposed skin in muck from the forest floor – *anything* to make her feel like a wanton slave.

She turned at last to see what he was doing. He was on his feet and facing her, looking at his phone. For one adrenalin-bursting moment she thought he was taking a picture of her plump bare bottom, but it transpired he was just looking for that same elusive message. His member had already been stored away and he was apparently done for the day. She felt suddenly foolish, bent over as she was, with him not even caring. She pulled her clothes back up and sat in silence while the burn in her cheek slowly subsided.

She packed up and they walked home again, with little said between them. A few days later and he was gone, off back to college. They didn't talk much in the interim and he didn't want to be dropped at the station, let alone to be waved goodbye. He didn't even text to say he had made it there OK. She tried ringing him but got nothing. So that was that, she had been dumped.

Dominic remained the only hangover from the 'Disappearing Youths' story that never was, a reminder that everything about that so-called mystery was a damp squib. She latched onto the tale out of desperation, having had another local story crumble before she had even managed to move into the village. One of the reasons she so coveted a place there was Haydn Shady, an unlikely-named villain who had taken possession of a big property on some of the estate lands outside the village. He was a shady character indeed, suspected of extortion and fraud at the very least, plus kidnapping and murder if you believed the gossip. He seemed omnipotent although he was seldom spotted. He was large, with a completely shaved head, and he always wore sunglasses, the myth being that no one had ever seen his eyes.

The manor house he stayed in was originally leased from the aging Baron who owned nearly all the land around. Somehow, through threats it was believed, Shady had then managed to purchase the house outright, along with many acres. The original theory had been that he needed the privacy to oversee his nefarious business, and he needed the land to safely bury the bodies of his murdered enemies. Bit by bit he seemed to eat into the estate, purchasing parcels of land here and there so that many of the tenant farmers suddenly found themselves at the mercy of a new and far more ruthless landlord, one prepared to raise their rents without scruple.

All this was juicy enough gossip for any aspiring journalist, although it was a story most would fear to follow, given the reputation of the subject. The plot thickened when it transpired that a new road had been proposed, a bypass that would run through the estate lands. The old Baron would never consent to such a thing but he held only a small area that could still stop it from happening, and it seemed Mr Shady was more than happy to allow the purchase of his newly gained land for a whopping sum, far in excess of what had been paid for it.

Everyone waited with bated breath, sure that the villain would bully or threaten the poor Baron and get this remaining land. The new road would have seen the whole area ruined. Ancient woodland would be levelled. Noise and traffic pollution would increase, spoiling the general atmosphere for ever. Most of the farmers would be driven out and the village would die a slow death, peopled only by the commuters who may have silently been pleased with the faster routes onto major road networks. Mimi, following the story over the months and years as closely as she could from her flat in Oxford, decided that she couldn't bear to see the area she so loved desecrated. This would be the cause to champion, the story that would show her mettle and talents and make her a heroine to the locals – who might reward her with a house there on the cheap.

However, another hero beat her to it. A few months before she secured her room at the Spinster's house, the equally mysterious Pieter Bakkers stepped out of nowhere to help the ailing Baron. He was a powerful businessman who seemingly could not be bullied. He saved the day by buying up much of the estate's remaining lands, promising to restore it to its former glory and never to sell off any further land. The loss of these ancestral lands and properties was tempered by the knowledge that they would be in the hands of someone with a genuine desire to keep the estate and restore it to its former glory.

Bakkers 'discovered' rare butterflies breeding in the meadows that the new road was set to go through, and quickly ensured the fields were designated as Sites of Special Scientific Interest, which meant that they were legally required to be maintained as they were. The proposed road plan was dead in the water. Mr Shady was no doubt grossly put out that his scam had failed but, rather than fight it in the way the villagers thought and feared he would, he instead decided to accept an offer from Bakkers for all the property and lands he had screwed from the Baron.

The price paid was apparently more than generous, an offer that simply could not be refused, although how anyone knew this, other than the protagonists and perhaps a single solicitor, was unclear. Maybe grateful locals were just quick to swell the legend of their saviour. Whatever the truth, Mr Shady sold up and slipped away without a word, leaving a new lord of the land in place, one who saw to it that the farmers were charged a fair rent again and that the village would never again come under threat.

Mimi was elated that Shady had been defeated but sad that her story had evaporated along with him. She would have loved to do a piece about the new hero but the man just seemed to be a ghost. No one ever saw him and no one could understand his vast generosity. The only explanation was that he was a true philanthropist, a lover of tradition and beauty and of the quiet, perfect villages quaintly nestling so far from his South African homeland. He made sure that buildings were properly maintained and, where necessary, renovated. He provided money for the church roof. He used his influence to ensure the post office stayed open, at a time when so many others fell under the axe.

Like most South Africans he was rugby mad, and he also came to the rescue of a local amateur rugby club who found themselves without a home. Not only did he assign an area to be used as a pitch, and build changing rooms and even some seating for the crowd, he designated other estate buildings as the clubhouse, to be used gratis by the team members for functions, and as a centre for the players to participate in outdoor leisure pursuits such as cycling and hiking, all great for building team spirit.

It was rumoured that the man himself secretly watched his new amateur side play, although no one seemed to know him by sight so no one could confirm this. It was said that he was away almost permanently on business, but it remained unclear why he never showed himself in person. Perhaps the weight of being so much the hero was too much for a genuinely generous man to carry. All dealings were overseen by an estate manager, and journalists' requests for interviews with the Great Man were politely declined. Mimi knew she would win few friends by trying to unmask a beneficiary who wished to remain anonymous.

With the status quo returned, the village lapsed back into its tranquillity. Mimi even found herself a little isolated, particularly in the winter months. Her naughtiness seemed to increase exponentially with her boredom, and since Dominic was usually otherwise engaged or unreachable she had to resort to her fingers to sate her needs. Once in a while she found herself alone in the house and could dig out the carefully secreted vibrators. But on most nights the landlady stayed resolutely at home and Mimi came close to tearing out her hair with the frustration of not daring to reach for her toys. One overheard buzz and it would be all round the village before breakfast.

Her fingers were willing substitutes, seemingly working to their own plans as soon as her bedroom door was shut. Soon even the thought of another night in her room trying to avoid the Spinster's incessant chatter had the strange dual effect of making her chest heave and her pussy tingle with anticipation. She seemed to spend all her leisure hours lost in either sticky-fingered escapism or guilt at her own wantonness. Her fantasies became more extravagant and drawn out, her head full of images of her being pleasured or, more commonly, abused by ever greater numbers of the most immoral people imaginable.

She tried to escape the slavery of masturbation by focusing on anything that might involve her in social life and keep her from her room and her mocking sex toys. She scanned the local paper for events or clubs she might join – anything that might prove more enticing than frigging while thinking about being held down and desecrated. Then one day she saw it, a barely noticeable advert in a little box buried within the classified section of her own paper.

'The *Ana Lucia Plan*: a magical way to lose weight. For girls 18–30.'

Mimi didn't know if the figures referred to size or age, nor had she ever heard of this Ana Lucia. But that wasn't the name that struck her most. The one below it was; the one given as the contact, with a phone number beside it: *Morgana Innamorato*. Mimi thought the name so exotic that she repeated it over and over in her head and then felt compelled to say out loud, just to hear it roll off her tongue. The Spinster broke off from her TV-induced trance at the sound of the words, a deep frown forming as if it were sacrilege for that name to be spoken under her roof.

'She's a witch,' she said, and meant it.

The landlady felt that no other qualification was needed and went back to her soap opera. Mimi's imagination had already been captured and so, ever the journalist, she probed further. Apparently the charge had been levelled against the woman and had never been denied. It was said that she ran a coven from her house tucked away within the estate lands, and brainwashed accomplices to help her ensnare other victims. Wicked rites were performed including ritual sacrifice. Curses were laid upon any who dared to go against them. Money was extorted from landowners all around the county in exchange for spells to bring good crops and healthy livestock. Worst of all, it seemed, was her refusal to let women either too old or too fat into her slimming club to learn the magical weight-loss secrets of the *Ana Lucia Plan*.

'I've tried to join several times,' huffed the portly spinster, 'but she don't ever allow it.'

Mimi smiled to herself, convinced now that Miss Innamorato was no more evil or insane than any of the villagers. Her heart was pumping though, enlivened by unfounded tales of sorcery by an exotically named local beauty who ran a Fat Class that banned overweight old women who talked too much. That kind of club, Mimi mused, was one that she definitely needed to seek out. And so she did.

2

He watched silently, stroking his pointed goatee. He liked the goatee. Very few could carry off such a devilish beard, and he was definitely one of them. Not only did it bring length and sharpness to his already strong jaw, but the sheer *blackness* of it seemed to make his steel-blue eyes even more piercing, if that were possible. His eyes defined him. They were mesmerising to all. Once people stared into them, and this was something they couldn't help but do, his word became their command. It had been so since his earliest days.

'Take that prick from your mouth and move on to the next one,' he said, and she did.

He could see that *her* eyes were bright, manic even. He allowed himself a smirk of satisfaction. Always look at the eyes. All truth is stored there, on display to everyone, all of the time. His were the only exception; his only ever said, *Be very scared*. A silver thread of saliva joined her lips to the erect penis she had just been sucking.

The wet shaft bore testament to the fact that she had avidly swallowed the whole slender length of it. She was breathing loudly and still staring hungrily at the erection as if she wasn't yet ready to stop feasting upon it. Then her focus changed as she saw the next one waiting in line. She grasped the just-sucked prick and used it as a support whilst she shuffled sideways upon her knees. She even kept hold of it as she sank her mouth onto the new prick and let out a loud moan of joy.

A little darker blue and his eyes would have had a different effect on people. He might even have been considered angelic – by those who judge character by physical appearance. As it was they made him a demon. They were vivid ice-cold coronas around a black oversized centre. The ring was pale but intense, captivating and unique but unnerving. If they reflected his soul then he must be a man with a heart of steel. Was it too much to say that if they had been just a little darker blue he would have had a completely different life?

People always defer to size but he had been put on a pedestal way before he grew so large. From his earliest years he learned to dominate his peers, to create a mysterious power around the eyes. He soon began to feel contempt for those around him, for the way they grovelled and blinked and looked away. He became a manipulator, a tyrant, a bully. What else is there to do when people allow it so freely? He was nearly six and a half feet tall when he finally stopped growing. Never gangly, he was always wide and solidly built. He learned boxing after he left school and could have been professional if he hadn't considered the sport beneath him. He just wanted to know how to use his fists most effectively.

At university he joined a club that taught sword-fighting. Not wimpy fencing, with its weird tight mummy-suits and camp *touché*s, but genuinely useful ancient techniques, like how to wield a broadsword in anger. The club was full of *Dungeons and Dragons* freaks and those obsessed with Arthurian legend. He scared the life out of all of them. They called him 'the Kurgan' after the villain from the *Highlander* film. The comparison swelled him. He made himself a mock-up of the Kurgan's armour, fashioned from black leather and chainmail taken from others at the club. In secret he would dress in it and parade around in front of a long mirror, swiping his sword whilst he imagined himself as the immortal demon-warrior. He enjoyed it so much that he would pull out his engorged penis and masturbate, still snarling and swiping thin air with his blade as he splashed the glass.

The girl's head was now bobbing up and down on the new prick as she tried to ingest as much of its length as she could. Her arms were reaching out to the sides, grasping and stroking the erections there, one already sucked, the other the next in line. Her audible appreciation of the cocks was ever growing and she stuck her bare bottom out as if hoping to lure another one inside her. Perhaps one of the lads of the line would have been aroused enough to want to oblige her, had they not all been chained to the wall with their hands secured behind their backs.

He studied the pristine white skin stretched over her chubby behind. The treatment had worked well. He remembered this one had had at least five small but prominent moles on her buttocks, a tiny constellation across her milky cheeks. Now there was no sign. When he finally came to bend her over and parted those cheeks he would find the darkness around her holes all gone, the openings and the delicate skin between them almost as pale as the hemispheres of her bottom.

The cryosurgery to eliminate the darker pigmentation was expensive, especially as he had to send his newly initiated girls to a clinic in the States for the treatment. However, it was worth it for the speed and thoroughness of the job. The results were always outstanding. As soon as his girls were accepted into his Sacred Order they were given a combination of whitening pills and creams for daily use, imported illegally from Europe, Japan or America. These helped lighten the moles and other surface blemishes but the process was slow. Sometimes minor surgery or a cleansing blast was required. He needed his girls pristine, as flawless as the statues of the bacchantes of antiquity. The legends all said that these girls had been perfect, and so they should be for him now. His status demanded no less; his *prick* demanded no less.

Those legends mostly told of the bacchantes' voracious sexual hunger, and this girl was doing her best to honour that tradition. She was still loudly trying to engulf the one penis whilst running her closed fists swiftly up and down the straining lengths at either side of her. She clearly couldn't get enough and here were six hard beauties all in a line, just for her. His massive member would make it lucky seven. His was the last she would have seen, some weeks ago now. That had been the day of her initiation hunt, when she had watched him stretch and fill a virgin *c lus* to its limits. At that point, she truly became his.

He might one day let her feel the same joy that plundered bottom had felt, but not today. Other, slimmer erections would go there but not his monster. It was something to be used sparingly, to make sure she always hankered after it and yearned for the chance to feel it stream inside her. In the meantime there were many other ways to ensure she stayed within the fold until he no longer had use for her. Today's ceremony, officially called *The Cleansing*, though more commonly known amongst the girls as *The Spattering*, was chief amongst these ways. This was another day she would never forget.

She had been jetted back only the day before and given a night to get over her trip. Earlier she had been overseen by Morgana, who always prepared her girls in person. She would have been bathed and then soothed all over with lotion. No depilation was necessary as during the stay at the clinic electrolysis was also undertaken to ensure no more hair grew around her privates. Priestess Morgana would have talked all the time about stiff pricks. They would have looked at glossy magazine pictures of lovely erections and discussed them in great detail. Throughout her long schooling period in this Order the girl would have been denied all flesh cocks. Once initiated, there was the promise of as many as she could take, starting that very day. She would have been dying for them.

She was now not only slurping at the prick before her but going back and forth to those in her grasp to slap them hard around her face, a sure sign of her surging lust. Morgana had clearly made her desperate for these beautiful youthful erections. Even though the Priestess never allowed them inside her own body she knew the fevered longing they could inspire. She would have inspected the girl's crotch closely, making sure the lips were pale and the surrounding skin porcelain-smooth and geisha-white. She knew nothing less than perfection would do. She would have spat upon the crotch, blown gently upon it, maybe even teased it with a flickering tongue-tip.

Then she would have got the girl on all fours and inspected her, telling her that her newly bleached holes were finally deserving of her Lord's huge, unmatchable erect *mentula*. She would have sluiced the girl's backside with a slick clear oil, perhaps holding a small vibrator to the girl's pubis as she expelled, being careful not to let her come. Towards the evening, when the girl was squirming, she would have been plied with wine and given access to the Priestess's potions. By this time she would be almost rabid with lust and would have to be handcuffed to ensure she didn't ravage herself. As a final torture, the Priestess might well have had one of the many sex machines brought in so that she could straddle it and pummel her own *cunnus* at the highest speed, whilst the chained-up girl watched and drooled and shrieked in desperation for her turn.

Her insatiable appetite was currently showing no signs of abating. He ordered her to move along the line and he sensed her disappointment that this was the last of them. He could see why she had such carnal hunger. The pricks were fine specimens, no more than average size but all sleek and rock-hard, all with fine upward curves. He felt the saliva gather in his own mouth at his sudden urge to join her on his knees. The temptation was strong but momentary, and he quickly dismissed it from his mind as far too demeaning an act for someone whom these people worshipped as a deity.

Odd; he had once thought such cravings alien to him. Although he had always been in awe of his own body he had never thought it was from a general love of the male form. He initially only envisaged an order of lust-crazed females to worship him. However, the practices of his coven were based upon those of the Roman Bacchanalian cults, and the records declared that around 188 BC their most feted leader, the High Priestess Paculla Annia, had indeed ordained that men be admitted for the first time. Her orgies were considered incomplete without males present, all committing the lewdest sexual acts, mostly upon one another. Since Paculla Annia was now reborn and living amongst them, in the form of Morgana Innamorato, it seemed essential that he follow her original instructions.

Deeper research persuaded him that the Roman gods and richer mortals did indeed employ male slaves, and commonly used them for sexual purposes. However, they never took the passive role, which they saw as a specifically Greek habit. Such slaves, or catamites, were typically young. His searches were restricted to athletic youths in their very early twenties, or fresh out of college. He needed them virile, primarily gay so that they would lust after him as much as any female, but still horny enough to grow stiff and be used by Morgana's girls when necessary.

His catamites were kept essentially as slaves, enjoying none of the privileges the girls had. They were there to do donkey work, to act as muscle, to bring authenticity to the orgies. Only after a while did he realise they could also be used for his gratification. Since he demanded of himself a daily minimum of three ejaculations, the boys came in handy when Morgana's girls had been shut away for the night. He treated them roughly. The Romans frowned upon the thought of love between males. He certainly didn't want them to feel like they were anything other than receptacles for his lust. But sometimes, when he was gripping those lithe thighs and pumping hard against their muscular buttocks, he thought he adored them every bit as much as the soft, marble-white rumps of his girls. The shame of it burned afterwards, a secret he could never allow to be discovered.

It posed a problem: what would he do with the boys when he was finished with them? They were hard to find and thus precious, but they couldn't last for long. They would become loose and grotesque. Morgana had her treatments but none was a cure. He kept telling himself he would have to devise a way of dismissing them from his service without fear of them revealing the secrets of the Order. After all, they had been lured there and then locked up and used – what would prevent them from betraying his illegal practices, the kidnapping and enslaving, the secret lust for athletic male bodies? He already knew there was only one feasible answer.

The girl had done a marvellous job. The pricks were all still hard but the ones at the start of the line would not stay that way for long. It was time to move on to the ceremony proper. He had her get off her knees and recline upon the raised dais covered in cushions. He refilled his goblet with claret and crossed to her. She was allowed two mouthfuls of the wine in case she was dry from all her sucking, and to make room in the goblet. He topped it up with olive oil poured from a terracotta jug and then used his long index finger to mix the liquids together.

She was smiling and licking her lips although she had no clue what was to happen next. He had her lie back with her hips raised off the platform by a cushion. He spread her knees and saw the delicate lips of her bare puss. What beauty. There was no lewdness here, just a study in sweet, spotless perfection. He took the goat horn from beside the pewter claret jug. It was ringed at the large end with silver, but while other examples were also similarly tipped, his was cut so that the very end was missing, leaving a small opening. He pressed the tapered end onto her soft quim and she reached down to part the lips, allowing him to feed the horn inside her. She gasped and closed her eyes, although this meagre penetration would never be enough for her.

He tipped the contents of his goblet gradually into the horn, allowing the bright-red viscous liquid to drain inside her. She knew not to spill a drop. When his goblet was empty he handed her the small bowl of raspberries and instructed her to fill herself. She let out a gasp of pure lust and proceeded to do his bidding, holding herself open with the fingers of one hand and feeding the berries one by one inside her puss with the other, careful not to let the liquid inside her ooze out.

As she continued her task he stripped to the waist. Strange, he was always desirous that his catamites see his bare torso. Although he was twice their age he knew his stood up well in comparison. It was far larger than theirs and firm with muscle. The skin was still smooth and free of hair, just like theirs. It was a suitable body for a god, one that they would long to have pressed against them.

He released the slaves so that three could get on their knees and use their mouths to keep the other three hard. They all knew better than to coax an ejaculation. Doing so would lead to humiliating and most likely painful punishments. The sight of them going about their expert business was enough to ensure his prick was fully engorged when he released it. He so often fucked like this, with his chest bare, his black riding boots and animal-hide britches still in place, his cock and balls unleashed from the buttoned fly. He liked the way the still-fastened leggings framed his huge manhood, the dark background making it stand out even more. He liked how his tanned torso looked so sleek and firm under its sheen of sweat, particularly in the flickering light of a fire. And he specially liked the way that leaving his lower half covered made it all seem so impersonal, so full of urgency and free of tenderness.

He already had his hair tied back. Sometimes, if he was having a prolonged, wild fuck, he would free it from the band for effect, letting it drop back to his shoulders. His hair was jet-black and glossy, only slightly oily in appearance. It parted at the front to leave his large expanse of forehead bare, and flowed down either side of his face, framing it like curtains. Along with the goatee it created a swashbuckling look that pleased him. It was a good thick thatch for someone in his early forties and quite a change from what he was used to.

Until fairly recently he had been completely bald. He had been that way since his last days at university, when he had shaved it to mimic the Kurgan in his last, most frightening incarnation. It made him look brutish and ugly, especially with his cold eyes – but it made him feel even more powerful. People could barely stand in his presence; they all cowered around him. He realised his bald head, bony and white as a polished skull, was as good a calling card as any. His eyes were what had always marked him out but their effect was almost too shocking. They wouldn't allow him to survive an identity parade. They needed to be used only when necessary, revealed at critical moments so as to have the same withering effect on his adversaries as if he had pulled out a gun.

He first shaved his head on the day he was ejected from university. He had celebrated his new look by punching a tutor to the ground for awarding a low mark to an essay he had put minimal effort into. He didn't care about his expulsion. He had only gone to university to teach himself how to use his brain properly. He found that academic qualifications were just that: academic. He realised that there were better ways to make money than through kowtowing to the strictures of society. If university taught him anything it was that that the youngsters of today, and of any day, thirsted for more than knowledge. With the birth of rave culture and all-nighters, everyday youth wanted something more than a few beers down the pub. They wanted drugs, in great quantities. So he decided to make it his life's work to give them exactly what they wanted. And he did far, far better out of it than they ever would.

Now he was safely within the confines his own realm the Ray-Bans could come off and the eyes could again be revealed to give him his full power. The way the girl regarded him showed her overwhelming desire to be put to his sword. Her eyes were fiery, wild, and her mouth was open in a wicked grin. She was in awe of all she surveyed as she busily stuffed herself with the raspberries. Some of the ooze inside her had already leaked and ran blood-red onto the cushion beneath her. He judged she was now full enough and bade her stop. He grasped his prick and moved slowly forward so that she knew what was coming. She breathed harder, gasping with the anticipation, parting her thighs even wider to welcome him in. Her fingers stayed at her crotch, ready to hold herself open to aid his penetration.

It was not his favourite position but it was the only way she could take him this first time. He guided the fat head of his prick up between her pale lips and saw an immediate trickle of her red juice upon it. As oily-wet as she was she still had to stretch herself apart as he pushed slowly forward. When the whole glans had been engulfed he steadied himself, grasping tightly under her hips to make sure she stayed exactly in position. He could feel that the mixture inside her was warm, so he knew she was ready. He then plunged inside her in one beautifully controlled thrust. It was slow at first, then built steadily into an unstoppable lunge, finishing with a loud wet slap as his balls and crotch met her soft opening.

Her wails increased as he drove into her, culminating in a shriek as he slammed home and forced the first burst of oily juice from inside her. He could feel the squash of fruit within, the tiny explosions as he filled her so suddenly and crushed the berries. He felt the splash on his belly and knew his balls would be dripping with the blood-red concoction. He saw the spatter shoot up her alabaster thighs, the oil making it cling to her skin before it gradually ran down.

He withdrew slowly so that she could witness his full length thickly covered in the gleaming claret mixture. Her eyes were wide and she was trembling with bliss. He drove home to the hilt once more. Another great splash of fruit juice shot up her inner thighs, leaving small lumps of the broken fruit upon her pristine white skin. She wasn't just trembling now but shaking. It had to be the nastiest thing she had ever seen, and he knew she adored it.

He gave her several more thrusts until her cream started to take over and make the secretions too opaque to look like fresh blood. Then he withdrew and replaced her upon the dais. He manoeuvred her onto him and she was quick to impale herself once more, sliding down hard upon him to expel the remnants of the pulped fruit. She felt tight still, clenching his shaft as she eased herself up and down or rocked against him to press her swollen bud into his crotch. He grasped her plump bottom to aid her movements, squeezing the soft flesh as hard as possible. He *hated* skinny, bony arses. He hated huge, flabby arses too. They had to be just right, and this one was, which is why she had been initiated in the first place.

It was good to watch her with her head thrown back, those perky breasts bouncing up and down. He could eat those tiny, sugar-mice-pink nipples. In fact he just might. Everything about her was good enough to gulp down.

He put his arms around her and gently brought her down, arresting her bouncing movement. Her eyes had lost their fire and were glazed with ecstasy. He pulled her flat against him, still buried inside her. Her breasts squashed into him just above his belly and he could feel the hard points of her nipples pressing upon his muscle.

He revelled in the fact that even tall girls like this still felt so small beside him. Her face was against his chest and she would be able to hear his heart pounding with divine passion.

She had forgotten all about the lads but now it was time to bring them into play. His hands went back down to her buttocks to squeeze them again and to ease them apart. Without even delving into her he could feel it was slippery from the oil enema that Morgana had earlier administered. He gave terse commands for the lads to stop their sucking and gather around him. They stood in a semicircle regarding her, all slowly stroking their erections and awaiting his command. He pointed to the eldest of the lads, the first he had brought under his wing.

'You,' was all he needed to say.

The lad climbed onto the platform and crouched down behind her. Although all the slaves were primarily there to service rather than take their own pleasure, during the various rites and orgies this lad used his seniority over the others to ensure he dealt out just as many buggerings as he received.

She couldn't even squeal any more; her only audible emission was a gust of breath from her open mouth. The Master knew that she would have been wishing for *him* in her tightest passage.

He let the first lad pump away until his initial rapid pace showed signs of slowing. Then he was ordered off and the next lad took his place. Each took their turn above him as she flooded his prick and drifted ever closer to unconsciousness. Each was replaced as soon as their pace flagged. She just lay there and took them all, burbling her new-found bliss. Each fresh lad could enter more easily. The last, the newest recruit, taken in barely a fortnight before, slipped into her with no pause whatsoever, even though it might have been the first time he had ever committed this delicious act.

Once they had all been through her he eased her off and left her face-down upon the platform. Although it looked as if she might expire if she received any more pleasure, he wasn't quite done with her yet. He pulled her hips back so that her bottom was at the edge of the platform, moved his way between her thighs once more and plunged deep into her sex. She had no resistance to offer. This was his favourite position: like a beast from the rear, holding her cheeks open, his heavy balls slapping her intimate flesh.

She found her voice once more, emitting a piercing scream that told of her joy. He roared in triumph as his balls tightened painfully with the force of his ejaculation. She was completely spent, beyond euphoria. He clutched and waggled his softening prick, like a fat python in his hand.

The girl would be taken back to Morgana and granted a good two weeks' respite. It would be a chance to stoke her rude passions again. When she was once more granted licence to have sex she would be mad for it. She would do it with rabid abandon, fuelled by drink and Morgana's herbal brews. She would dance until possessed and then erupt with sexual fury. He considered no sight more wonderful than that of a young girl utterly lost to wantonness; these seemingly pure girls, with their faultless white skin and their neat, delicate, innocent-looking quims, all suddenly transformed into lust-filled savages; their young perfect rumps, as smooth, ample and apparently guilt-free as those of the bacchantes who adorned his Lalique vases, suddenly being squashed and ground into the face of their victim, or driven down with shuddering force upon a hard cock or anything else that might do for one.

He knew all about the Bacchanalia from his classical studies at university, although back then he had only vague dreams of rekindling these ceremonies. It happened more by accident. By his mid-thirties, part of his burgeoning business empire included the promotion of club nights aimed at students in university towns. He used a DJ who did a surprisingly good set of goth/dance music mixes that seemed to wow the new wave of emos, who were far more into having fun than the morbid soap-dodging goths of his college days. The nights grew in popularity – especially because it was strictly forbidden to bring in drugs. Doormen were very thorough with their searches and woe betide anyone trying to smuggle gear inside. Once in, however, and suddenly all manner of drugs were apparently on offer, all of good quality and at very fair prices, available from certain shady-looking gentlemen who just happened to be in the employ of the promoter.

One night he was watching as the DJ was whipping up the crowd. One girl, with short pink punk hair, clearly under the influence, suddenly decided that the only way to truly embody the excitement of the music was to take her top off. She jumped around waving her hands in the air, her little tiny-nippled tits bouncing free. Then her red tartan miniskirt was off and she was leaping around, singing her head off, in just shiny black Doc Martens boots and a pair of short, pink, lacy knickers.

It was the most arresting sight he could remember. She looked wild and free and gorgeous. Some of her friends seemed to be going to follow suit, but this girl was getting too heated and as she bounced around to the music her hand went down between her legs to squeeze at her crotch. Even this he would have allowed but the girl was too pumped up to keep it at that. When she took her hand off her crotch and thrust it inside her knickers, he clicked his fingers and his bouncers went into action.

He had the girl immediately ejected from the dance-floor and thrown across his office desk, where he gave her what she was literally crying out for. It was probably

the most frantic fuck of his life. Her frenzied shameless-
ness was a real turn-on. He loved the fact that she had
publicly stripped and paraded her half-bare arse even
though it was plump enough to be marked by little
dimples in the surface. He adored her young white flesh
when she was bent over in front of him. It was nearly
glorious. Only her fatly lewd, dark-lipped cunt made her
look too lascivious to be perfect.

It was only after she had been turned out onto the
street that he wished he had taken more time to study
this girl and make more use of her. He missed her flagrant
disregard for morals. He decided that he must encourage
the same in others. He began running similar nights
after hours in a pub he had recently acquired, which
he renamed the *Bag o' Nails*, in honour of the ancient
Bacchanals to be restaged there. The nights were only a
partial success. He hired young prostitutes to get high and
dance around and then strip off, in the hope of encouraging the paying female guests to do the same. Although
the flyers on each table showed pictures of nymphs in
unabashed action, the local 'nymphs' all seemed too reti-
cent. The nights mainly consisted of the prostitutes being
manhandled by fat middle-aged men in leather trousers.

He didn't like the lack of spontaneity, or the fact that
the street girls looked so rough and used. He wanted real
girls, ones driven by lust for flesh rather than for money,
ones like that pink-haired punk at the club. He started

advertising in select publications for 'witches and bitches' to attend his Bacchanalian nights, promising free drinks and even accommodation. For once he didn't even care if the nights only turned a small profit. He just wanted to watch a room full of horny young females getting naked and wild. The thought of 'normal' girls being driven into a frenzy made him insatiable.

One evening a couple of nubile goth-witch bitches showed up. The night ended with them simultaneously fingering one of his barmaids while she pinched her own bare nipples, under his instruction. He was about to service both these girls but they told him they belonged to their Priestess and pointed into the shadows. In the gloomy corner was their Mistress, one Morgana Innamorato. He took out his erect cock but she refused it, the first female ever to dare do so. Notwithstanding this awkward start, they soon got on well, kindred spirits as they were, although it helped that she granted him his wish and let him have both the bitches, side by side, over his desk.

Whilst he pounded the girls from behind, Morgana told him of her worship of the god Bacchus, how she was the reincarnation of Paculla Annia and had her own coven of orgy-loving girls. These girls loved their Priestess but they needed a god. It was obvious by the way he had these bitches creaming and screaming that she meant *him*. He was, after all, a huge-cocked, bald-headed giant with captivating, chilling eyes. It was clear she would never in her life meet anyone more imposing and extraordinary, more suitably *divine*. If he agreed to be their focus of worship, they would give him all the private Bacchanals he could handle. It seemed the ideal set-up.

However, as always, there was a catch. She told him of her problem in keeping her coven together, of needing to find somewhere for them to act out their rites in secret. She owned a cottage in the grounds of an ancient estate, but the landlord was rightly suspicious of her activities. She feared eviction, especially as the landlord was in dire financial straits and was under pressure to sell off some of the estate, which could have proved difficult with a renowned witch living there. If she was thrown out the coven would dissolve, ruining years of careful planning. That's where *he* came in, their god and saviour.

He agreed to discuss helping, once Morgana had agreed to suck his balls and put her finger up his backside.

'I am your god, after all,' he said with a smile.

It warmed his cold heart to get this mad Priestess on her knees. Nonetheless, a partnership with her certainly appealed. She was more ravishing than any woman he had seen and her love of the more licentious practices of classical civilisation was uncannily close to his own. Anyway, if his full, prosperous life was missing anything then it was surely an on-tap bevy of lusty witch-girls to service him. It was about time he was showered with the adoration he deserved. He liked how pure these girls were with their pale skin. They reminded him of the pink-haired punk that he had so stupidly let slip. Morgana gave one of her wolfish grins and told him it was all due to the potions she fed them. He liked that word 'potions'. It meant they were on the same wavelength.

Morgana then stood and slowly stripped, showing off her Amazonian figure and flawless white skin. There was not a mark upon it. Her breasts were large, firm, with small pink nipples. There was flesh to her but no excess anywhere. Her belly was smooth and indented with a deep button. Her pussy was hairless and cute, a little dark line splitting her soft mons. Her hips were wide and her bottom was the most perfect he had ever seen – plump, with a lovely round curve and no suggestion of sag despite its weight.

'I am ageless,' she said. 'I have spells that can make me look this way for all time. Even in this current incarnation I am over four hundred years old.'

With anyone else such talk might have been met with a jeering response, but for one who considered himself the Kurgan made flesh such talk of immortality only fired his soul.

The girls were now at the feet of their Priestess. He decided he had to have her and grasped her arms and pushed her onto all fours. Her peachy bottom was so smooth and sweet-smelling he was almost overwhelmed by the need to sink his teeth into it. His fat erection was only millimetres from her delectable sex when she suddenly looked back over her shoulder, fiery-eyed. She babbled some incantation and pointed at his erection, and he watched it helplessly deflate.

He sneered as she nonchalantly got up and dressed, telling him that she was someone he would never have. He wasn't beaten yet, though.

'If I can't have you,' he said, 'then I must have the next best thing. All your girls must have exactly the same body as you. The big breasts I can live without, but the skin must be as pure as yours, the pussy as pristine and neat, the hips and rump exactly the same size as yours.'

He was clearly enjoying this plan to become their god, and so it was agreed. If he would provide the base, Morgana would attract the girls and build the coven. She would oversee and teach the girls, and they would in turn worship him. He was to pay for the upkeep of the coven and was obliged to respect their rites and ceremonies, but he could avail himself of the girls however and whenever he chose. As a parting gift Morgana reversed the spell and left the girls to tend to his erection.

She went back to plan her new coven and he, this oddly named Haydn Shady, went about looking into the estate he was to try and buy. Initial research suggested it would be a suitable kingdom for him to rule over. Then an unscrupulous town planner disclosed that part of the estate was on the route of a proposed bypass. If certain other permissions could be gained for the road's construction, then handsome offers would be made for these lands. Purchase of the estate could therefore prove extremely lucrative. This was information he decided to keep from his new friend the immortal witch.

That meeting had been a few years ago, and whilst he had let his hair grow and now sometimes had to pluck a few grey strands from his new goatee, she had not changed in the slightest. The coven had grown, some fully-fledged bacchantes had been created and others were in training to join the ranks. His manhood was in a permanent state of arousal and the rudeness of it never bored him, not even for a second, helped perhaps by Morgana's Lust Tonics. The bacchantes led a life of simmering desire, which was stoked into a frenzy every few weeks during ceremonies or ritual punishments.

As their god, it was down to him to ensure their continued happiness, along with his own. As a stickler for accuracy, he was keenly aware that in classical tradition the practice of the Orders revolved around the ravaging of strangers. His own Order was falling short in this respect. So far their circle was closed, and orgies involved only members of the extended coven. Time was now pressing to find outsiders to lure in, if a way could be devised to maintain the secret. He was sure he could think of one. He already knew a tried and tested method. All he needed was a suitable candidate.

Thus his ears pricked up when Morgana told him of a new female interested in joining up to the *Ana Lucia Plan*. The Priestess had spies everywhere so background on this girl was not hard to find. She was pretty by all accounts, and heavy-hipped enough to be crafted into the kind of female he needed. Morgana would no doubt want to train this girl properly, hungry as she was for any new potential followers. However, this female was already in her mid-twenties, older by a couple of years than even the longest-serving girls. He wanted none past 24, at the most.

Worse still, this female was a journalist – a two-bit journalist, but one nonetheless. He didn't trust anyone connected with publicity of any kind. He didn't need natural snoops. Morgana was less cautious. She thought all girls equal and there for the turning. She wanted them for herself, he knew that. The bigger her coven, the greater her power. Well, he would keep her sweet for now. Although this female could be gently introduced to their Order, she was to be kept strictly at arm's length. No matter how much Morgana wanted her in, he would thwart all such requests, keeping the female on the periphery just to ensure she was easy to lure in. When the time was right he would give his girls what he knew they craved. He would give them a pretty outsider to hunt down and tear to pieces. This female journalist would be the first one they didn't have to spare.

3

'Turn around and show me your behind,' Morgana said.

Mimi blinked mutely at her, totally taken aback. If she had had a million guesses she would not have picked those to be the first words this witch-woman would say to her. The sight of the crimson-haired beauty was disarming enough without this introduction. She seemed to have come directly from the set of some sexy horror movie entitled *Stereotypically Gorgeous Vampire Witches with Sumptuous Milky-White Cleavages who Unfailingly Make Your Heart Stop*, or something like that. Anyway, what did she mean by 'show'? What, literally bare it for her, right here in front of the class? Mimi fleetingly thought about summoning up a joke but the woman was impatiently tapping one finger on the desk and didn't look like she wanted to crack a smile.

Bizarrely, almost magically, Mimi found herself complying, turning to face the seated girls and bending forward from the waist until she was nearly forming a right angle. Incredibly, she even reached back and pulled up her top slightly, so the view of her bottom in tight jeans would not be impeded.

'It is large, is it not? It sticks out,' the woman observed, matter-of-factly.

Yes, I have got a fat backside, thank you very much. Glad you've brought that to the attention of the whole world, thought Mimi, her cheeks flushing as she saw the sadistic glee sweep the faces of her classmates. Miss Morgana didn't seem at all perturbed by the embarrassment her brusque honesty was causing.

'Are others drawn to it? Do your men like to finish upon it?' she asked.

Finish upon it? Did she hear that right? Was there any way that could mean anything other than what it seemed to? Now Mimi was incredulous. As her eyebrows shot up, her mouth fell open, as if the two parts of her face were linked. Potential answers stopped short in her mouth, making it sound like she was panting erratically on her last breaths. Some kind of rebuttal seemed appropriate but how can any statement begin 'I've never been so insulted' when you're voluntarily sticking your bottom out for a woman you first clapped eyes on about a minute before? Does a dignified reply actually exist when you are bent over in front of eight giggling fresh-faced females, all of them complete strangers, whilst being asked to comment on whether your male lovers like to come all over your fat bum?

'Well, yes, they do seem to,' was the answer she eventually mumbled.

'It will always be large because of the jut,' Morgana unfeelingly continued, actually prodding the proffered bottom a couple of times. 'The firmness of the fat gives it good shape, at least, but it will dimple the surface texture and take away any smoothness. That will never do. Your bottom has great potential but is too much of a spread to be perfect. We need weight off your hips to accentuate the roundness of the buttocks, and greater muscle tone to compensate for the loss of fat. If we can keep the curve and eliminate sag you will find a great many more admirers, men and women, desperate to ravish you from behind.'

Mimi flushed even deeper red. She knew she had audibly gasped at the word 'ravish'. Having been plainly informed that, should she join this class, the primary objective would be to make her bottom more desirable, she now didn't know what to do or say. However, the woman had apparently not yet finished her appraisal, and was pressing gently at the small of Mimi's back to keep her bent over.

'Obviously society in general would always ridicule its size,' Morgana was now saying, 'but the lustful spirits of this world would adore it. And who cares for society's approval? Of course, if you wished it to stay exactly as it is I could teach you a spell to make it irresistible to all who saw it, whatever its appearance. However, it is not an easy spell to perform. You have to mix an exact recipe based on heather honey and liquorice root to spread upon the skin. You must stay in the woods, naked by day, for two whole weeks, with the mixture upon your bottom, even within the crack. And the incantation will not work unless every inch of your behind is covered by insects feeding upon the honey, and that essentially requires a colony of bees or wasps. It can get a little, shall we say, *stingy* in the sensitive areas.'

The woman was now not just prodding the bottom under inspection but running her long black-painted nails lightly over the expanse of stretched denim as she talked of feeding insects. The grazing contact sent a shiver across Mimi's skin and she knew her face might easily betray how much she was enjoying it. Despite this public humiliation she was glad she was still being bent over, and gladder still that the woman was doing all the talking.

'There are downsides to having an irresistible bottom,' Mimi was informed. 'You may find the attention constant. You will be groped and pinched wherever you go. It will drive your admirers mad with lust. Certainly your lovers will want to plunder your tighter hole. It will undoubtedly become a focus of their penetrations.'

Well, when Mimi decided to get some background for a possible article on the supposed witch and her weight-loss plan, she had no idea the class would be so instantly revealing. Despite this contrived and frankly baffling rudeness, Miss Morgana *was* undeniably bewitching. As the pressure lifted from Mimi's back and she found herself being slowly righted, she could easily see why the girls were sitting here so attentively.

'You may join the class for a while,' the witch said. 'That desk at the back is free. What is your name?'

'It is Mimi, Miss.'

Why had she called her 'Miss'? She wasn't in school now! Why did she feel so inferior to this beautiful but clearly unhinged woman? Why had she felt such a sudden and undeniably pleasurable twinge between her legs when this woman had squeezed her bottom?

'Mimi? That is a very selfish name, is it not? Go and sit down then.'

Mimi automatically did as instructed, chastised and confused, her face colouring even more vividly than before. She was keenly aware that all eyes were on her, trying to get a view of the big bottom that had been the focus of the lesson so far. She would have loved to wiggle it defiantly at them but instead she rushed to hide it on the wooden seat behind her allotted desk. A selfish name? That comment had smarted, made her chest flutter with indignation. It's not *Me, Me*, it's *Mimi* – as in the heroine of *La Bohème*, her parents' favourite opera. It was disconcerting to have this rebuke from the woman who had just been touching her with such tender familiarity.

Bizarrely, it seemed suddenly very important to Mimi that this bewitching female look fondly upon her. Glancing around the room she felt a sudden pang of envy, noting that she was quite probably the oldest of the girls, and not necessarily the prettiest. Even if her underlying motives were to potentially expose the woman as a charlatan witch, Mimi still strangely wanted to be her class favourite.

She had a sudden image of herself still at the front of the class, bent forward facing the girls. But she was naked this time, with her wrists tied to her ankles. In her mind's eye Morgana was raking the taut skin on her bottom with those long nails, pinching the flesh hard, eliciting gasps from all, giving each peachy cheek a slap in turn. Then Mimi imagined the Witch's grin spreading and the little slaps becoming a hail of stinging smacks that exploded upon her bottom. She pictured herself shrieking with the pain but taking it all, hurt by the spite of the woman, humiliated at being treated like this in front of the others, yet so proud that she had been chosen above all.

'Are you listening?'

Mimi jumped in her seat, realising that the witch was sternly addressing her and that the other girls were once again stifling giggles at her expense. She blushed again and mumbled her apologies.

'You had better get on the treadmill first, if you can't even stay focused for two minutes.'

Once again Mimi found herself shrinking at Morgana's chiding tone. She was confused and disorientated and stood hesitantly before following the woman's eyes to the piece of gym apparatus in the corner. The class was being held at the rugby club buildings that had been built within the estate grounds by the new beneficent owner. She was familiar with the place, having been there a few times to support Dominic when he was playing for the First Team. This building was next to the refurbished changing rooms and was designed for after-match gatherings. Next door was the well-kitted gym, although the only piece of apparatus this Fat Club had seen fit to drag through for its use was the single treadmill Mimi was now standing upon.

The witch set it in motion and Mimi, with her back to the girls, started off at no more than a gentle jog. She was still very conscious of the movement of her rear end, and that all eyes would be upon it. Having put her to her exercise, her teacher now apparently forgot her.

'The potion I will teach you today is to enliven the *c le* ,' Morgana was saying. 'When ingested it increases their output threefold and their power tenfold.'

There were gasps and more giggles from the girls. Mimi didn't know if this *c le* was a muscle or perhaps some kind of fat-busting cell of the digestive system, or indeed why its mention created such mirth. She rather suspected the girls were laughing at her wobbling bottom, now that she was beginning to struggle with the pace of the treadmill. Morgana remained uninterested in her, focusing instead on the importance of first mixing the basil with the clove before burning the candle exactly half-way down and adding three drops of wax to the potion. Mimi tried to listen but she was flagging and sure the treadmill was speeding up of its own accord. The witch's list of unknown roots and leaves, and the odd ways they had to be added, all became too much for her to digest. However, the thought of losing weight just by drinking some herbal brews certainly seemed preferable to this enforced exercise.

'You are slowing down.'

Suddenly the witch's voice was behind her, startlingly close. Mimi felt ridiculous that she was so jumpy and so apparently incapable of keeping up the gentlest of exercises. She started to put in more effort but decided she'd had enough humiliation for one day and announced that she wanted to stop. The splat on her backside was immediate, so unexpected and sharp it took a couple of seconds to register its sting. Mimi looked back in panic, forced to continue on the treadmill or go flying off the back into a graceless heap. The witch was holding a flat paddle made of black leather, conjured apparently from nowhere. She had smacked Mimi's arse!

'Stopping won't get your hips any firmer! Do you want more?'

Mimi didn't know what to say. The sting had been sharp but the thought that she could be publicly beaten by this woman somehow seemed to outweigh the dread of pain. She redoubled her efforts in silence, but Morgana was not placated and stayed put, ready to deal more blows of encouragement. It seemed ridiculous. First there was talk of weight-loss by drinking potions, now exercise enforced by flogging. Mimi started to pipe up but as soon as she did another slap landed and she was ordered to concentrate. This second blow was worse. Not because it was sharper, but because Mimi had squealed at the impact. Not screeched or shouted, but *squealed*, like she had enjoyed it.

Her legs were spent now and she wanted to turn and tell the witch to leave her alone, but her head was jumbled and her face was burning with the exertion and the embarrassment of her situation. She couldn't get off with any dignity unless the machine was first stopped for her, so she just had to go on. It quickly became a cycle: trying to keep up, then flagging, then getting a cheek-wobbling smack that enlivened her again. She was being spanked, genuinely, for the first time in her life.

It was terrible and the panic was rushing through her, but her puss was getting so, so hot. She had the sudden thought that the woman had somehow read her mind, seen her fantasy of being beaten upon the bum. As Mimi sobbed and gibbered the girls openly laughed. The pace seemed to be getting faster all the time, although no one was touching the machine. Her leg muscles were burning as much as her rump, but still she went on, desperate for it to stop but unable to make this happen, perhaps not even wanting it to end.

She was on the point of collapse but the slaps were coming one after another, across both cheeks, driving her on. The pain was almost indiscernible now that her bottom was so numb, but the heat between her legs was ever more noticeable. She was so het up that she thought for one terrible moment she was actually going to climax uncontrollably from her panic and humiliation, right there in front of the class. Then suddenly the treadmill was slowing to a stop. She got off it but still held onto it for support, bent forward with exhaustion.

The tears were still on her flushed cheeks. Her mouth was open and a thin thread of viscous saliva was dangling from her lips. She was shaking. Her head wouldn't clear and she didn't know what to do. She didn't need to. The witch moved in to her, so close she felt the crotch at her throbbing bottom and the breasts squashing against her back. She felt an arm come around her waist, a sneaky move on the blind side of the girls, the hand slipping down to jam between her thighs. One finger buried itself in her crotch and pressed hard, magically finding her clit as it pulsed against the constraining denim. She almost collapsed but the woman held her up.

She could feel breath in her ear. The witch was going to say something comforting to her, something loving. That's what happened in her fantasies. Miss Morgana would whisper that it was all right to be turned on by torture and public sexual humiliation. She would say something to the watching girls that made this whole bizarre episode OK. She would absolve Mimi of any guilt, explaining the squeals as something other than the joy of being openly spanked.

But it was not to be. Instead the witch quietly hissed, 'You want me to do that to your bare arse, don't you, you naughty slut?'

Mimi felt one more clitty press that sent the bliss shooting through her, and then the woman had backed away and was commanding her to sit. She could offer no response at all. With one hand covering her tearful eyes and the other clutching her sore bottom, Mimi wobbled back to her desk on legs that would barely move. She couldn't recall a more mortifying episode in all her life. Worse still, as she played it back in her head she knew it would have sounded to her audience exactly like it had felt to her: like she *loved* it. Then there were those witchy words, hissed in her ear. The truth was that Morgana had read her mind again. She *did* want it on her bare arse. At the end, when she had all but lost control and the shameful joy of it was getting too much, she had been desperate for her jeans and knickers to be pulled down. She had almost cried out for it. The urge to feel the sting on her unprotected skin had been desperate. She had wanted to hear the dull sound turn sharp. She wished the girls could have witnessed her naked juddering rump, the red patches on pure white skin.

She couldn't quite explain what her body had been crying out for, but it was like she had needed to explode. She had wanted to scream. She had wanted to pee, massively. Most of all she had wanted a *huge* prick inside her from the rear. Or if not a prick then fingers, or a whole hand, things that under normal circumstances she could never dream of taking inside her body – and not just in her pussy but in her virgin bottom. She had wanted to be filled way beyond anything she had ever experienced.

She had wanted all the girls behind her, pinching her, slapping her, squeezing her desperate clitty so cruelly. Even now that the girls had been forced to wipe the happy sneers from their faces and refocus on their tutor, Mimi still wished she had the strength to risk further humiliation, to bend over bare-arsed in front of them all and let them do their worst.

The blood was banging in her ears and all the noises of the class were muffled. Her vision was tear-blurred and everything seemed to be going on as if under water. The girls had gone back to their potion recipe and were copying down the witch's words. They had the herbs and leaves on their desks, and were examining them, drawing them so that they could later identify them as well as their properties. Mimi's desk was empty except for a blank sheet of paper and a pencil. The girl next to her was speaking and passing over a sprig of sweet-smelling herb. Mimi couldn't quite hear the words yet through her cloth ears.

Now, as the class continued writing their notes, they were being called up one by one. For the first time Mimi realised the girls were dressed identically, in black tracksuit bottoms and red T-shirts. It had to be a dream. Each girl stood before the witch and pulled her top up so that her belly paunch could be inspected and prodded. Then they would pull down their tracksuits to expose a bottom confined within a pair of tight black cotton short-style knickers, and the witch would measure them at the fullest part. Finally she would check the firmness of the hips and give her one-word verdict.

'Elixir,' she was saying, and the latest just-scrutinised girl was turning with an elated smile and skipping away to her desk. Her hearing was returning to Mimi now and she realised the girl at the next desk was still talking to her, still passing the herbs over for Mimi to memorise.

'You have to do the recipe,' the girl said. 'It's to make your boyfriend's balls grow bigger and shoot ten times harder.'

The joyful thought of this was visible in the girl's bright

eyes. Mimi had thought the *cōleī* Morgana had spoken of was some kind of muscle, but it appeared to mean the testes. A potion to make your boyfriend ejaculate ten times harder – that's what she was meant to be learning.

'How does that help you get slim?' she said, suddenly incredulous again, more herself, the only sane one amongst the madness.

'You can lose weight through Increased Carnal Proclivities,' said the girl. 'And if your boyfriend ingests the potion and you ingest his seed, it makes your magic stronger too. All the male slaves have to drink the potion. Anyway, we don't have to be *slim*, we have to be *just right*. Some even need fattening up. Priestess Morgana will decide.'

'Elixir,' Morgana again announced, and the latest just-measured girl turned around, beaming her excitement.

It was all too much for Mimi. The questions were buzzing around her befuddled head, all jostling to be the most imperative.

'What slaves?' she asked, and received a look in return that suggested she was more than stupid.

'Our Lord Bacchus provides us with male slaves, as is the custom. Rumour has it they are all really *fit*.'

The girl was giggling again now, her eyes alive with the thought of these good-looking slaves. 'He gets them from round here but they are all totally buff. They are kept on the other side of the estate but when you are trained and ready you can have them as many times as you like. You've got a really nice bum, by the way. Can I lick you when we get to playtime?'

'Elixir!' Morgana proclaimed once more from the background, and another girl smilingly returned to her desk.

Mimi's head was now close to spontaneously combusting. So many questions yet no clue where best to start. She could only manage a small nod in reply to the other girl's request. It had been so simply put, as if she had merely asked to borrow a pencil. The thought of being taken by this pretty thing amid some kind of public ceremony was threatening to make Mimi dissolve. The situation was now way beyond surreal.

'Who is your Lord?' she finally managed to say, but in her head this girl was already behind her, and her jeans were coming down.

'I've not seen him yet because I'm too new,' said the girl with a shrug. 'But some here have and they say he's got the best thingy in the world. They say he comes so hard you can feel it burst in your belly. When we are trained we might get to have him *inside* us, not just in our mouths. He is really big and has eyes like ice. They can turn you to stone, apparently. But it's his sexual power we are here to worship, not his eyes.'

So it *was* all just a load of rubbish: ice-eyed classical gods who happened to have shifted their heavenly realm to deepest Buckinghamshire. It was a pity to break the spell, especially since all the girls here were so obviously transfixed by it. Mimi wondered how the so-called Priestess, still happily proclaiming 'Elixir!' to each newly measured girl, profited from the whole charade. She hadn't even charged Mimi an entry fee for tonight.

It seemed like an elaborate fabrication to enable a bum-obsessed, clearly deranged (if rather delicious) female to play at being a witch, to let her strip a few chosen young females to their knickers and deal out an impromptu spanking here or there. Yet the girl had said others had seen these slaves, and the word 'kept' had been used, suggesting the slaves were there under duress. But how could these supposedly local males possibly be held there without anyone in the vicinity noticing their absence? Suddenly her blood ran cold. The Missing Lads Case – the story she thought was not a story.

'Purging!' Morgana loudly announced, cutting through Mimi's latest onrush of thoughts. The happy chatter all around died instantly and was replaced by gasps. The atmosphere of nervous excitement was instantly palpable. The girl at the front had not turned with a smile as all the others had done. She was standing with her hand over her mouth, looking shaken and pale. Yet *all* the girls looked pale – how had Mimi not noticed this before? This one definitely had the widest hips to have been measured that night. Her bum was pronounced, though not as much as

Mimi's own. Whatever this 'purging' meant, the bottom seemed to be the offender. By the look on the girl's face she was to get something much less pleasurable than the elixir promised to the others.

A hush had descended. The last girl had not returned to her seat but had gone to stand in front of the witch's desk, her back to the class. She was in trouble for sure, and all the others were glad about it. Mimi was going to ask her neighbour what was going on but Morgana was suddenly right there in front of her, bending forward to say in measured tones that class for her was over and that it was time for her to go. The witch backed her statement with a little smile and a nod, to show there was no room for negotiation. Despite the strangeness of this gathering, all Mimi wanted to do was stay and find out what was coming to the chosen girl, what other bizarre rituals were due to be played out that night.

As Mimi reluctantly left the room, her bottom seemed to her miraculously unharmed, merely glowing with residual pleasure. She knew her departure was being monitored so she duly got into her car and drove off some hundred yards or more until she was around a bend and covered by a stand of trees. There she pulled over, got out again and hurried through the blackness back towards the small square of light showing from the single small window at the rear of the clubhouse. Despite her earlier exertions, her need to witness proceedings got her there quicker than she could have hoped. The window was too high but an upturned discarded beer crate proved an adequate booster. She tentatively peered in, getting a view almost identical to the one she would have had from her desk, and almost fell off her perch with surprise.

In her absence the girl at the desk had been bent over it, her tracksuit and knickers in a heap on the floor. Standing on one side of her fat, stuck-out rear end was one of the other girls, holding a large pewter jug. On her other side was Morgana, the long red robe she had been wearing now pulled up around her middle as she placed what seemed to be some long object into a harness at her crotch. Mimi had seen strap-ons during her internet searches, so there was no doubt what was to happen. However, what then stood out from the witch's crotch was no ordinary dildo. It looked more like some kind of animal horn, with a gentle upward curve. It was smooth and tapered, although not to a point, as if the end had been snipped off.

The witch said something and her helper tipped the jug and carefully poured out a thick, bright liquid, blood-red in colour, all over the naked arse of the victim. The liquid gleamed and clung to her skin, sticking and covering the rump, sliding ever so slowly down the backs of her legs.

In all the excitement, Mimi had failed to notice that the witch had now removed her outer gown and stood in only heels and a black basque, her buttocks almost entirely on view except for the top portion covered by the harness at her waist. And what a bottom she had, simply the most glorious one Mimi could imagine, the most exciting thing she had ever witnessed. She had always quite liked the sight of other girls but never lusted after any. Now, suddenly, this bare female bottom was the sexiest thing she had ever clapped eyes upon and she wanted it more than anything else, ever. She didn't even know what to *do* with it – smother herself with it, taste it; *anything* just to be worshipping it.

Mimi was totally transfixed as she watched the witch hold the girl by the hips and drive herself forward against the punished rump. Back and forth the witch went, her full, white, peachy-soft arse cheeks so firm they barely wobbled as they slammed the horn home. It was a rough fucking that transfixed all witnesses. More and more Mimi was tempted to smash the glass to get to the witch's bottom, to *give* herself to it. She didn't know whether the victim was having puss or bottom filled but she suspected – hoped – it was the latter. She even forced her hand down the back of her jeans and knickers to find her own tiny hole with her finger and pushed it in as best she could, just to have some idea of the joy the purged victim was now feeling.

At last the Priestess left the girl and perched on a desk on the other side of the room, whilst her victim lay spent.

Two other girls were summoned to Morgana's side and she kissed them lightly in turn. They worked away at her back and then, to Mimi's delight, the basque was lifted away and the witch was left with her breasts free. If her bottom had been a revelation the breasts were every bit as captivating. Mimi heard herself sob with the desperation of not being able to touch the witch. She knew the juice that had been leaching from her all evening would now be visibly soaking her denim-covered crotch. Her pussy felt absolutely molten. Never did she think she could be so hopelessly attracted to another human being, let alone a female. She was utterly spellbound.

Morgana again kissed the girls who had stripped her, more forcefully this time. Then she was pushing them down and they were seeking her nipples. Mimi watched, eaten up with jealousy, as the Priestess closed her eyes, gasped and threw her head back. The two girls sucked hard, clutching and squeezing the beautiful firm breasts as they feasted. Morgana had to pull them off by the hair, such was their hunger. She held the soft orbs herself, one in each hand, holding them in triumph, her fingers rising to pinch the nipples. Then Mimi saw it. Again she hit her nose on the glass as she instinctively peered in for a closer look.

There was a small drop at the end of one teat, a pure white tear of milk from the witch's nipple. Morgana took the drip onto her finger and raised it to her lips. She closed her eyes as if in rapture and let out a laugh of glee. The two girls looked hungrily on as their Priestess coaxed more drops from her teats, squeezing and pulling at them so that the drips flowed faster.

Two more girls were summoned up and they pushed the others aside and fell upon the tits to gorge themselves. Again they drank as if it was their lifeblood and both had to be forcibly pulled away to give the next two their turn. The girls who had been given the first taste of the witch's milk then began to forcibly kiss this next pair, as if hoping to steal the last remnants of the precious liquid from their lips. That word came instantly back to mind: *elixir*.

How Mimi wanted to taste it. She didn't care if it bewitched her or even cursed her. The next two were now gorging themselves, their cheeks hollow with the force of their sucking, the supply seemingly endless. Morgana still had her eyes shut and her mouth open in a wide smile, gasping from time to time at the joy of being feasted upon so hard. She pulled them back by their hair to tease the girls and both instinctively sucked harder upon the nipple, catching it in their teeth, such was their reluctance to lose it. Mimi saw each teat stretch impossibly before pinging clear of the biting grip.

As soon as Morgana released her hold of the girls' hair they were back suckling again. Their greed clearly gave the witch much pleasure. She stroked the girl's backs and kissed the top of their heads tenderly. She whispered to them in turn and they responded by pulling down their tracksuits and knickers to get their bottoms bare. The girls each grasped and crushed the firm flesh of the breast at their mouth, their urgency seeming to increase as they felt their Priestess's hand sliding down behind them towards their bare behinds.

Morgana buried her fingers into them from the rear, two digits pushing between the squashed mounds of their buttocks, seeking their warmest place. Mimi could see from the way the girl's eyes screwed shut in pleasure that the fingers were inside them. Imagine having that beautiful woman's slender fingers filling your melting pussy while her sweet milk flooded your mouth.

The situation was building. In tasting the milk the girls were by no means sated, merely more aroused. The four who had already suckled were kissing each other hungrily, their faces wet from their passion. The two still feeding did so with ever greater greed, especially now that Morgana's juice-slippery fingers were pumping in and out of them with vigour. The one still to have her turn, Mimi's recent class neighbour, was standing with the small of her back pulled in, knees tight together and one hand pressed hard to her crotch, as if trying to hold back a deluge. Mimi recalled the 'playtime' this one girl had referred to. She couldn't wait to witness it.

As Mimi unzipped her jeans, ready to shove her hand

inside her knickers, there was a loud crack from below and she felt the crate beneath collapsing on one side. She scrabbled at the ledge for a hold but missed, bashing her fingertips instead on the underside of the thin ledge. With nothing holding her there it was impossible for Mimi to remain in view from the inside. She should have disappeared from sight the moment the plastic gave way beneath her. However, she seemed to take ages to fall, like she was hovering cartoon-like in thin air. It was long enough for her to see the Priestess's eyes open from their rapture and focus upon the window. Enough to see the feasting girls release their suction grip in surprise.

Then Mimi was sprawling on the ground. Panic was coursing through her once more as she tried to fathom whether she had been seen. If she had been back far enough from the window then surely she would have been shrouded in darkness and invisible from the room. But she remembered the cold of the glass on her nose and the spread of mist on the pane from each panting breath. She was up and running. There was no time to move the broken crate and it would have to remain as damning evidence. If she was quick they might not get out in time to see her disappear behind the far treeline. From there her car was not visible and her escape would be masked.

She thought she heard the distant sound of a door opening but she couldn't be sure. Was that voices? She seemed to be running in treacle. Despite the adrenalin flooding through her, she was moving far slower now than when she had run to get to the building in the first place. They would surely see her and identify her as the spy. Then what? She needed to be gone but she couldn't cover the ground. It was like the treeline that spelled safety was on a conveyor belt, always moving away from her. It was going to be worse than just being seen and identified. They were going to run her down and catch her, right here. She was sure she could feel them at her back but she couldn't bring herself to look. It was like a gathering force, a gush coming unstoppably her way, a tempest or a wave building behind her and catching her. She could feel the *whoosh!* in her ears and expected to be smashed to the floor at any second.

Then, as if someone had chopped out the final agonising twenty yards, she was suddenly there at her car, slapping her hands sharply against the roof to halt her momentum. The noise of the chasing force behind her died instantly. Rather than the expected massive impact she felt nothing but a breath of wind through her loose blouse, passing warm against her skin. She looked back and there was no one, nothing, just black silence and the same small distant square of light from the clubhouse window.

She drove off, cringing at the noise her starting engine made, taking the first hundred yards to freedom slowly and with no lights, constantly checking her mirrors. Nobody appeared in them. She had got away. Then she remembered the eyes of the Priestess the instant before they had disappeared from view. They had widened slightly, fired not with surprise but with excitement. They had shown recognition.

At home, Mimi had to masturbate twice in quick succession before she could even begin to get her head straight. She forced herself out of her room and into the lounge with the laptop, knowing the Spinster would be gone for another hour. That time would pass in a blur of frantic masturbation if she didn't pull herself together and concentrate. Beneath the crowding thoughts of the beautiful witch and her coven of lusty girls there were serious matters to think of. If they were going to come after her she needed to be armed with all the evidence against them she could find. There was talk of mysterious godlike figures and male slaves. If the last bit was true then it could mean a story to make her name, one that might even make the nationals. She typed the title *KIDNAPPED!* at the top of her page.

She had to focus on the scraps of information she had gleaned. If there was even the slightest truth in what the girl had said in class then it had to be followed up. Firstly, who *were* these girls at the class? She had never seen any of them before and by their accents some at least were clearly not local. So where did they come from and where did they go afterwards? They couldn't all stay with Morgana. What were they being taught at the class, since weight-loss didn't seem to be the primary objective? Also, there was the mention of a 'Lord'. If he existed, who was he and how was he able to lurk unseen within the estate? Sure, the owner was nearly always away and the Big House was mostly shut up, but an estate manager oversaw things, even if it was a huge territory to cover. Most importantly there was the mention of slaves. Even if it were untrue, her neighbouring classmate had clearly believed they existed.

She began to scour her borrowed library books for any clues, but the thoughts of Morgana were ghosting back, like she was compelled to think of her above all things. She was so beautiful, from head to toe, so completely captivating. This immediate, overwhelming crush upon another female was inexplicable. Mimi had fantasised about making love to another girl maybe ten times in her life, yet she felt sure she might have to double that count in this single evening. In fact, even as she sat there her eyes were closing and her breathing was becoming fitful and she knew she was swiftly losing the battle to avoid frigging herself off right there in the front room before the Spinster came back.

'If kidnapping's your subject then you're in the right village.'

Mimi jumped a mile, the hand that had been heading inexorably towards her crotch shooting up guiltily to cover her little yelp of surprise. She hadn't even heard the Spinster come in the front door, let alone into the room. Thank God she hadn't given in to the reckless voice in her head urging her to go and get the little bullet vibe out of its hiding place. She mumbled a few things about investigating local rumours, mainly to try and cover her embarrassment. Fortunately the Spinster was raring to give her thoughts on the subject.

'It's that Haydn Shady, you mark my words. Remember I know Mary Trimble and she knew Sergeant Butler *very* well, if you catch my meaning, and he always said Shady was renowned for his kidnapping. None of them ever found, he says. *And* he's back round here, though some reckon he never left. Hiding out, they reckon.'

The sound of the villain's name had Mimi's belly tingling. First the missing lads, now Haydn Shady, the two subjects of stories she had thought buried, now both mentioned in the same evening, and apparently linked. However, if there was one thing the Spinster was renowned for, it was for talking shit.

'What do you mean, he's back?' Mimi asked, now a little more composed.

'Don't forget I know Old Aggy and she says she saw him. Her son was driving her over Hughenden way last week and she saw the man himself riding his horse on the back roads. She might be completely dotty but she says it was definitely him. No mistaking them eyes, she says, and she should know.'

'What's wrong with his eyes?' Mimi asked, trying to dredge up any forgotten references to the villain's appearance.

'Old Aggy was the only one I know to have seen them. He always wore dark glasses, but she used to do pruning in the orchard for the old Baron and when the land was sold she just kept on doing what she always did. One day she walked slap-bang into Shady, took him totally by surprise. That's when she saw his eyes. Cold as ice they were, almost turned her to stone.'

Mimi could feel the blood fizzing in her veins.

'Tell me *everything* you know about witches in the village and Haydn Shady,' she said.

The Spinster gave a little look that seemed to say, *oh, so now all of a sudden you are interested in what I have to say when before you never gave me the time of day,* but the instinct to gossip was just too great to ignore. She pulled up a chair, put her hand on Mimi's forearm and launched into her speech.

'Well, now ...' she began.

Mimi tried to listen, she really did, but those thoughts of Morgana kept coming back. Every time the word 'witch' was mentioned, the vivid images popped back into her head, however much she tried to drive them out. She couldn't help seeing the witch as a sexy and overwhelmingly enticing figure. Nothing the Spinster said could stop the images of Morgana behind her, with her horn at her waist and her basque enclosing her curves. Mimi had no idea why she was so taken by this mysterious witch, or why she wasn't planning to run a mile now that the connection with Haydn Shady had given everything a decidedly sinister dimension.

The witch was almost certainly coming for her soon. Danger was looming large and she seemed unable to drag herself away from it. If it had just been her journalistic instincts taking over then perhaps she could have forgiven herself, but in truth she knew she was driven by a sexual urge she had never felt before. Instead of heading for cover, she decided that the thing she *must* do, as soon as possible, was pay another visit to the ravishing Priestess.

4

The Master reclined on the velvet-covered chaise and gripped his erect prick at its base, holding it upright so it could be regarded with awe. He felt a rush of power and pride and exhaled in a snarl. Looking down his naked torso, all toned and oiled, and seeing this huge weapon, he knew why they all worshipped him with such fervour. It would be impossible not to. He did enjoy clasping his own prick. It was a constant smug reminder of why he ruled over these minions. Every time he gripped it he thrilled at how it filled his palm, like it was the first time he had ever seen or felt it. He couldn't believe the rigid thickness of it, as wide as his own strong wrist.

In truth he was sure it had grown bigger over the last few years, perhaps somehow through pride. Maybe it had expanded like any muscle that was constantly worked. Possibly, just possibly, it had grown through Morgana's secret handiwork; a spell maybe, or a potion slipped in his wine – she was certainly very fond of spiking his drinks. Strange, he couldn't remember how large it had been in the years before he joined the coven as their god. He was sure it had always been big, but *this* big? Perhaps the spell only made him *think* it was so huge. Or maybe the spell made everyone who looked at it think it was huge, when in reality it was of far more meagre dimensions, which is why it could fit into the tight passages on constant offer to him. He didn't care. As long as everyone gasped when they saw it and trembled at the thought of taking it, he was happy.

'Would you like me to suck you, my Lord?' said the girl, looking hopeful.

'Dance for me,' he replied brusquely.

The slave girl bowed her head in obedience and rose to her feet. There was music in the background – there was *always* music – just loud enough for her to pick up a rhythm to gyrate to. She closed her eyes, lifted her arms above her head and started to move from the waist, incorporating some of the belly-dancing moves that the witch had taught her. God, that witch knew how to seduce. Even when she wasn't here her hand was in everything, an echo of her taunting presence. It seemed like hers was the only *cunnus* in the world his great prick had not been inside, and since hers was also the most beautiful his failure to slay her with a weapon all others found irresistible mocked him relentlessly. She never explained why she refused him. It drove him to distraction and they both knew he would not rest until he had been inside her. Of course he would have to rape her to do so, and he was supremely comfortable with this. In fact, since she teased him so mercilessly, he now wouldn't want it any other way.

He knew full well that some of the potions she slipped him made him long for her. Although her spells gave him this constant nagging need to see her, he had taught other parts of his brain to be glad when she wasn't around. Times like these, when she was elsewhere training her new girls, provided much-needed respite and a chance to indulge in his powers without being judged. Down here in the converted basement beneath the Big House he was sealed off from her, if only temporarily.

When he had purchased this place from the old Baron he immediately spent a vast sum renovating the disused servants' quarters and wine cellar that constituted the huge subterranean basement. He envisaged it as a bunker, a private refuge to escape the law, or his enemies, should they ever come looking for him. Visitors not in the know would never dream what lay beneath their feet, and even if you did know you could spend hours and never hope to locate the secret entrance. First he had seen it as a place to house the coven girls, but Morgana insisted they live under her jurisdiction. He therefore converted the stable block on the far side of the estate to act as their quarters. The basement, he decided, would instead act as his Pleasure Palace. There would be his private chamber, a small dorm for the planned handful of male slaves, kitchen and toilet facilities, and the Fuck Room where he currently sat, designed to house his miniature orgies.

The whole place was soundproofed at great expense, so from the outside the house would seem uninhabited, although below stairs it could be a hive of wanton activity. He barely needed to use the rest of the house if he didn't want to. It could act solely to create the impression of an abode for a legitimate businessman. He had the plans of the house redrawn so that no cellar appeared. A future owner might never even know of its existence. He could almost continue to live in it without them knowing he was there, although he might have to turn the sound down on the giant speakers that filled the Fuck Room with rave music. One day, centuries from now, some archaeologists might unearth it like a new Tutankhamun's tomb, and wonder at the power and sexual prowess of the god who created it.

The girl removed her top to reveal her ample breasts and pushed them together as she bent forward towards him, showing off a cleavage that his cock might like to be enveloped in. She seemed to be doing less of a belly-dance now and more of a lap dance, which was probably what she did to make money before he found her. Now she was in his care, so money was irrelevant. He paid all her expenses, charged no rent and kept her in food and clothing, as he did with all the coven girls. He even purported to pay them a retainer, a generous monthly sum paid into a special account that could be accessed if any ever decided to go back to a 'normal' life. He occasionally let them see how much they were accruing whilst living this life of pleasure. Little did they know that the accounts were all bogus and would only ever pay out to him. In the grand scheme of things the amounts he supposedly paid represented only a tiny fraction of his vast wealth, and he could well afford to pay them for the delight they gave him in return, but he just *had* to double-cross them. He couldn't help himself.

The dancing girl turned again, wiggling her knicker-clad rump and pushing it in his direction. Her fingers looped around the thin sides of her underwear. She had a big behind, bigger than what he considered perfect. There were even signs of some dimpling in the portion of the cheek poking out of the bottom of her knickers. She was looking over her shoulder at him, the lust evident in her eyes. The eyes then dropped to his groin and her bum went right out, in time with the downward movement of her hands, so in one deft move her arse was suddenly bare and stuck out, a mere two feet from his face.

The sex was puffy and poked out proud of the large thighs, as if it was desperate for its own sight of his erection. The buttocks were lewdly apart and he could see the oval of her dark, as yet unbleached anus. It looked nothing but rude to him. Seeing the direction of his glance, she made a show of licking her finger and reaching back to wipe her saliva around her little ring, before pushing just the tip inside. Then she removed her finger, gripped her cheeks with both hands and splayed her cheeks apart. The message was clear: *please do to me what you did last time*. That last time she had been amongst bushes, impaled upon Morgana's silver dildo whilst he entered from the rear and gave her the fucking of her young life. Whilst yesterday he had enjoyed the initiate from that same ceremony, tonight he had the victim of the hunt. He had a different treat in mind for her.

This girl had received that punishment for failing to come up to his demands in physical appearance. After any punishment the victim spent time under his jurisdiction to recuperate, and so he could decide when she was fit for a return to the training classes. By the look of her she was not ready, and perhaps she never intended to be. While she was there he hadn't yet used her personally, but he had farmed her out to some of his rougher business associates.

This particular girl was fast becoming the thin end of the wedge. He had already realised that some of the trainees deliberately attracted punishments so that they could be put to the hunt. Some returning victims might have told the others in guarded whispers of his beautiful cock and how he used it on them to teach them their lesson. If they *wanted* to be punished they wouldn't focus on getting perfect for him. They just wanted sex, with anyone, when their sole aim should have been readying themselves for him alone. There was no incentive to train, to get their bodies in shape, to take their role seriously. He couldn't risk sending them for bleaching when they might balloon in size on their return. They would remain fat nearly-witches, and he was fuelling their indolence every time he fucked them.

It wasn't like they didn't get fair warning to behave. If they failed to keep to the allotted regime they received a first warning, and had to undergo the ritual of purging in front of their classmates. If they still failed to come up to scratch they received their second and final warning in the guise of The Pounding, a rite he himself had dreamed up. This was done here in the Fuck Room, with all the Order present to witness it. The victim was placed on a treadmill with a leash around her neck bound to the control panel, so that she was pulled forward. She therefore had to run in an uncomfortable manner, bent forwards, which thrust her bottom out. The pace of the treadmill was not excessive but her problems were compounded by a fucking machine positioned at her rear, with a piston arm leading to a thick black ten-inch dildo attachment that buffeted the entrance of her well-oiled sex. The speed of the treadmill was set to gradually increase, so she had to maintain her pace with the prick slapping in and out between her labia.

God forbid she should stop or be unable to keep up, because she would be sent flying back onto the hard false prick and the hammer action would drive it into her. If she could not regain her footing she would be held there by the dildo and would have to seek out the little blocks at the side that acted like stirrups to keep her in position, bent forwards with her rump out as the prick pistoned its full length in and out of her body. The punishment went on as long as he decided necessary, and while she was in the stirrups the bacchantes were allowed to step forward and do whatever they wanted to her.

Incredibly, some girls still did not think this enough to put them back on the straight and narrow. Some had transgressed again, and thus found themselves the victim of The Hunt. This ritual was the most mystical, the most talked of and longed for. All the coven girls were desperate to be a part of it, although it seemed that some were so desperate they were willing to forgo the thrill of being a hunter and engineered it so they became the victim instead. This was hardly the point of the training classes. One serial offender even had to be prematurely promoted to the ranks of the bacchantes, because they did not know what else to do with her after she had been put twice to the hunt. That highlighted the folly of his system.

However, in essence, he loved the hunt. He saw it as the pivotal rite of their Order, where the bacchantes let themselves loose and let their primal spirit come forth.

It was where they were closest to the myths and he felt most divine. He wanted to give them *real* victims to hunt, not bitches who craved it so much they barely ran. There was no sense in using his own trainees. He had therefore decided this particular girl was not going back. From now on, the hunted girls would be exempt from a return to training. They would still worship him, and be desperate for him again, but he could use this in other ways. If they weren't prepared to dedicate themselves to him in the way he wanted, they would be used entirely for his ends, not for the good of the coven. He would use them as sweeteners in his less legal business deals, perhaps traded. He had a lot of Bulgarian business associates who had great use for pretty girls with big bums, so perhaps she would end up with one of them. Until then she would be used when the need took him, like now.

An athletic figure dressed in a toga came into his periphery but he didn't take his eyes off the girl's bottom.

'More wine, Master?' said the slave.

Why couldn't Morgana's girls be more like his slaves? His did everything asked of them without question. They played their roles to perfection and knew their place. The one he had picked out to serve him tonight was his new favourite, the young Dominic. He had liked him the first moment he saw him. He had felt his prick stiffen at some suppressed thought, and had to send Gavin back out with the new charge before his bulge became obvious.

It was Gavin the Head Slave who had found Dominic, and he had surpassed himself. It had been via the rugby club, as usual. He wasn't sure quite why so many of these well-educated, fit young rugby-playing lads were so comfortable with their sexuality and so willing to experiment, but they were and he wasn't going to argue. Gavin had said it would be a source of rich pickings, and he should know. He was then captain of the rugby team, the type of sporty, intelligent, good-looking lad that all the girls fancied and all the guys looked up to. It was seemingly impossible not to form a crush on him. His penchant was for rough sex, especially with him on the receiving end. Very few had given him what he craved. Very few dared. He considered most too beneath him to let them try, until Haydn Shady came along.

The Master let the slave fill his goblet. The lad's hands were trembling, a combination of excitement and trepidation, no doubt. The slave was trying not to regard his Master's body, but could not help himself.

'Do you like what you see?' the Master said, nodding towards the girl's stuck-out rump, although both he and the slave knew he was really referring to his great prick.

'I do, my Lord,' said Dominic the slave, 'very much so.'

The Master sneered and took a gulp of wine.

'Sit on me,' he commanded. 'Backwards.'

It was music to the girl's ears and she let go a little whimper of joy. She straddled the chaise and lowered herself down onto his prick, which he was still gripping at its base. He grunted aloud as her slick lips kissed his swollen tip and spread to engulf him. The warmth was glorious and he reminded himself that this surely eclipsed any feeling he could gain from another man.

She squatted over him, breathing hard, trying to relax herself enough to sink down. However, this fucking was not designed for her benefit nor would she ever have the chance to feel him inside her again, so the Master impatiently put his hand on her shoulder and pressed down hard to force her upon him. She took half his meat before the girth arrested her movement. She cried out. Her juice dribbled down his shaft onto his tight, smooth ball sack. He pushed again and down she slid until her bottom was squashed to his groin. She dutifully arched her back and leaned forward, so he could be afforded a view of her stretched sex.

She rode him, slowly at first, waiting until she had opened up. He could tell from her noise that she was already nearing ecstasy. As she relaxed she was able to increase her tempo and force, so that her buttocks could slap against him. The shuddering jolt through her flesh was mesmerising, but her bottom just did not have the pristine beauty of Morgana's. The skin was not white but pink, and not even uniformly so. His prick actually twitched, enjoying the imperfection because it made her somehow more real. However, his disciplined mind pushed the thoughts away. Yes, she was good, but she was not good enough to deserve *him*.

The slave still positioned at his shoulder was breathing more heavily now. A quick glance to the side revealed a billowing in the fabric covering the slave's crotch. That was one very good thing about this particular lad: he was seemingly incapable of keeping his prick down. It was obvious that he was drawn less to the sight of the girl and more to the glimpses of the Master's cock. The Master allowed himself a smile of satisfaction. The view was indeed compelling. The stretched skin of his member was smooth and lightly tanned like the rest of him. It was seemingly gossamer thin and covered prime muscle. This meat was thick enough at the base to balance a goblet upon, when he was in the correct position. In fact, one of his games was to do so, and to have a girl on all fours ride his shaft with backward thrusts and make him come, without spilling a drop of his wine.

The girl was squealing now, as well she might, since he was filling her so completely. He *knew* this was what all the girls wanted above all. They wanted to be stretched open beyond what they believed possible. They wanted to be spitted to their bellies on the fattest pricks. When they were full, they wanted even more. He knew this because he took all his pointers from porn sites and magazines. He always had. It had never entered his head, even for a second, nor would it ever do so, to ask one of his conquests what *she* liked. Why the fuck would he? He had a huge prick, so he *knew* what they wanted. He wasn't interested in love or tenderness – just pure, raw, filthy fucking. If he offered a huge cock, rode them hard and with great stamina, and then showered them with his beautiful hot seed, they would want him for ever. If they came in a panting, semi-conscious heap then he knew he would be a god in their eyes, and that swelled his ego. Fucking was, after all, not about two people but about *him* – about how magnificent *he* was.

When he felt her juice pooling at his arse he knew she was ready for more proof of his magnificence. He reached around for her breasts and clasped them, pulling her back so that her weight was against him. She had to adjust her feet, placing them on his thighs to get more purchase as she wriggled upon his cock. She still didn't know what she was about to get.

'Do you like what you see?' said the Master again to his slave.

'Yes, my Lord,' the slave replied, although the tent at the front of his toga already demonstrated his excitement perfectly.

'Slide your *mentula* inside her, above mine,' the Master commanded.

He heard the slave's breath falter, but the lad still went immediately into action on his word. The toga was pulled up to expose the bare, slim erection and the slave grasped it at the base. He straddled the chaise and hunkered down, pointing his prick at the little piece of darkness below the clit. The Master felt the slave's warm balls sink down upon his own, then the heat of the smaller erection against his shaft.

The girl warbled loudly as the lad pushed into her, but the Master was only concentrating on the feel of the smooth glide of prick against his. It was a scintillating friction, travelling all along his length as the cock was pushed slowly into the girl to stretch her even wider. He could feel the pulse of the slave's lovely erection, even detect the underside of the silky exposed head now just touching his sensitive, stretched frenum.

There was a pause while the girl relaxed after this further invasion and the slave adjusted his weight so that he could find scope to move. The slave began a slow in-and-out thrust, sliding back and forth over the Master's prick so that every vein and detail could be felt by the other. The Master couldn't see the slave's face, which was maybe just as well, since eye contact might have been perceived as affection between them. He didn't want the slave to have any inkling how much he was enjoying the feel of him.

It was the first time he had committed this particular act, having studied it closely many times on porn websites. Although it could be taken as an act of utter depravity, with no homosexual overtones intended, he was still only prepared to do it in this relative privacy. He had selected this slave in particular, not just for his slim, smooth prick, but because he was clearly a submissive, and, once sworn to secrecy, would never dare blab about these proceedings to the others. In truth he also picked him for his handsome face and fit body, but those reasons were quickly pushed back into the darker part of his mind.

The Master waited for the slave to find a rhythm and then he joined it, pulling his hips downwards on the slave's out-stroke and then pushing them up as the cock above his was driven back inside the girl. Thus they were fucking her in tandem, two hot pricks together forcing her as open as she had ever been. She bathed them in her come as a reward. The Master clasped the girl's breasts again to give him extra purchase. He stretched the nipples hard, like the bacchantes did to their Priestess.

Such a thought made him lust again after Morgana. His inability to have her drove him to distraction. It made him fuck the other girls harder and come with huge, wrenching force, but it also made him want to tear his hair out. Sometimes, quite often these days, he simply wanted to kill her. He might well have done so already, had he thought it possible. But how do you kill an immortal? The sudden anger he felt for the Priestess and her teasing ways made him pinch the girl's nipples even harder as he sank his cock as far into her as he could.

The slave reacted to this stronger thrust and matched

his Master's force and speed. The girl was saturated now and the Master released his grip on her breasts to hold her behind the knees, pulling her thighs wide apart. The movement inside her was still difficult but the feel of the other prick on his more than compensated for it. He could hear from the slave's sighs and panting breaths that he was enjoying it enough to be close to a climax.

The rod above his slipped out without ceremony. The slave was quickly at his side, his jerking prick pointing skywards as the girl grinned at it in her euphoria. She unhurriedly took hold of it and snaked her tongue out over the tip twice, three times. It was exquisite torture and a demonstration of incredible willpower, since she was drooling so much she must have been dying to swallow him. The Master was almost furious that she should tease the slave so, but he gave her no orders, so intent was he to watch the way she teased and then engulfed the prick and gently sucked. It was a method that had the slave crying out and weakening at the knees, a style to be admired and remembered for future reference. Her hand movement on the shaft remained frustratingly slow. Could the Master possibly grasp the slave's prick and toss him swiftly into the girl's mouth? Was there any way this act could be seen as something other than gay desire?

As it happened the girl beat him to it, suddenly sending her fist at blurring speed up and down the iron-hard cock as she closed her eyes and sucked. The slave yelped like a girl as he unloaded into her, throwing his head back and grasping his own buttocks. It was clearly a powerful eruption but she took it all and didn't let him back out until he was on the verge of collapse and his now softening prick had been entirely emptied. All the time she had sucked him she had still ridden the Master, jerking her hips back and forth in the hope of forcing him to spray her insides. He had to admire her wantonness. If bitches like this could be so utterly rude before all the magic had been instilled in them, before they could be properly indoctrinated by a love of the Dark Arts and the ways of Paculla Annia, then was there really a need for a Priestess to guide them at all?

The Master lifted her up off his hard prick. She would have been happy to have milked him there and then, and he might have liked the release while the thought of the slave's cock against his was so still vivid. However, if there was one thing he had learned about being a god, it was to never come just because you wanted to. Always make it memorable. She needed a rest but would be granted little. The Master took her over to one of his Fuck Tables and laid her upon it, face down.

This particular piece of apparatus was one of his favourites. About the size of a pool table, it had different layers that could be removed from or added to the surface, depending on the desired function. It was currently stripped down to its base layer. It had a padded top in black, and restraints in each corner that he used to secure the girl. Towards the centre, where the girl's crotch was now hovering, a little square was cut out. Half of a disc protruded some two inches from the surface. This disc was like a small solid wheel, no larger or wider than one found on a skateboard, and made from soft, slightly ridged silicone gel. Beneath the table surface a spindle ran through the centre of the wheel to turn it, and the spindle was driven by a small motor. The wheel sat in a sump housed below the table top and filled with oil, so that as it turned its surface was always replenished with lubrication. The Master chose olive oil as his lubricant, since it was what the Romans would have done, had they invented such a table.

The Master pressed a button and the wheel began to spin, quite slowly at first. The girl's crotch was mere centimetres from it. She would feel the breeze its rotation produced upon her clit. She was still too turned on to be able to bear such extreme, relentless pleasure, but soon her muscles would tire and she would drop into contact with it. Then she would have to strain every muscle in her body to keep herself in position, to ensure she kept precise contact with the oily surface of the wheel so that it spun freely beneath her, just buffing her clit. Too much contact would be excruciating, maybe even harmful. Of course, this was only half the battle. To add to the torture he could position a fuck machine at the foot end, its long arm attached to whichever dildo he thought she deserved. She could be pummelled for as long as she could stay conscious, while the spinning silicone grindstone constantly dragged more and more orgasms from her ravaged body.

Or, instead, he could mount the table and fuck her himself, his weight of thrust driving her crotch hard into the wheel with repeated shocking intensity. This is what he chose to do, not just because he needed his own finish but because the slave was still there to witness it. He slipped into her from the back with minimal effort and she felt gloriously hot inside. He would have to hold himself above her and not press down, but this was a good thing, since it would show off the tensed muscles in his arms and thighs. His chest was in light contact with her back and his groin was pushing into the flesh of her soft bum. She squealed as the clit buffer did its work, and he could smell the taint of the slave's seed on her breath.

It would not be a long fuck, because even his stamina had its limits. He would use his hips to slide in and out of her and his forward press would hold her crotch to the wheel. She would come every half dozen times he thrust inside her. Better still, it would dawn on the slave that this was a position a man could take another man in – not with that spinning wheel perhaps, but elsewhere, in the Master's private chamber, for instance. The slave would jealously envisage himself in the girl's place. He would see his Master's measured strokes, feel the girl's rapture at being filled by him. It was deep and gentle and incredibly intense, almost an act of love by the Master. He balked at his own need to feel compassionate in the eyes of this slave, although he could not deny the urge was strong. He hated this flaw in his character, this weakness. He even closed his eyes and silently cursed Gavin for finding Dominic in the first place.

Everything was Gavin's fault. If not for him, the Master would never have been tempted away from the delights of female flesh. The young rugby captain claimed he could turn any straight man and that seemed to be the case. He had been working on the estate during the summer break from university, when it passed into Shady's hands. He went personally to meet the new owner, to argue a case for being kept on. Somehow he ended up with Shady's stiff bare prick in his hands. The villain, in a sudden burst of shame and rage, had struck him. This only fuelled their lusts and Gavin had left with a gash above his eye, his job secure, and a mouthful of his new boss.

Shady was quick to see that Gavin was a prime candidate to be the first slave of the coven. Myth dictated that men were present at Paculla Annia's bacchanals, and he needed his own private entourage if Morgana was to oversee all the girls. It helped him get more power back from the witch. It was Gavin who volunteered, after

112

only a little gentle persuasion, to bring in more boys. It was also his idea to write to his parents, telling them he was safe and not to come looking for him, which became the template for masking the disappearance of all the new recruits. Gavin remained the only male to have had the Master in his arse. Shady's shame at his own latent homosexuality burned terribly and the slave bore the brunt of this fury. Worse for Shady, he knew it meant Gavin held some power over him.

The Master fought back any more such instincts. He allowed certain slaves to suck him and he justified it to himself as being part of the orgiastic fervour, of the coven's ways. He resisted urges to do the same to his slaves, although some, Dominic especially, tested his resolve to its fullest. There was no way he could give in to his urges. He told himself it was just another of Morgana's curses, undermining him by making him want other men. To give in to what he seemed to crave most, to have Dominic's slim, wonderful prick up inside him, would be the ultimate emasculation. The coven would never forgive him for it, nor could he forgive himself. They wanted a warrior-god, a bitch-devouring Kurgan, not some effete prick-lover. The thought of his growing desire for his slave made him shrink inside, but it still made his cock swell.

He increased his thrust and the girl had to tense and push herself back to avoid having her clit crushed against the wheel. He gritted his teeth and thrust harder. The shuddering girl shrieked but he didn't let up. The sound of her bum cheeks slapping against him momentarily blanked out his thoughts of men. When he had eaten his fill he would go after Gavin and make him pay for corrupting his mind. He was getting way too big for his boots because he knew too much. Well, there were ways to sort that out once and for all.

The Master felt his balls tightening as they readied to unload. The feel of the girl's arse and *cunnus* was proving enough to take him to the edge after all. He stupidly allowed himself a glance towards Dominic and noticed that the slave's prick had grown again. The sight of that erection and the knowledge that it had gone hard again out of desire for his own sent the Master into a climactic passion. He was barely able to pull out.

He would have liked to finish inside her for the extra intensity of orgasm, but he wanted his ejaculation to be seen. It showed him at his most powerful, blasting his heavy jets of come all over his adoring girls. Also, the internet had taught him that, just as girls loved to be filled and fucked hard, gay lads loved the sight of huge cocks.

The bitterness filled him even as his last drops showered the girl. He climbed off and tersely ordered the slave to free the girl and take her away. She had to crawl out on her hands and knees. He had a flashback of his final thoughts just before he erupted. He quickly chased them away but not before he recognised the image of himself on his knees with Dominic pumping him from the rear. He felt angry and confused, not for the first time recently. He had an urge to bring the fucking machine into play, to get a dildo the size of Dominic's prick onto the piston arm and lie on the Fuck Table himself, to get it out of his system once and for all. However, Morgana would *know*, since she somehow seemed to know everything, and she would make sure his secret counted against him.

He had to gather his thoughts and make sense of them, make a plan of action. He had to reassert himself, because he could feel things slipping away. Primarily he had to stay as a god, because he could not exist without the constant adoration. The coven needed a god to make it real, so to maintain his position he need only ensure that the rites and beliefs of the coven were strictly adhered to. He had always thought that he needed the Priestess to make this so, but was that actually the case?

Morgana brought the magic, but then she taught it to her girls and they could teach others. Yes, she was the incarnation of the High Priestess, but now they had an actual *god*, the Beast of Depravity made flesh to worship. He could get new coven girls. He didn't need Morgana for this. He could even get slaves, now Gavin had shown him the richest source. Gavin had to go, that was for sure. He would be sent on holiday as a reward for good service. It would be a skiing trip, to Bulgaria, one he wouldn't come back from. He would keep the other slave lads for now, just in case.

The thought of getting rid of Morgana made him shiver. How could he live without the person he most needed and most craved? What if it was only her potions that fuelled his never-flagging desire, fired his dirty imagination, made his cock so mesmerising to all? But then, what if it was only her potions making him feel so dependent upon her, so in love with her? What if it was her making him feel as desperate to fill his slaves as he was to fill her, presumably so that she could stoke her own power and alone enjoy the pleasures of the bacchante girls?

The witch was certainly as conniving and power-hungry as she was beautiful. She had already broken their original agreement. She had promised him immortality but now held back from bestowing it, claiming the time was not right, when they both knew this was merely an excuse to retain a hold over him. She had promised to bring him girls *exactly* in her own image, but they never were. Some were close but her perfection was clearly impossible to recreate. If he couldn't have her double then he had to have her, but this was never allowed. He knew she *made* him desire her more to keep him at her side, but then, if he could never have her, was he not doomed to ever greater frustration? And if he could not have her, then why stick with her to be constantly reminded of the one pleasure eluding him? Was the witch the pivotal element of the Order, or was she now a redundant trouble-maker who mocked him daily with her refusals?

His mind was made up. It was time to enforce his will. The Order would be run by his rules from now on, not Morgana's. He would ruthlessly eliminate anyone who threatened his position, including smug Head Slaves, snooping fat-bummed journalists, even High Priestesses if it came to it. The witch had to be brought to heel. It was time for her to give in to him. He would take his pleasure at last, and thereafter whenever he wanted to. He knew he could not kill her, but then he was also shrewd enough to have gathered that Morgana was for some reason tied to the estate, and apparently unable to move away. This is why she had brought him here and made him stay under such a cloak of secrecy. He could move the entire coven to a different location, leaving her behind, but he feared she had spells in place to prevent this happening. He had, however, one more ace up his sleeve, and if the witch was not willing to give herself up to him then he was just about ready to play it. If he could not kill Morgana, or move her coven away from her, then the only alternative was to take her home away. He could do as he wished with the coven once the witch had her power base ripped from underneath her. And it just so happened that he knew of a very good way to do this.

5

Morgana slowly sucked the first two fingers of her left hand and then eased them deep into her warm sex. Her mind was full of the journalist girl. She knew she was The One. She had spied on her from afar before she had turned up for the first class but she hadn't realised just how similar she was to the one great love of her life. The hair was different and this new girl carried a little extra weight, but the face was almost identical. They could have been twins. They *must* have been twins. Only they couldn't be, because her previous lover had died of consumption nearly a century and a half before.

The sooner she could get this girl close to her the better. She knew *he* was after outsiders for sacrifice. His attention to the details of the legends seemed pathological. Either that or he was just using the legends as an excuse to vent his more disturbing carnal desires. While she needed to build, he was seemingly more intent on destroying what they had. It was as though he knew that the more girls

118

she controlled, the more her power intensified and the less she would need him. He wanted girls to be ripped and torn by the others. He wanted a fast turnover, some variety. He wanted the fear of him to fuel their lusts. He offered outsiders as their reward, thinking this would bring them closer to him.

She often cursed herself for seeking him out in the first place. However, magic was seldom done by pointing wands or wiggling your nose. Some took a huge amount of resources and time. Many situations were only served by using hard cash, and he was able to provide that. It was not the first time in her long history that she had needed to seek external help. Her coven always needed a god, such was the love of cock she herself had to fill them with. It was complex, but she was a being of pure lust, and so were her followers. Orgies could not survive on cunnies alone. Pricks were needed too. Unfortunately that meant serving a god who put himself first, even above her. These gods never quite understood that essentially they were only there to aid her continued existence.

She took her fingers from her quim and sucked at the juice. She never tired of her own taste. How could she, when she had given herself such sweet nectar? Her girls thirsted for it. They would jump into fire for one more taste. Of course *he* was always after it too. He wanted all of her, all of the time, and she didn't help by pouring her libido-strengthening elixir of John the Conqueror root into his ear whenever he slept. However, she needed to keep him focused and sometimes potions were the best way, especially now he seemed increasingly intent on breaching the arses of his slaves rather than any of the delightful quims on offer.

A delicate balance existed between Priestess and God. They needed each other but their motives were intrinsically different. He was desperate to fuck her. At times it seemed like his life depended on it. Hers actually *did* depend on refusing it. Many times she had resorted to spells to prevent him raping her. One time she had forgotten to paint on her third eye before she slept and had woken just in time to see him between her thighs, his great prick about to descend. She was only just able to transform it into the helpless, tiny appendage of an infant before it slapped harmlessly against her. Of course she turned it back once the danger was averted. He never seemed to begrudge her using these powers. It just made him more determined to have her.

He didn't realise that to fuck her was to kill her. Only she knew that as soon as any man breached her *cunnus* to the hilt all her powers would be transferred to him. She would lose everything and he would gain it all. Her immortality would be immediately lost and since she was so ancient she would wither and turn to dust on the spot. The spirit of Paculla Annia would leave her, to be reborn in another place, within another person. She,

Morgana, would be no more. The soul she carried would continue, but she would know nothing of it, condemned instead to everlasting darkness.

Before the High Priestess died, over two millennia ago, she had laid this curse. This greatest female paragon of decadence, the woman who had allowed men into her private circle to share in her banquets of debauchery, suddenly found how thankless males could be. They were jealous of her power and wanted her dethroned. Under a guise of being fearful of the rise of female influence in politics, men embarked on history's first recorded witch hunt, and High Priestess Paculla Annia was their target. When finally seized, she was tortured and raped by a series of those very politicians who claimed her sins were the worst evil. Before she expired she swore to return to haunt them. She would live once more to mock their hypocrisy by encouraging ever greater sin. She vowed never to let any flesh cock inside her again, and mankind would be driven mad by being robbed of this exquisite pleasure.

Morgana carried this soul, born inside her along with the secrets and knowledge of magic that the High Priestess had died with. She would go on living in whatever guise she chose for herself, as long as she never betrayed the soul of Paculla Annia and let a male inside her. It proved hard. As much as she adored female flesh, temptation often threatened to overwhelm her. His was one of the hardest to refuse, not that she would ever tell him that. He thought she just refused him because she was a stick-in-the-mud lesbian, and he was determined to break her. Of course, if he knew he would get all her power if he succeeded, he would never rest for a second until he had done so.

At least he accepted her abilities without question. Most thought her deranged. A local doctor had once tried to get her sectioned, but look where that had got him. The consensus was that her pagan practices were spawned by nothing more than an excess of drink and drugs, which fuelled her inherent wickedness and nymphomania. Many scoffed at her claims to have lived for so long. They would exclaim with incredulity, 'But we knew your mother, God rest her tortured soul! We brought the fresh towels to your cottage the day you were born! You used to go to school with our children! You would steal the sandwich from their lunchbox and replace it with a frog from the village pond, and then say you had magicked the sandwich into the frog! We were with your mother the day you drove her to madness – the day you were expelled for pulling Tilly Cartwright's knickers down in class because she said you had burned her cat!'

She just laughed at them. They knew none of this. It was all a fabrication she had planted in their minds. They didn't understand the powers she had to make them believe whatever she wanted them to. Sure, she didn't quite understand them herself, and couldn't remember casting most of these memory-warping spells. And true, her memories of her long existence were now clouded and sometimes seemed more like dreams than reality. However, clearly the *soul* within her fully understood all of its powers and it made sure all the intricacies were covered on her behalf, by magic. *It* clearly acted for her, ensuring certain realities never came to light. The soul of the dead Priestess didn't want them knowing the truth. It didn't want another witch hunt.

A few locals took her for what she was. Despite the scoffing, a couple of the old farmers still paid her good money for the spells she cast to ensure a good yield. Once upon a time the girls of the village would come to her for potions to rid themselves of anything from colds to big feet. They would beg her for spells to cast over the good-looking lads in the hope of getting them up the aisle. There were plenty of them, now in old age, that she had taken sexual favours from half a century before. If they wanted her potions she would make them bare their backsides and bend over to take her fingers. If they came in twos for protection she would make them strip their knickers and rub their cunnies together before she handed anything over.

All of these had forgotten this now, or claimed to have. They were the ones who denounced her the loudest. They said she was a deranged fantasist, a deviant with evil at her core, a siren who tried to lure innocent girls onto her sinful rocks. She was a pervert, they said. She caused babies to be stillborn and put dead rats in people's drainpipes. When they woke to find their garden blooms all withered and brown, it wasn't the unexpected frost, it was *her*, drinking evil potions and urinating upon their flower beds. To think she had once given these women their first orgasms.

Of course, while they aged she stayed young, and there were other generations that had their first kisses with her, felt her fingers inside their virgin quims. But now the girls were fewer. The new influx was of rich executive types with either very young families or kids that had grown and gone. The incomers didn't know of her. No one cared for the old tales or knew the traditions of the village. No one sought her out to hear if the whispers were true. So the money that used to pour in had all but gone too. When she had enlisted *his* help, she had by necessity bowed to his wish for girls only in her own image. This had cost her most of her already scant coven. She was forced to start almost from scratch.

The new girls came from far and wide. They were goths and Satanists of a new tradition, hedonists and thrill-seekers who cared nothing for morals or reputation. He found them for her through clubs and contact websites. However, he didn't realise that powers were diluted the further you went from home. She was tied to this village, to this cottage where she was born. She could stray, even for a few years, but her strength would dramatically wane. Last time she had gone for too long her lover had died in her arms coughing up blood, and there was nothing she could do to prevent it. No matter what threats she faced, she *had* to stay at the cottage, the source of her power. She had to surround herself with local girls, to lure them in and breed the magic.

She was one of the few who realised that magic was a living force. Some, like her, could even hear the constant buzz of it as it whipped and swirled around the ether, rushing into the bodies of the believers. The more believers, the faster it swirled around them and the more power it generated. The magic moved easier around the bodies of the locals because they were born emitting the same resonance. Whether we know it or not, all of us are tuned in to the individual forces of magic and nature that swirl around our home. In compact areas, like villages, this expands to encompass every dwelling, every street and wood and field within its boundary. In towns and cities it becomes ever weaker, mainly because there are so many outsiders not tuned in to the same resonance. If you stay long enough, you will eventually subconsciously tune in. Homesickness is caused by the conflicting magic of a new place. That indefinable comfort you get whenever you return home is actually the feel of the magic you are naturally tuned into, re-entering your body.

Some, like her, knew how to be one with nature and utilise the powers of the magic. However, she also knew she was tied to it at its source. Her home was under threat so she was beholden to *him* and his ill-gotten wealth. That weird-eyed, fuck-loving devil who liked boys ever more each day and wanted to rip apart the fat-bummed local girls. Without her home she was lost. If she could not surround herself with the same girls, her power would diminish. The new ones took ages to train and to tune in.

Bit by bit he was draining her strength, prising her fingers from their grip on supremacy. She could not act boldly against him because if he was removed, or forced to act in bitter revenge, he had ways to ensure the dreaded road might yet be built and she would find herself evicted. Her home would be gone for ever, buried beneath four lanes of tarmac. She would be finished. There was no spell great enough to defeat the power of greed in the guise of progress.

Mimi was her last chance. Not only was she the image of her last love, but she had been born there too. The timbre of the magic between them was *exact*. She had felt it the moment the girl stepped into her class. It was stronger still when she stroked her big bottom through those tight jeans. She could feed off that magic. It would make her instantly stronger. The closer she was to this girl, the greater the power she would gain, just as it had been with her last great love. With her she might be able to ride out the storm and then start again. Forming a spell to draw Mimi in was therefore paramount.

She had already pulped the damiana leaves with the deer's tongue. She had burned the photo she had found and crumbled the ashes into the pestle to blend it into the mixture. She took her two fingers from inside her and saw that she was ready. She put her sticky fingers into the pestle so that the mixture coated them. She scooped out more and held herself open with her other hand so she could plunge them back in and get the mixture deep inside her. She stirred the fingers around and whispered the girl's name. She took the cut ginger stem and wiped it six times across the hood of her swollen sex, so that it might burn hard whilst she rubbed herself. This was to represent the passion she intended to visit upon the girl whose name she still whispered through her gasps.

She took the stolen thong from the cupboard beside her. She would have liked to say she had used spells to spirit this scrap of underwear from the girl's room, but actually it was the fruit of good old-fashioned burglary. That morning she had waited until the Spinster had gone out. She had instantly found the spare key in the potting shed, hidden inside a ball of twine. Mimi's room had been small but neat. Everything had been tidied away from the prying eyes of her nosy landlady. Morgana noted the borrowed library books on witchcraft lying on top of the laptop. So it *was* snooping and not a genuine desire to lose weight that had brought the journalist girl to her class. She had searched the larger chest first and found the photo album buried in the bottom drawer. She had removed one candid snap of Mimi smiling back over her shoulder at the camera. In it her bottom looked big and inviting.

Morgana had then searched the wardrobe and located the jeans the girl had worn to her class the night before, identifiable by the stitched and bejewelled butterfly design on the rear pockets. She sniffed at the crotch but even with her heightened senses she couldn't discern much beyond the smell of denim. The base of the wardrobe was stacked with shoeboxes. Inside were pairs of high heels in all manner of colours and varieties. Where this girl got to wear them around this village was a mystery. Other flat shoes were there but out of boxes, except for one very ordinary-looking pair that sat on a layer of scrunched-up paper. The Spinster might have been fooled by this but Morgana was not. She slipped her hand under the paper and smiled as her fingers closed around a familiar shape. Further investigation revealed not only a rabbit vibrator but a little bullet vibe in chrome too, along with a small bottle of lubricating gel.

As well as the sex toys, the shoebox also hid a well-thumbed paperback. The cover showed a beauty's face in close up, pulling an expression of joyful surprise.

Behind her was a shadowy male form, as if this stranger had found her prone and was forcefully doing her from behind. The book was a collection of short stories entitled *He Made Me Do It!*. Morgana had held the book up and flicked through the pages to see where it naturally opened. Again she allowed herself a little smile as the book popped apart on pages describing a woman's ravishment at the hands of a gang of thieves. The no-holds-barred passage was within a story entitled *Dragged to the Woods*. Naughty, *dirty* Mimi!

The smaller chest revealed a plethora of lingerie. The drawers were full of tights and stockings, and tiny undies in all colours, presumably to match the shoes of the day. It seemed that journalism was a job for flirts who expected to be stripped to their smalls at any moment. The laundry basket yielded more underwear. She had pressed a few pairs to her nose and some gave off Mimi's scent. She needed blood ideally, but none carried any sign. Perhaps, as the two of them seemed so in tune in some ways, Mimi already had the same cycle as Morgana, like all but the very newest of her coven girls. However, Morgana couldn't wait another week before returning.

The thong she had selected was lilac in colour. It had been on top of the pile so it was reasonable to assume it had been the one worn to the class the night before.

Morgana had laid them on the bed alongside the jeans and then stripped naked. She had taken the trouser hanger from the jeans. She had raised it to her chest to check the distance, and slid the two plastic gripper-clips inwards slightly to get it perfect. Then she had pinched each gripper-clip open in turn and closed them over her stiff nipples. The clips bit tightly and she had yelped, but it was a good kind of hurt. She took the metal hook of the hanger and put it into her mouth. Lifting her head meant pulling the hanger upwards, which meant tugging harder upon her swollen, trapped teats.

She had splayed the lips of her quim apart and grasped the pillow Mimi slept upon. She had straddled it and sunk down to press her sex to the portion of material where the girl's head would rest. She wanted her own sweet scent to be there, to be breathed in as Mimi slept. It would make her irresistible to the girl. As she humped the pillow to spread her scent, she had repeatedly jerked her head back to stretch her tortured nipples. A few little squirts of her milk had been wrenched from them, caught by the plastic of the clips before dripping onto the pillow. If she had been discovered at that very moment, she would almost certainly have been carted off to the funny farm most already claimed she should be in.

Those same lilac knickers were now being carefully pushed up inside her. Her clit was throbbing from the contact with the ginger and she was ready to invoke the spell. She was on her back, with her knees raised above her breasts. The thong was now fully inside her and her puss lips had closed up to conceal it. She began her incantation. It was one to draw the subject in and make her fall in love. It started slowly, with Morgana trying to hold back and say each word clearly, but the thought of the girl naked and the itch in her clit made her fingers hurry. Soon she was gabbling her words over and over and her fingers were a blur at her crotch. She came with a shriek. She was sure the girl could not now escape the pull.

She smiled with satisfaction and was still congratulating herself when a knock came at the door. It shouldn't have been any of her girls. The bacchantes were at exercise class and the trainees were forbidden to come to that part of the estate. It would be one of the Lord's slave boys, delivering some petty instruction. Perhaps she would make the slave suffer a bit; shoot the messenger, so to speak. If it was that new boy Dominic, the one the Master seemed to have taken a particular shine to, perhaps she would order him over the kitchen table and fill him with a huge dildo, just to get there before *he* did. It would be nice to steal his thunder. It would be nice to ruin his boys the way he seemed hell-bent on ruining her girls.

She pulled her long dress back down and bounced off the bed, keeping the thong inside so it could soak up her juices. The spell wouldn't work otherwise. She made a few hasty adjustments in front of the mirror and decided she would definitely give whichever annoying slave he had sent a taste of plastic up his sorry arse. She was annoyed with *him*. He was being a prick about Mimi, out of spite. He had ordained that she be allowed into class, but only to be prepared physically. She was not to be given any secrets of the Order. He gave Morgana a month to get her into shape, after which time he would reconsider letting her in. It was lies, she knew. The fact that he wanted her in shape as quickly as possible meant he wanted to use her for his ends. If he had any intention of allowing her into the Order he would have done it from the outset. So his designs upon her body were clearly for more nefarious reasons.

He clearly had reservations about the girl's background and her motives for wanting to join Morgana's bogus slimming club. Almost certainly he had plans to make her pay for this snooping. Morgana herself had no qualms about bringing someone as potentially problematic as a journalist into their midst. All she knew was that she needed this girl close to her, very soon, sharing all her secrets, sharing her love. Whatever *he* said, the girl had to be brought close because Morgana's life depended on it. And the girl's life probably depended on it too.

The knock at the door came again, louder this time, impatient even. The cheek of it! She would fuck this bastard slave all over the estate. She adjusted the deep V at the front of her hastily donned dress to ensure her breasts didn't spill free as she opened the door.

'What the hell do you want?' she was saying fiercely, before she had even seen who was there.

Mimi blinked at her, looking a little taken aback.

'I was hoping for a chat,' she said nervously.

Morgana's face lightened with a wide smile, and her pussy clenched on the sodden stolen panties still inside her.

'My, my,' she said, 'that *was* quick!'

6

Mimi sat as instructed and surveyed the room. It seemed a little early for wine but the witch had brooked no refusal and was out in the kitchen pouring them each a glass. Perhaps a little alcohol would help calm her nerves. She felt confused and groggy. Her efforts the previous evening to gather information had melted away. She had excused herself from the Spinster's company while the old woman was still nattering, and once in the safety of her room she had stripped and leaped into bed. Her fingers were inside her before she'd even hit the mattress.

She had endured a night of fitful sleep and vivid dreams of Morgana, broken by spells of sleepy, almost forced masturbation. In the morning she had tried to recall all the things the Spinster had said, tried to tally it with the information she had gleaned from her books and the internet. It was important stuff, she knew it was, but the thoughts kept morphing into images of Morgana with her dress pulled up. She hadn't felt this lost in somebody since her earliest crushes. She would have liked to believe the witch had slipped her some kind of love drug. However, she knew the infatuation was simply sheer lust for a gorgeous, authoritative woman, one who fed her pupils from her breasts and spanked miscreants, and kept sex slaves for her girls' enjoyment.

Yes, sex slaves and Haydn Shady: this was really a serious matter, so why couldn't Mimi focus on the bigger picture? Morgana was seemingly harbouring a villain of the highest order and that made her just as dangerous. Trifling with her was clearly not something to consider. An approach of any kind was foolhardy. Mimi needed to concentrate on her leads and build a story to expose possibly the worst criminal activity this area had ever seen. Caution was paramount, but the longer the day went on the more difficult it was to keep the witch from her mind. She decided, against all logic, that she would go to her after all. She would ask some tough questions, the ones she had said over and over in her head to get them right.

Now she was sitting here those questions seemed to be locked behind some frosted glass in her mind. She had quite forgotten why she had felt impelled to abandon caution and rush to this woman's house at a speed that saw her bouncing off kerbs. She felt a little dizzy. The butterflies were alive in her stomach, like she was awaiting her first kiss. She should have run but she was already in the web.

The witch looked every bit as appealing as the night before. She wore a full-length red velvet sleeved dress cut down the front almost to her belly button. Plenty of cleavage was on view, the breasts huddled together and held in place only by the tightness of the dress. One sideways tug and they would have fallen out bare. It took all Mimi's willpower to keep her hands in her lap and not slide them inside the dress to cup the warm soft flesh. Heaven alone knew where Morgana got such an item of clothing from, unless Top Sorceress had just opened their first branch in town. It was a totally inappropriate garment for lounging around at home in the early afternoon. However, Mimi wasn't doing much better, clad as she was in her normal workwear combination of skirt and blouse, but with fishnet stockings beneath. She hadn't planned to be here but now that she was her attire felt very unbusinesslike and wholly provocative. She had to calm down and see if she could gather her wits, or she would be there for the taking.

The front room didn't automatically shout 'witch'. Mimi had hoped that by turning up unexpectedly there would be evidence of Morgana's dark practices all around. But there were no lambs lying sacrificed on stone altars, no scary stuffed cats in jars or broomsticks propped in the corner. The chocolate-brown leather suite was disconcertingly modern, as were the rugs that lay on the flagstoned floor. At least the fire was open and sooty as if in constant use, and there was a big black pot sitting in the grate, perhaps all the better for boiling witchy potions in? There were no pentagrams daubed in blood anywhere. The walls, apart from the exposed stone around the fire, were all plain magnolia and looked recently painted.

The decor was certainly eclectic. One window seat was decked out with wax-covered wine bottles and pewter holders housing well-used candles. Other furniture was sparse, just a couple of antique-looking side tables. There was no TV, just a row of old books on a ledge to provide entertainment. One wall had stag antlers hanging upon it, while another had a huge, ornately framed portrait of a pretty young woman in period costume. Mimi was struck by the uncanny similarity between herself and the subject of the portrait – or was she just imagining it? It didn't seem like the type of picture a woman of Morgana's age would choose, but then again how old *was* she? Mimi realised the witch could be anywhere between twenty and fifty. The bearing of absolute authority suggested maturity, yet the flawless soft skin and firm body could scarcely belong to anyone much out of their teens.

The woman came back from the kitchen and handed Mimi her glass. She then sat down, not on the single chair, but right next to Mimi on the two-seater, so close their legs were almost touching. The room was small, certainly not large enough to have the girls from the class staying there. In fact, if she was concealing anyone there at all, she was doing a good job. There was no sign of a man's touch or belongings. No sign that a villain was hiding out there. Ah, yes, Haydn Shady, the man she must keep in mind because he was the key to this all. Already he was fading. Mimi was instead thinking of the woman's sweet smell, citric and slightly spicy, warm but not overpowering. It didn't seem like a sprayed-on perfume, more a natural aroma, as if she had mixed so many potions and burned so many candles that her whole body now exuded the vapours. It was just one more thing to make Mimi's guard slip.

'I see you are here on business,' Morgana said, indicating Mimi's clothes.

It was too bad that Mimi couldn't now remember what that business was. She felt intoxicated but she hadn't yet touched her drink. The woman's eyes seemed more intensely green than they had the night before and Mimi found it very difficult not to be transfixed by them. Perhaps it was the heavy black eyeliner and mascara making them stand out. The flawless white skin of her face was natural, not aided by makeup at all. The wide lips were set in a smile but painted blood-red. Mimi needed to get a grip fast or she would be sunk. She raised her glass but somehow mistimed her sip and ended up having to take a big gulp to avoid spilling some down her front.

'No need to be nervous just because I know you want your bare bottom spanked,' the witch said with a smile.

'I never said I wanted –'

'I assume you have come here either to interview me for your paper or because you want to be my lover? I suspect you *think* it's the former but deep down your soul knows it's the latter. Do you wish to become my lover?'

It was an utterly disarming question and Mimi's resolve was rapidly being scattered. She had wanted to seize the initiative. She hadn't quite worked out a viable pretext for being there asking difficult questions without having to admit she was a journalist. She had hoped a bullish approach would put the woman in the corner and have her spilling the beans before she knew what had hit her. However, the witch seemed to be expecting the visit and already knew of Mimi's trade. Now she was talking about becoming her lover, as if she also knew exactly what her visitor had been fantasising about all the previous night. Blushing furiously and stumbling for an answer was only going to reinforce this conviction, but that's all Mimi found herself doing. How the hell could she bat this question away and somehow regain the ascendancy?

'I'm not a lesbian,' she eventually said, trying to sound curt but in fact sounding hesitant.

'You don't have to be a *tribas*, my darling. It is almost impossible for *anyone* not to yearn for the softness of a woman, her gentle nature, her beauty. Females fall for me all the time. Some think I must cast spells upon them. But did you know that heart-stealing magic is the most difficult to perform? Once upon a time it was simple. Nowadays, with all the one-night stands and lies and non-commitment, the heart is so much less easy to fool. It instinctively hides and protects itself. It takes strong magic just to find and touch it. Yes, I have spells to make you dream of me and even to make you come to me. I can make you lust after me as easy as pie, but I want more than that from you. It is your heart I want but I cannot just take it. You have to give it to me. So, what you have to decide is: do you want to give me your heart?'

'So you admit you're a witch, then,' Mimi blurted, unable to say anything else.

'Ah, yes, I forgot you have so many questions to ask me, for your *exposé* on the Wicked Witch. Well, ask away. Would you like me to put my fingers inside you whilst you do so?'

The words alone were disturbing enough for Mimi, without the addition of the witch's hand on her knee. Her composure was crumbling fast. She was desperately trying to expel vivid images of her skirt being pulled up past her stocking tops, of her legs open and her eyes shut, of her fluttering breaths and little gasps as she felt the woman's fingers stirring deeply around inside her. She wanted to say no in answer to the witch's brazen question, but she knew if she opened her mouth it would only come out as 'Yes, please'. She tried to sift through her scrambled thoughts to find one of her own questions that she had earlier memorised, but they had all been chased away. She had been rendered mute, giving the witch the opportunity to press home her advantage.

'Ask me any question you like, my dearest, and I will slide my fingers inside you,' Morgana was saying, closing in so that Mimi could feel her breath warm against her cheek. 'It will make the interview so much more pleasurable, don't you think? It will be your first step towards becoming my sweetheart.'

The hand on Mimi's thigh was slowly moving upwards, the nails gently grazing the nylon of her stockings to make the skin below tingle. The fingertips came to the hem of her skirt but this proved no barrier. On the hand went, ever so slowly, inside the skirt now, upwards to the thigh. Mimi could summon no words to stop it.

'To be my lover you must be prepared to give up everything you know. You must give in to darkness and your soul will never be the same again. But our love will be the purest and most exciting of all, and it will last for ever. I will give you pleasures that you cannot even imagine. We will live wild, taking whatever we want from whoever we want. I will nurture you and protect you and feed you, and all you will have to do is anything I say.'

Mimi hadn't really been listening to the words, too busy willing the fingers that now lay inert on the warm bare thigh just past her stocking top to resume their upward journey. But the words 'feed you' had sent a shiver through her and she had emitted a little gasp. The image of the girls suckling hungrily at their Priestess's breasts came hurtling back. Why was this idea so resonant? God knows she had never felt the desire to taste another woman's milk before, but now gorging on the witch's elixir seemed the most sumptuously erotic thought imaginable. Those wonderful firm breasts were now pressing into her own, the witch having responded to Mimi's gasp and moved closer still.

If she was to regain control of the situation, now was her last chance, but she didn't have the strength in her legs to stand and break free of the embrace. She didn't have the willpower or the inclination to tell the witch to stop. She could have just stonewalled the attempted seduction, just proceeded to ask her questions as intended. But to ask any question was to ask for fingers to be buried inside her, and there would be no going back from that. Mimi had nowhere to go, no words to retrieve the situation, no power of resolve over desire. By her own admission the witch was dangerous, but at that moment lust was chasing logic away. So Mimi just shut her eyes and waited for the kiss.

It didn't quite come. She felt the brush of the witch's lips upon her own, a feather touch, back and forth three or four times. Mimi realised her lips were pushing out seeking a fuller contact. This was a sure sign that she had already yielded, regardless of what good reason might have told her. Some part of her wanted to believe it was the witch *making* her feel this way. That, at least, would have excused this immediate and utter capitulation. She had an image of herself falling, but she was sure the landing would be soft and she wasn't scared. Still the witch just kept up her light, teasing contact, occasionally applying just the slightest pressure of her lips to Mimi's.

If the ploy was to make Mimi desperate for the kiss then it was working. She found herself squirming in her seat, moving her hips forward to bring her crotch into contact with the witch's fingers. Her skirt was stretched as tight as it would go, so Mimi lifted her bottom slightly and slid the material up her legs to give the witch all the freedom of movement she required. There could be no stronger hint that Mimi wanted this woman to take her. Still it didn't happen. Mimi was fizzing with the anticipation. She wanted to say it out loud, to give her consent. 'Fuck me,' she wanted to say, just like all those porno girls did so freely. 'Put your fingers inside me and make me come.'

Predictably her thoughts didn't pass the witch by. The fingertips that had been frustratingly inert since she had pressed her crotch against them suddenly awoke and traced a nail-tip journey up her cotton-covered slit. Mimi exhaled hard and warm into the witch's open mouth. Teeth closed on her trembling bottom lip and held it momentarily, exerting just a little biting force. Any second now and Mimi would surely feel the tongue in her mouth and the finger sliding inside her. She couldn't wait. The material at her crotch felt damp and constraining. She could picture it moulded to the curve of her mound, the dark split beneath defined and visible, ready for the taking. So why *wasn't* it being taken?

'You have to give in to me first,' the witch whispered. 'To be my lover you must first promise to live exactly as I. When you give yourself to me you give yourself to a whole new world, for all time. Many will fear and shun you. Most will think you belong to Satan, not to me. But mine you will be and everything from then on will be about pleasure. You will never know sadness, boredom, grief or loneliness again. All you will know is bliss, and that bliss will never, ever feel any less great than at that exalted time when you first knew it.'

The nails were still tracing tickling lines over her crotch. Mimi parted her thighs wider, hoping to encourage the penetration she was all but crying out for. She knew that while the cotton was stretched taut over her bulge, at her opening the string of the thong would be gathered and wet through, an ineffectual barrier against any invasion. She was ripe for the picking but the witch first wanted her to promise things she couldn't even comprehend. All this talk of being eternal lovers, of giving in to another life, it was sending her head spinning almost as much as her lust. The witch couldn't actually mean it, could she? Surely it was just part of some extravagant fantasy? After all, there wasn't actually any such thing as *magic*, was there? Yet here Mimi was, somehow drawn into the danger against all good sense, transfixed by a female her rampaging desire had no way of resisting, playing with a fire she had no hope of controlling.

The long black nails were on her bareness now. They had found the delicate skin of her pussy and were sending electric tingles deep inside her. She shifted in her seat and pushed her hips forward but the witch was quicker and kept her fingers from slipping inside, ensuring her teasing touch never abated. Mimi's effort to impale herself upon the finger was met with an amused 'tut tut' and a little chiding bite on her bottom lip.

'I need you to promise yourself to me,' the witch said. 'But you have to *mean* it. The magic will never work unless you tell the truth. I need only your promise, that's all – oh, and of course I need to taste a single drop of blood from your little *landica*.'

On the final word the witch's eyes had widened with the excitement of the thought, and her nail had flicked upwards, right over Mimi's throbbing, sparsely covered clit, demonstrating exactly which part of the anatomy the drop of blood was supposed to come from. Mimi heard her own whimpers but still couldn't find an ounce of resistance.

'Don't be scared,' the witch was saying, 'it takes only one little prick – the last you will ever feel at your puss. It won't hurt much. And it might be only one drop but it will feel like the most wonderful gush you could imagine, like bliss. Then you will be mine and I will pleasure you. Did you know I have the magic to make my tongue feel like it's all the way up inside you? Think of it, as deep as anything you have ever had, a snake within you! My girls say it's the best feeling they have ever had.'

Every time Mimi thought she could gain even the slenderest hold on her thoughts or the situation, the witch's next words rushed such notions away. Now Mimi was totally lost. It was like torture. She knew she was in danger but she wanted this woman beyond all desperation. She would happily have granted anything to have those fingers inside her, had this just been a frivolous game of passion. However, it was not just part of a fantasy. The witch was serious.

How could Mimi *honestly* promise something when she had no comprehension of how to do so, or what that promise entailed? You can't just say, 'Yeah, good old Satan, I'm going to start worshipping him from now on!' Witchcraft, magic, it was all nonsense, wasn't it? You can't just suddenly say you believe in it after all. You can't just suddenly turn bad when all your life has been about being good. The witch was asking Mimi to give her something when the taking of it was impossible.

Perhaps she could get away without making any promises. Ask a question and those fingers would be inside her, that's what the witch had said. Why then was her usually inquisitive mind unable to summon a single query from the blankness? Mimi knew it was the witch's doing. It was some kind of spell to make her think more deeply about the situation. It was blackmail to make her consider commitment and love over wantonness. The witch wouldn't just *fuck* her; she needed some old-fashioned assurances that it would actually *mean* something afterwards, for ever. It should have been a noble idea, but it just drove Mimi mad.

It was teasing of the worst, most frustrating kind, and now it was getting worse still, because the witch was climbing onto Mimi and that irresistible cleavage was being flaunted just inches away. Mimi was being straddled. Her thighs were still open, still forced apart by the witch's hand between them. The fingers were still at her opening, teasing but not giving her the plunging penetration she so badly needed. The witch was smiling down at her, feinting to kiss then drawing back. Then her free hand was at her dress front, sliding inside the deep V to cup one of those delicious breasts. As the hand came out, the breast came with it, first to be squeezed, then to be freed, to bounce naked, so close to Mimi's open mouth.

The witch unceremoniously pulled out her other breast and both were bare and fabulously inviting. They proved

147

too much for Mimi. She knew she couldn't resist and was past caring whether her desire was merely being induced by some kind of witchy spell. She certainly couldn't wait around for any more provisos to be made to thwart her. She reached up with her mouth, found a nipple and sucked it in to hold it until her hand got there to grasp it firmly. She could picture the girls in her class feasting so hard upon them, and she immediately tried the same. The nipple was erect and long, but didn't feel as fat in her mouth as she had imagined it in her fantasies the previous evening. It also wasn't yielding milk as it had in her dreams. No matter how hard she sucked, the longed-for burst of elixir wouldn't come. It almost made her weep.

Mimi knew she must look desperate, and from the smile on the witch's face she was enjoying the frustration. Both breasts felt weighty and firm in her hands, like they were full of milk, but nothing would come, however much she squeezed them or pulled at the nipples. To make matters worse the witch went on lightly running her fingernail up and down Mimi's still covered sex, sending tingling waves through her but not sating her needs.

'When you are my lover you will be able to drink my elixir,' said the witch.

More teasing, more blackmail. Mimi understood the implication. The witch clearly knew how intoxicating was the thought of feasting from her, so it was safe to assume this sudden breast fixation was instilled by another magic spell of sorts. She felt rising anger jostling with frustration. She tried some tenderness, swirling her tongue around the teats and then attempting to coax out the liquid with gentle squeezing of the breasts. When that didn't work she went back to rougher treatment. She pinched each nipple in turn before closing her lips around them and sucking as hard as she could. Still nothing. She bit at them and stretched them taut between her teeth. She felt a sudden hot burst of jealousy at all the young bitches in her class the previous night who had the technique to milk their Priestess where she did not. Why was their sucking so much more efficient than hers? What did they do to deserve the exquisite treat?

'My elixir is like the sweetest cream, like condensed milk,' the witch taunted. 'All my girls say it is the most wonderful taste they can imagine.'

The jealousy jangled through Mimi once more. Why did she have to act with love while all those tarts got to feast out of raging lust? Anyway, why was the witch talking of love when she clearly liked surrounding herself with a whole harem of sluts? Exactly how many girls were there? She should ask her that. She should ask: exactly how many fucking girlfriends have you got that you want more than me?

Mimi didn't exactly phrase her question like that and she only got part of it out anyway. Almost as soon as her question began, the fingers at her crotch made light work of the tiny strip of sodden material defending her pussy and slid deep inside her, turning her words into a loud gasping moan. The sound was cut off by a kiss, at long last. Mimi hoped the talk of rash promises was now over, but as soon as she pushed out her tongue to find Morgana's the woman pulled away.

'There are many girls,' said the witch, 'but you can never be one of them. Our Lord and Master won't allow it. The ones you saw last night are merely trainees, but once I have taught them they will become my *bacchantes*, the nymphs of the wood who worship lust in all its forms. They will live to get drunk, to gorge and to fuck.'

As she spoke the witch brushed her lips over Mimi's once more and then held up a breast and pushed the elongated nipple back into Mimi's mouth for her to suck upon. The two fingers inside her were as deep as they could go, stirring slowly in circles that opened her up and made her stream. Her engorged clit was pressed into the soft mound of the witch's palm but although the contact was most welcome it was not enough to take her over the edge. Mimi tried to grind into the palm but she found her hips unable to move. She was at the mercy of the witch and her teasing words.

'My girls,' Morgana said, 'are not just your everyday, modern party girls. Once they might have been but now they are way, way beyond that. When they have learned from me they become wild beings, driven frenzied by desire. They have no allegiance except to the Dark Arts and to the God of Ritual Madness and Ecstasy. Theirs is the Cult of the Souls, and they feed the dead with blood offerings. They feed themselves with my magic and then feast upon cock, quim and arse alike. They crave anyone who makes their pussy wet, and any who refuse to join their orgies will become the sacrifice. They fall upon all non-followers like a pack of werewolves and there is no escape. No silver bullet kills them, not even the one you own and press against your little clitty to make yourself come.'

Mimi squealed at the surprise reference to her little vibe and at the light stroke of the witch's thumbnail across the hood of her clit as it was mentioned. How could the woman possibly know about her secret toys unless she was a mind-reader? What other secrets had she stolen? But her mouth was full of the soft flesh of the witch's breast, her jaws forced apart to prevent further questions. She felt the two fingers inside her twisting and wiggling around to release another wet flow before settling into a rhythm, slipping in and out of her. The feeling was wonderful but Mimi wanted milk. She wanted her mouth flooded with the liquid as she was brought to a shuddering climax. She wanted to flood this beautiful Priestess and drink her down at the same time.

'Our Master knows all about you and what you are,'

Morgana continued, impervious to Mimi's needs. 'He knows about your snooping. He wants to make a sacrifice of you. He wants to throw you to my girls so they can tear you apart in their fuck-fury. There will be no escaping them. Once they are set upon you they will hunt you down and take their insatiable passions out upon your body. Put simply, my sweet, they will ravish you to death. Since you cannot hide from them, nor be one of them, your only hope is to rise above them. Your only hope is to become my lover. You have been prying in the wrong place and now Darkness is coming to find you. Your only remaining choice is whether to become a part of it or be smothered by it.'

Mimi felt the fingers slide from her puss. The woman brought them up to her lips and greedily sucked them clean. Mimi could smell her scent upon them. It seemed such a rude act, one she might have shrunk from had anyone else done it, but the witch's open greediness for Mimi's juice made it completely scintillating. It was almost enough compensation for having her desperate pussy left empty. The witch's threatening words should have killed the passion but they made it burn even hotter in Mimi's belly. Perhaps it was the spell that had been cast upon her, or perhaps it was the underlying belief that the fantastical talk was just part of an intricate seduction. Most probably it was the fact that Mimi now wanted this woman more than anyone or anything ever, and nothing else seemed to matter, especially not the pussy-wetting thought of being ravished to death by a bunch of wild pagan vixens!

Mimi was kissed again and she tasted the tang of her own desire on the witch's lips. Then the woman was pushing her breasts back inside her dress and Mimi realised with a panic that the witch wasn't bluffing. She was bringing an end to this little tryst when it was barely past the teasing stage. It should have been a relief. Mimi should have been grateful she had been released before she was plunged way too deep to ever surface again. Instead she felt almost bereft, like a great prize was being wrenched from her grasp. She needed this woman to make her come. She needed to engage her again while the heat was still between them, let passion take over so that her climax was assured.

'Let me lick you,' Mimi said.

'When you are my lover,' Morgana replied.

Mimi let out a single involuntary sob. She felt utterly helpless. Somewhere at the back of her mind a sensible voice was telling her to seize the initiative back, to realise that her current burning need was caused by a maliciously cast magic spell, not nature. The witch was trying to put her off, to distract her from asking questions about Haydn Shady and his criminal deeds. That's what she had to do: pull herself together and ask some tough questions, ask about the kidnapping of young men to be used as slaves.

'I want to give you my bottom to spank' was what she actually said.

Mimi felt the breath catching in her chest. Her hand automatically came up to her mouth and she blinked three or four times in silent disbelief at the words she had spoken. It was easily the rudest, most suggestive thing she had ever said to anyone. She could feel the heat of embarrassment flush across her cheeks. The witch was giving her a look of sympathy but it didn't make her feel any less ridiculous. Worse still, she really wanted the spanking. Hearing the words out loud, even from her own lips, had caused another little gush of excitement to flow from her puss. She wanted to force the issue, to hide her shame by crawling across the witch's lap, but she couldn't make her muscles move.

'When you can *properly* give yourself to me, come to me and tell me that once more,' said Morgana. 'Until then, you have to go. I'm not refusing you just to tease. To be my lover you must commit to me completely, or the magic will never work between us. You cannot be just another of my girls. We cannot just fuck. With us it must be all or nothing. If you give yourself to me I promise you will never regret it, but if you don't I cannot promise that I can save you from the coming danger.'

The alarm bells should have been ringing, but still Mimi wondered if she might yet force her frozen muscles into action and turn to offer her bare bum to the witch.

Morgana didn't wait to see if this could happen. She rose and crossed to select one of the books from the row on the ledge. It was small, bound in leather so dark it was almost black. When Mimi took it, she felt a spark from it hit her palm.

'Read the first chapter,' Morgana said. 'It will explain the teachings of your High Priestess. It will show you how you must act from now on. Keep me in mind at all times. When you are ready to be my lover you must perform the Rite of Surrender the night before you come to me. Take this candle. You must show your *c lus* to heaven and put this inside you. Look.'

The witch took the book and opened it to show a crude drawing of a naked girl on her back with her hips raised completely off the floor, so her bottom was pointing upwards. A lit candle was sticking straight up from her body. The subject had her knees splayed so that her pussy was visible and open, meaning the candle was being held by her anus.

'You may need to lean against the wall to do it,' Morgana said, clearly seeing Mimi looking aghast. 'Light the candle and say my name and think of us naked together, kissing and touching. Hold yourself wide open so that the drips of the hot wax can fall right inside your *cunnus*. As each drip lands say out loud, "Priestess, I give you my heart and soul." When the thirteenth drip has landed inside you, snuff out the candle before any more drips can fall, get onto your hands and knees, push the candle as far inside you as you can and then rub your little *landīca* for all you are worth. Do it as fast as possible and think of me doing it to you. Keep saying that you love me until your climax comes. Your orgasm will be six times wetter and more intense than any you have previously had, but don't worry because that will be the norm from that time on. Find me the next morning. I will know that you have performed the rite so I shall be expecting you. I will strip you and perform the Rite of Satiation upon you, and then I will give you that one little prick and take your single drop of blood. Then you will be mine. We will be free to make love for all time. I will even spank you, if you want. On that first day you may ask me for anything your heart and body desire.'

As she was speaking, the witch pressed the book back into Mimi's hands and guided her out of the door into the afternoon sunshine. She blew her a final kiss and then shut the door before any more words could be exchanged. Mimi stood for maybe two silent minutes just staring at the door, running over the witch's last words. It should have been the biggest load of mumbo-jumbo imaginable, but Mimi was buzzing with the excitement of it. She pressed the book and the slim candle to her chest as if they were the most precious gifts on earth. She was picturing giving herself up to the witch, casting aside her beliefs and feeling the singe of burning wax inside her womb. It suddenly seemed such an easy thing to do.

She didn't even make it off the estate before she was compelled to pull up by some trees on the long private road, recline her seat, get her high heels up onto the dashboard and thrust two fingers up her hot, saturated puss. She masturbated and moaned out loud, repeating the witch's name, hoping her words carried back to Morgana's cottage. She felt possessed. Her knees were wide apart and her hips were off the seat, coming up in desperation to meet the upward thrust of her fingers. She wanted to rip her blouse open to bare her breasts and pinch them as she had pinched Morgana's. She wanted to slap her own wet quim, hard. She wished the girls of the estate would sniff her out and watch her before prising open the doors to ravage her.

She couldn't see straight for ten minutes after her orgasm. She had to stay there, panting hard, sitting on her hands to stop them creeping back and starting all over again. Even with the release nothing cleared in her mind. Wanting Morgana was still paramount. It was one hell of a spell the witch had placed upon her but if all she ever felt was this driving urge for rudeness of the dirtiest kind then she could live with that. She even wondered if she could fall in love quickly enough to be back at Morgana's by the morning, so they could carry on immediately from where they left off.

The spell shattered with alarming speed when Mimi

eventually arrived home. She hadn't even realised she had opened the letter. She had hung her jacket over a chair in the kitchen and poured herself a Diet Coke from the fridge, all on autopilot, her mind still full of Morgana's beauty. She must have seen the letter addressed to her and opened it because there it was in her hand. She hadn't recognised the handwriting on the envelope but it was immediately obvious the author was the mother of Dominic, her ex-boyfriend. Inside was a copy of another letter, written by Dominic himself, telling his parents that he had not gone back to his studies but had gone elsewhere, though where remained unspecified. They were not to worry, he told them. He was safe, so they were not to try and find him under any circumstances. The mother, in understandably frantic tones, was entreating Mimi to reveal anything she might know about Dominic's disappearance.

Mimi found herself shaking, her head suddenly clear of the nonsense of her lust-crazy afternoon. The heat of her desire was replaced by a chill. She knew nothing of Dominic's plans, but remembered his aloofness during their last meetings and particularly his distraction that final day they spent together in the woods. He had been checking his phone constantly, as if awaiting a message or call. He hadn't wanted a lift to the station, presumably because he had no intention of boarding the train. Of all the things Mimi didn't know, she *did* know one thing with crystal clarity: Dominic's disappearance exactly mirrored that of the other local lads. Wherever they had gone, he had gone too. Mimi strongly suspected that place was a lot nearer than everyone imagined.

Suddenly the Missing Lads Case was a story after all, and threatened to have far more sinister overtones than anyone in the village could possibly guess. Haydn Shady was almost certainly behind it and that meant danger. The missing lads had been either tricked or tempted into what others had clearly referred to as slavery. They were surely in peril and she had to find them. Murder was not inconceivable, including her own; the witch had intimated that very fact.

She shivered again, this time at the thought of how close she had just come to the jaws of the trap. She wouldn't make the same mistake again. She would do her job, unearth the facts and take her case to the police – just before she broke her exclusive to an enthralled public. She needed evidence, of course, or the police would laugh her out of town. She needed to return to the estate. She would jump back into the fire to track down Dominic and free him, to find evil Shady and the hordes of lust-mad witches. First, though, she had to pleasure herself, right away, because the images of Morgana's gorgeous milky breasts were creeping back, and there was no way she could defeat the compulsion to make herself come thinking about them.

7

'There is to be an orgy tonight,' Gavin said, looking a little wearied by the prospect. 'The Master has ordained it.'

Dominic felt a familiar stirring down below. He was not sure he could ever grow tired of such things. It was words like 'orgy' that had made him give up his studies so quickly to come here in the first place. Yes, it was short notice, as Gavin was pointing out, and yes, it wouldn't fall within the usual lunar cycle, but if it was OK with the Master then Dominic wasn't going to complain. He was still very new to this ritual. He had been told all about it in hushed whispers. He then had to watch more than one without being allowed to participate, before finally being granted his place. It was everything his ever-erect cock was crying out for: hard, dirty, copious, indiscriminate sex. Yes, some of the couplings he enjoyed more than others, but spurting into any body was always a joy, male or female. Best of all, Gavin was there, and that meant there was always a chance.

It was a shame the Head Slave did not seem to be as excited. Hopefully this would change when the hard prep work was done. Of course, Dominic would help out as much as he could and not just because he was told to. Even if he were not under orders he would have gladly helped, simply because he had a massive crush on Gavin and had done for many years, since the moment he first saw him. He would do literally anything for Gavin, anything just to be in his company for a few fleeting moments. He would gladly give up everything – his heart, his studies, his family – and he had. It was perhaps more accurate to say that he was in love with him, even if the feelings were not as yet reciprocated.

It had taken less than five minutes to want him for ever. Back when Dominic first joined the rugby club Gavin had been the captain of the First Team. Dominic was three years his junior and not old or strong enough to be promoted beyond the Reserves. He immediately set about putting this right. He trained every day, almost obsessively, building up his skills and his body. Of course, it helped that it meant seeing Gavin more often.

It was disconcerting, at first, having to admit to lusting after another male. Before, he had allowed himself only a few minor crushes on teachers and the father of a friend, and only occasionally masturbated while thinking about other males. He put his feelings for his captain down to an incredible respect for a guy with such fortitude and intelligence, such grace and, yes, beauty. But *respect* doesn't generally make your heart ache and your belly flip. Eventually he had to accept the truth, even if the sight of female nudity could still make his cock hard.

Joy swept him when he was finally picked for the First Team, only to have his heart spattered a fortnight later when Gavin mysteriously disappeared. No one knew of their captain's whereabouts, or why he had gone to ground having just finished university with such high honours. Dominic waded through dark months, his head spinning. It was as if his best friend had died or gone away, rather than a guy who barely spoke to him and seldom looked at him when he did. He vented his sadness through masturbation and sex, since his prick had a mind of its own and mourning was most definitely not on its agenda. He never forgot his captain, though, and many times, whilst he slapped against the soft rump of his girlfriend, he imagined being her, with Gavin behind dealing out the fast, deep, ball-slapping fuckings.

Other lads disappeared too, including one he had talked to about Gavin, maybe confiding a little too much about his feelings for their ex-captain. Dominic knew that it could not be coincidence. The other lads had to be with Gavin. His relief at knowing he must be well was countered by his jealousy. So imagine his elation when, out of the blue, nearly two years after he had gone,

Gavin was suddenly there again, beckoning him from the treeline, his silhouette as familiar as ever.

'Come with me,' Gavin had said and Dominic had agreed before he had even heard the terms.

He hadn't regretted his decision. The work was hard at times and the conditions were not quite as wonderful as Gavin had made out. However, he had taken to being ordered about, humiliated and generally derided – far more than he would have imagined. The Master was scary, but compellingly so. The bacchante girls were even more frightening and he was glad that for the most part they were kept segregated. Gavin had told him about the wild girls, but he hadn't told him just *how* wild they were.

The others wound him up with tall tales of the bacchantes' depraved deeds: capturing stray slaves and tying them to trees, queuing up to slam their bare arses back against the captive's erection, taking him in either hole, one sucking his balls while the others rode him, another slicing his balls off as he was coming, all of them whooping for joy as he bled, dancing around at his cries, one still with his balls in her mouth. It was surely all lies, but the reality was not too far distant. Just a brief contact with them and you might come away with welts and bite-marks in your flesh. They were insatiable and wonderfully pretty, their Priestess the most beautiful of all, and they nearly turned him back on to women – until he clapped eyes on Gavin again.

His ex-captain had mentioned the orgies, of course. They were always going to be a big selling point. That day when Gavin had secretly returned, he had led Dominic through the trees to one of the enclosed barns and sat him on the hay bales. Out had poured all the tantalising stories. He told him about a new, incredible life that was on offer to him.

'We get properly paid for it as well – big money too!' his hero had enthused. 'You won't have to scrape around just to repay student loans. I've seen the account state-ments. In a couple of years I'll be able to buy a house outright! It's the best job in the world!'

He had spoken mostly of the orgies, about how *anything* was acceptable; in fact it was encouraged. He said it was for the most open-minded of people, those who didn't mind showing themselves off in front of others.

'You don't mind having your dick out in front of other blokes, do you?' Gavin had said, and while he said it he was fishing around inside his fly and then pulling out his already swelling penis. As Dominic was saying that he didn't mind at all, his words were trailing off and his eyes were growing saucer-wide as he watched the prick being slowly stroked and growing stiff in his companion's hand. Dominic was encouraged to prove his assertion, and soon both sat on the hay, slowly masturbating, admiring each other's handiwork. Gavin had made no move on him. He had just continued his tales of the Order and the orgies, about what Dominic could expect if he joined. It was an erotic tale in itself, well worth wanking over.

'I'm the Head Slave,' Gavin had said at one point, 'which means I get to order whoever I want to give me head!'

He had looked meaningfully into Dominic's eyes as he said it. Dominic had nearly spunked. Gavin had described the rude rites and practices of the Order, watching to see which turned the younger lad on most.

'They sometimes treat us boys like bitches,' he had said, and Dominic's sharp intake of breath had betrayed his excitement.

'You like it rough then, like I do?' Gavin had asked.

There had been no time to answer. Dominic had found himself being pulled across the older guy's lap and then sharp smacks were being dealt to his buttocks. That had sealed the deal in an instant. The pain had been greater than Dominic had imagined, but it was all the better for it. The mortification was exquisite, the blush bursting on both face and arse cheeks. To be so prone, so exposed, especially to another male, was quite the most exciting thing of all. Gavin hadn't just slapped the cheeks. He had aimed a few down the crack itself, so the fingertips were just making contact with the perineum, just grazing the balls, which were hanging down in the gap between his knees.

'Toss yourself off, you dirty sissy boy,' Gavin had said,

and Dominic had gratefully done as instructed, grasping himself and masturbating furiously, whimpering aloud as his sperm gathered and bubbled and then flew.

The finer points were arranged as Gavin fastened his fly again, too quickly for Dominic to beg to give a reward. The date was set. They would stay in contact by text only. Dominic had barely a week to become used to leaving his old life behind, but he spent almost all of it dreaming about taking Gavin into his mouth. It was a treat he had still not been granted, some weeks on now from that day in the barn, but he hoped it would happen soon, maybe even that night at the surprise orgy.

'The caterers can do some of our usual stuff, even at this short notice,' Gavin was saying, 'and I'll just go out to get a few Bargain Buckets.'

It wasn't quite what the Romans did but the girls would like it. They needed sustenance to soak up all the alcohol and to give them energy for their exertions. They liked messy food – greasy, meaty, hunger-sating mouthfuls that they could eat with their hands and gorge upon. No fancy titbits for them. Anyway, no knives and forks were allowed, since no one could trust the girls with such dangerous implements. Even the *thyrsus*, their hunting stick, was banned from the orgy.

The order of each orgy was set in stone. The speakers would start pumping out the music from the get-go. None of it was music for dancing sedately around handbags.

It was harder club beats; techno, drum and bass, dub-step, some high-tempo remixes of rock, goth and punk favourites. The *Macarena* most certainly did not get an airing. The girls would gather, sizing up what and who was in the room. They would line up and in turn toast their god, down a full glass of wine, then drop to their knees to give his proffered erection a little suck. Then there would be more drinking, mainly wine, since it was the choice of Bacchus.

The dancing would follow, interspersed with eating and more drinking. Some goblets were filled with Morgana's special mixtures, and the girls loved these. They fired their lusts and drew out the beast within. The dancing would become more raucous and the girls visibly more excited and worked up. You could feel it building remorselessly in the room, all that uncontainable lust. When it became more physical, when they started to rip at each other's clothes, the Master would give his order and the fucking would begin.

It was always timed so that they were beside them-selves with desire before they were allowed to take their pleasure. They mostly just went straight for one another, since, outside these sessions, they were banned from touching – a rule that drove them to distraction since they lived on top of each other. Then, as more alcohol and potions were imbibed, as the music drove them on, anything was possible. The slaves had to watch themselves, even if they had already paired off. Sex toys were used, furniture, anything. Whatever they were driven to was done, however rude. Only the Priestess and their Master were immune, and they could take their pleasures as they saw fit. Dominic had been shaking the first time he witnessed the girls in full flow.

Because of the noise of the clanking wine glasses Dominic did not realise that the two of them were no longer alone. A female had snuck in. He jumped as he saw the new arrival but her casual dress told him she was one of the trainees, not a bacchante, which made her only slightly less of a threat.

Gavin had spotted her now too and was regarding her warily. By rights she shouldn't be there, mixing with them. However, since slaves were considered the lowest of all, technically she held supremacy here, even if she were a mere trainee. Gavin questioned her and got some excuse about having to collect something for the Priestess, but she was already smiling archly and eyeing their crotches. The Head Slave was trying to warn her off but the girl was pent-up like all Morgana's charges, starved of sex and simmering with need. For all Gavin's apparent clout, there was nothing he could do here. The girl was coming at Dominic and he was backing up against the wall. Her hand was reaching down to cup his crotch and give it a light squeeze. He was already growing beneath her touch.

The girl took her cue and got inside his clothes to

bring his prick out. Once it was unconfined she watched it expand to its fullest. She gave a little squeal of glee and held him tight, not wanting him to get away. She called Gavin over and he had to oblige. She impatiently unbuttoned him to reveal his member, which was also twitching and filling with blood, despite Gavin's protests and threats. She had them stand side by side and Dominic realised it was the first time he and Gavin had touched since that day at the barn. Her eyes were wide and she had a big, open-mouthed smile to show how pleased she was. If this weren't enough proof, she undid her miniskirt and let it drop, then pulled her tiny thong aside so she could rub herself.

It was still a wonderful sight, Dominic thought, though not as wonderful as Gavin's slim, proud cock. The girl was having trouble choosing between them. She dropped to her haunches with her knees splayed, so that they could see her fingers rubbing at her clitty and then disappearing up inside her. She respected rank, taking hold of Gavin first and giving the head of his prick a hot, hard suck, pulling it out again with a wet pop and snaking her tongue over the tip. The Head Slave grunted, trying not to give any outward sign of pleasure. The girl noted his efforts and smiled wider, as if accepting a challenge to break him.

She gave Dominic his turn and the thrill of her soft mouth made him gasp. He felt fabulous, side by side with the person he most wanted, their naked thighs touching, sharing this pleasure. The girl was warming to her task, taking them in turn whilst still fingering herself. Their cocks were almost the same, nearly perfect twins. She couldn't choose between them. She gobbled one and then speedily engulfed the other, not even bothering to take her grip off Gavin to do Dominic. His prick was so close that it was resting on her cheek anyway.

Her need to do them both was evident and Dominic could almost see what was about to happen, although he dared not hope for it. She loosened her grip on Gavin's erection, keeping her palm close to the shaft but stretching her fingers out to try to gather in Dominic's shaft too. It had to happen now; they were just too close for it not to. She paused and lifted her head and then the cocks were touching. Dominic felt the shiver running over his whole body. He was willing her to do it, and she did. She went down on them both, stretching her mouth on their cock heads, trying to get them both in. She had wide lips but it was still tight. Nonetheless she squeezed their pricks together and forced herself down.

Her tongue was flicking over them both and she was doing her best to suck without being able to get a proper seal. She had stopped fingering herself and was now grasping their balls, trying to get her hand round both sacks to squeeze them. Her fevered grasp was almost painful but it was glorious too, since Gavin's balls were squashed against his. She was trying to force herself further down their shafts and it was bringing them even closer together. Dominic wanted to put his arm around his companion. He wanted to kiss him – it seemed like the perfect time. Courage failed him, but the image was in his head and it drove the sperm out of his bollocks, past her grip, into his shaft and ready for its final coaxing.

'Hurry up, bitch,' Gavin growled.

The desire showed in his voice even though his words were unnecessarily harsh. Dominic hoped it meant he was nearing his climax too. How fabulous to come together! He savoured the feel of their hard pricks side by side, their balls squashed close, their seed ready to explode in unison. Surely after this they must be thrown closer together? Gavin might not be pleased that the girl was taking such liberties but as far as Dominic was concerned he wouldn't wish himself anywhere but right here, right now. Gavin hadn't lied. This really, *really* was the very best job in the world, and there was no way Dominic was about to leave it for anything.

8

Barely a mile away, oblivious to Dominic's current favourable situation, Mimi was frantically trying to find the information that might help free him from the clutches of Haydn Shady. Aware that time was against her she was frantically sifting through her notes, rereading passages from the borrowed books and trying to remember all the Spinster had told her about witches. The more she delved, the more she was reminded that this wasn't just some frivolous role-playing game, despite what her brain kept trying to tell her. However, that same silly brain still insisted that there was more for her to do before she could go to the police.

All she had on Shady was the Spinster's theory that he was still around, but no actual evidence to back it other than the word of a dotty old bag. The idea was frankly incredible that he could stay hidden away, apparently able to perform his dastardly deeds and yet not be discovered by the patrolling estate manager. It didn't matter how big the estate was, or that as its previous owner he would know of all its most secret places, or even that the new owner was never there himself. *Someone* would have seen him. If he was this *Master* that Morgana had spoken of then where the hell was he? Only a god could be omnipotent yet remain unseen.

Mimi decided to concentrate on Morgana, probably because the witch was so difficult to shift from her mind. First, it seemed indisputable that she was indeed a witch, although what that meant in real terms was anyone's guess. The extent of her power, if she had any at all, was hard to determine. Everything surrounding her seemed to be myth. People damned her and attributed all sorts of evil deeds to her, but where was the proof? Morgana herself had spoken of her group of wild, lust-crazed girls, but where were they and what was their purpose? Again, why had no one ever seen them? She had a small group of 'trainees', but these were surely little more than hormone-driven, dirty-minded party girls who thought that dabbling in the Dark Arts gave them an excuse to be as wanton as their bodies demanded. There was no sorcery here. As far as Mimi could tell Morgana's only trick so far was to produce milk from her breasts at will. And, of course, to make one fall desperately in love with her. Or was Mimi's sudden, overwhelming crush just due to the woman's matchless, heart-stopping perfection?

Mimi dug deeper. There was no information to

be gleaned from the internet by searching *Morgana Innamorato*. There was nothing on the *Ana Lucia Plan* either, so it was safe to assume it was a fabrication, although why that particular name was chosen remained unclear. The witch's slimming club was seemingly no more than a front for some kind of sex class for supposed witches in training. Mimi felt an involuntary twinge in her crotch at just the thought of being in a wild sex club for girls. The penny was beginning to drop. Whatever else was involved, sex was at the heart of the mystery. Mimi referred to her borrowed copy of a translation of the *Malleus Maleficarum*, a medieval treatise that aimed to prove the existence of witchcraft and that females were the driving force behind it. She reread the sentence that had previously struck her most: 'All witchcraft comes from carnal lust, which in women is insatiable.'

Mimi's best guess was that Morgana was a nympho-maniac with a penchant for a certain kind of young goth girl, and that claiming Powers of Darkness was the best way to seduce such misguided souls. However, things were about to become more complicated. It seemed witchcraft was deeply rooted in the area from way back. There were reports that the ancient church in her village stood on the site where a coven once met, and had been built to thwart their evil gatherings. Her sources gave references to the arrests and trials around the early 1600s, towards the end of another series of witch hunts encouraged by King James I. No names were listed or punishments described, but the consensus was that Satan was alive in the area.

The first name Mimi came across was that of a Mistress Aventine Hill, a notorious local witch living in the mid-1700s. She reputedly taught the secrets of the *Bacchanalia* to Sir Francis Dashwood, and supplied girls for use in the rites of his infamous Hellfire Club, who met at nearby Medmenham Abbey and the caves at West Wycombe. The Spinster had also mentioned this Aventine Hill woman, although conversely she claimed she had lived towards the end of the nineteenth century and had owned the very cottage in which Morgana still dwelt. Many believed Morgana to be possessed by the spirit of this witch. Some thought she just liked the idea of that and played up to it, because she was perverted and deranged.

According to the Spinster, Mistress Hill had lost her lover after being driven from her home. She returned and in her anger she let loose her pack of wild animals to ravage all the prettiest girls in the village, tearing them limb from limb. She put a curse on the other villagers, which is why barley never grew in the fields to the north and why one lamb in three died before it was a month old – statements Mimi was unable to verify. She searched the internet for this Aventine Hill. She came up not with a person but with a place: one of the seven hills on which ancient Rome was built. Surely it was no coincidence that in the shadow of this hill lay a grove where bacchanals were once held, organised by one of the most celebrated deviants of classical history, the High Priestess Paculla Annia?

That truly set the alarm bells ringing. Searching for this name yielded little more than confirmation that the Priestess was most active around 188 BC and was famous for restructuring the rite of the bacchanals to make them more frequent, to make them truly no-holds-barred, and to allow men to join. Her ceremonies consisted of frenzied drinking and dancing and apparently indescribably dirty sex. Same-sex couplings were encouraged, and orgies with groups of writhing naked bodies were commonplace. Ever greater depravities were *de rigueur*. The young female devotees were like a pack of wild animals (like the pack Miss Aventine Hill once set in revenge upon the village?) and any who would not join in their demonic acts were ripped apart in sacrifice. All of this was done in the name of Bacchus, overseen by the insatiable Paculla Annia.

Mimi was sure she already knew the name. No, wait – she was thinking of that other Latin-sounding name, Ana Lucia, her of the non-existent Plan. As she stared at the name and unpicked it, she realised with a shiver that Ana Lucia Plan was actually an anagram of Paculla Annia. So Morgana clearly knew about Paculla Annia, maybe even styled herself upon her. It seemed the mysterious Miss Aventine Hill did the same, although the name was clearly an alias, so who was she? Was it plausible that there was no other connection between her and Morgana, other than living in the same cottage over a century apart? The common denominator in all three cases seemed to be the band of wild wanton girls, so if Morgana did indeed have some girls holed up somewhere, one could assume that she used them in orgies. To think that the witch wanted Mimi to be a part of all this!

Mimi suddenly remembered the book Morgana had given her. It seemed ridiculous that she had all but forgotten it in the panic of finding out about Dominic's disappearance. It was sitting there on the coffee table, looking small, black and benign, although it possibly contained all the answers she needed. The first chapter, so the witch had said, would reveal all. It felt cold in her palm, yet opening it sent a surge of nervous heat through her belly. The pages were of thick parchment, tinged with age. The text was in neat handwritten black script, the bulk of the words completely unfamiliar. If Mimi had recognised the language as Middle English she could have established that the book must therefore be between five and eight hundred years old. If she had had the time, the inclination and the means to study and translate the first paragraph, it would have told her that this was a copy from the original Latin of the Priestess's Book of Magick, converted into English when her undying soul found itself on these shores and took its first incarnation. That, at least, was what the book said.

Mimi had already gone past this passage, trying to find any familiar words or phrases that would give her a clue. As she followed the text with her finger she kept feeling a tingle in its tip, like a tiny electric shock, although she was careful not to actually touch the page. She felt suddenly cold, even though it was such a mild early-summer afternoon. Her extremities were freezing, her nose feeling like it might drip. Whereas the book had first been cold, now it was open it seemed to be getting increasingly warm, almost like a burn on her chilly hands. She had to quickly place it in her lap, and the warmth radiated immediately into her crotch and made her gasp. She found herself pushing down onto the page with her fingertip, to keep the heat pressed to her puss.

Morgana had claimed that the first chapter would explain everything, and although the text was almost impenetrable, Mimi realised that with concentration she could make sense of parts. It was studded with words she could recognise and that spoke for themselves: *lustful, fornicācĭŏun, ravishe, dēfŏulen, incantācĭŏun, be-horewed, slaughter*. In giving herself to Morgana, Mimi was apparently expected to *lŏve filth* and *abhominācĭŏun*, to *practīse harlotrīe* and make a *cunte-hoare* of *al yonge wymmen* and *beautēful maidene*. There were several things she must *worshippe* or *adŏure*. Primarily she should devote herself to Bacchus and deny all other gods. Thereafter the most pressing requirement seemed to be getting lusty with as many *damisēle* and *fair wenches* as she could, especially those whom Bacchus had gifted with a *glōriŏus rumpe*.

Beautiful behinds seemed to feature heavily in the text, more so even than the frequently mentioned *bāre brests*, although there were a few sentences about the latter that Mimi found particularly exciting. She picked out references to suckling and *norishen* on milk. Her heart nearly stopped as she read the phrase *drinke milk fro Þe prēsteresses brest*, knowing immediately it meant *drink milk from the priestess's breast*, although she didn't pick up on the subtlety of it, not realising that *drinke* referred to a magical drink, or a love potion.

The words were spinning around her head, conjuring wonderfully rude images. Her breath was heavy and she felt jittery. The book was now pressed tight to her crotch and was still seemingly emanating heat, but only to her sex. Although the rest of her was ice-cold her quim seemed to be on fire. The image in her mind was of a mild but constant flow of electricity passing into her, as if the book was unloading energy into her womb. She should have thrown it to the ground or at least closed it, but her hands refused to do either.

Steadfastly clutching the book to her crotch, she clumsily pulled off her jeans and knickers one-handed in an attempt to cool her raging loins. The heat only intensified on her bare slit and instinctively she pressed the spine of the book harder to her crotch. The tingle in her little swelling bud was immediate and far greater than could have been caused by pressure alone. She felt dirty and like she was not alone, but she could neither drop the book nor take her eyes off it to scan for any unseen presence. The book needed to be read; it was compelling.

Another urge was growing too, and she realised this was why she felt so jittery. The urge was to get out and return to the estate. At first she thought this was her own sensibilities, telling her she shouldn't tarry while her friend was elsewhere in peril. This couldn't be right, though, because logic demanded she gather evidence before any return, or at least try to work out who and what she was dealing with, to help form a strategy. Anyway, the impulse, she realised, was not to get back there for Dominic's benefit but to return to Morgana. The witch was to be avoided at all costs and she knew it. But she had already left her computer desk and was standing in a ridiculous position, bizarre enough to make her blush and wish she could stop herself. She was grasping the top edge of the open book and pushing it into her groin, which had forced her bare bottom out. Her free hand had gone behind her and she was gripping one cold bum cheek and pulling it outwards, to open herself up. Her knees were pressed tight together as if they were bound, and she was shuffling forward towards the bedroom door, eyes down upon the text. Still, even though she was stuck in this ludicrous manner, *still* she was trying to read the book, as if it was demanded of her.

Apparently the book itself would not wait for her. The compulsion to read was matched by the compulsion to get out of the house. She was naked from the waist down and clearly couldn't go out like this, so why was she heading downstairs? She told herself the book must have some kind of powerful homing device within it, a Morgana magnet. This was utter claptrap and she knew it, even though she was now in the lounge and aiming for the front door. It was simply her naughty mind, driven by the overwhelming itch in her pussy and her rudest fantasy of being naked and fucked in public whilst others watched. Just throw the book down and snap out of this shameful yearning to masturbate! Forget the beautiful witch and remember your poor friend!

She managed to pin herself down on the lounge settee, but her legs were apart and the book was still open and pressed to her crotch. She felt wide-eyed and mad, incapable of stopping the montage of breasts and bottoms, of pussies and beautiful witches, that was spinning through her mind. She was lucid enough to know that, if the Spinster came back and found her like this, she could never explain herself. She couldn't get up, though, because the book needed to be read and it just wouldn't wait. Holding it tightly against her bare lap, she turned the pages to see what else was in store for her as the witch's lover.

It stated that males, specifically young men, could be

used in acts of fornication, but roughness was the order of the day; *bēte his buttok* and *smīte his flesche* were phrases used. The *sinne of sodomīe* was lauded, and below were three illustrations, all crude line-drawings but with enough clear detail to put the point across. The first showed a male entering a female from the rear, the second a male entering another male, the third a line of standing naked bodies, a male entering a male entering a male entering a bent-over, smiling female. Mimi felt the current surging into her, gathering pace as each picture turned her on more.

Rationality seemed to have all but flown and she was telling herself that it wasn't just her dirty mind at work; strange forces were surely gripping her. Many times over the years she had been hit by a fevered need to masturbate, by a flurry of vivid images that drove her so much to distraction that she had been forced to do herself wherever she was, despite the dangers. This was beyond any of those urges. She was shaking from the thought that she would not be able to resist running bare-arsed and free through the village, so that she could surrender herself to the witch and declare her love.

Was it her imagination or was the book now pulling to the side of its own accord, trying to slide off her lap and make for the door? The need to keep it in place to read was still as strong and she pushed it even tighter to her. She gasped as her swollen, burning puss lips were breached by the little V at the bottom of the spine. The feeling of being watched by unseen eyes was greater than ever. She knew it was Morgana, and maybe all of her girls, all waiting for her to come to them.

The urge to get out of the house was now so intense that Mimi once more found herself having to forcibly resist. She slid off her seat and plonked her weight down upon the carpet, so that she was now sitting with her knees bent up, squashed between the sofa and the coffee table. She was panicky, almost manic, aware she was no longer in charge of her actions. She automatically turned the page and found another drawing, which sent a sweep of goose pimples across her already freezing body. It was of a very fat-bummed girl being chased by a group of naked females, each of whom sported what was clearly a large dildo harnessed to her crotch.

Mimi felt a sudden jolting chill in her own, enough to make her gasp. She looked down and saw that her free hand had found its way beneath the book. She had unconsciously pinched the flesh hiding her throbbing clitoris, and was now pressing hard upon it, presumably in an effort to sate the itching burn there. She couldn't pull her hand away. The shame of being turned on by this wicked book was withering. Worse was the knowledge that she might have to give in to her craving for masturbation, even though her friend's life was quite possibly hanging in the balance. And still she couldn't prevent herself from reading on, although she knew that each word, each picture, sank her deeper under the spell and increased her need to go back to the witch.

The next page had the underlined heading of *Sparagmos* and beneath it there was no text, only drawings to show that it referred to some kind of ritual sacrifice. Again, each new picture drew her in more, despite their grisly nature, which should surely repulse her. There was a decapitated sheep, still standing, with its wound spurting drops of blood that travelled in an arc to fall upon a prostrate naked female. There was a male on all fours being pierced from the rear by one male whilst at the other end an even bigger erection filled his mouth. He had, however, been cloven in two at his middle. Above the gap in his torso was a sword held by a floating hand to demonstrate how the death blow had been dealt. Mimi was now salivating.

Overleaf was a full-page drawing of a female held down on some kind of rack, her wrists and ankles secured by thick ropes so that she was splayed out in a star shape. The ropes securing her limbs were each secured to some kind of beast, bulls perhaps. These were running away from her, and the drawing showed that her limbs had in fact been ripped free of her body and were spurting gore. An oversized phallus complete with large balls had been drawn near her crotch, the head and part of the shaft buried inside her. At the sight of the prick in the tortured female's body, Mimi suddenly felt her two fingers release their press on her clit and slide up into her puss. The shock was massive. Her insides were roaring hot and the fingers freezing. The contrast was huge and seemed to wake every nerve ending at once, sending the pleasure shooting through her body.

'You dirty *cunt-whore*!' she cried out involuntarily.

She couldn't believe she had said it. She almost thought it must have come from one of her unseen observers, although it was clearly her voice. She didn't know who the insult was aimed at, so it had to be herself. She was almost sobbing with the shame of her words and at the overwhelming need to frig, but she couldn't pull her fingers clear. Instead she jammed them back up inside her, spattering the heat of her juice onto her freezing thighs. It was as wretchedly wanton as she had ever felt. She had a sudden mental picture of her schoolfriend who once claimed to have masturbated with an ice pop. She even had a flash of the two of them plugging each other with frozen lollies, and now she really did feel utterly possessed.

The fingers continued thrusting in and out of her but the cold did not dissipate at all. Still it burned her insides and sent the shockwaves of joy radiating through her body. She needed to be filled, though. Suddenly, fingers were not enough. If she could just make it upstairs then she could sink her dildo inside. Maybe that would be enough to calm her down. She shuffled sideways, the wrong way as it happened because she was now facing the front door, not the stairs. The urge to rush out was still massively strong, and the panic rose again at the realisation that she might not be able to stop herself shuffling on her behind out of the door and all the way down the garden path, so that she would be sitting bare-arsed, still playing with herself, in the road.

She dug her heels in. If she could just make herself come she might yet shake the demon from her body. She couldn't get up and run for her dildo because she knew she wouldn't get past the front door. The book was still in her lap, masking her fevered masturbation and begging to be read, to show her things to fire her dirty thoughts. Again her hands seemed to be working beyond her control, one plugging zealously at her puss, the other keeping the pages turning. She skimmed through the text at speed, catching mere words here or there, although the butterfly excitement was constantly building, as if her *soul* was processing and understanding whole passages, and exalting in them all.

Another drawing interrupted the text, beautifully clear this time. It was a detailed close-up of a fat-lipped vulva, with an engorged clitoris poking out. To one side a not-to-scale dagger was pointing at it, one drop of blood at its tip. At the other side, also not to scale, was a side view of a female head, the mouth open in a smile and her very long tongue curling out, trying to catch the falling drip. Mimi's eyes picked out a single phrase from the text, *lōn droppe of blod fro Þe kēkir*. She knew immediately what it meant: *a single drop of blood from the clitoris*.

'Yes! Drink from me!'

Unbelievably, it was her voice again, louder even than before, enough to be heard outside. Even the porn stars she so jealously watched were never this loud and lurid. She whimpered in her shame, but the licentious spirit was growing inside and taking her over, telling her to let go and abandon all decency. She was going mad with the desire to come. Oddly she wasn't yet scared, despite her lack of control over her own body. There was underlying comfort in it all, as if rudeness was something to luxuriate in, and to hell with what others thought of her. Morgana promised a haven for such alluring immorality.

It was a trick, she knew it. The witch was planting these thoughts to reel her in. Drop the book, it was the only way. But she wouldn't, she had to keep it open, pressed down upon the fingers working so furiously inside her. She had to make one last stab at breaking the spell. Summoning all her willpower she managed to drag her fingers from her puss, but as soon as they left her empty her body hated her for it and rebelled. Her heels had been dug in to stop her moving but her legs shot out in front of her, as if to make a break for freedom. She dug in again, but this time her bottom immediately rose up and came forward, moving her body towards her heels, and towards the front door. It was bizarre and unreal and her head was swimming. She was sitting hunched up, humping at the hard cover of the book now that her fingers were not giving her pleasure, delighting in the rude sensation of the long pile of the Spinster's rug tickling her bare anus. God, how she longed for that magic snake tongue right up her backside!

Her presumably possessed legs stretched out in front of her again and before she could stop herself her bottom lunged forward to meet her heels, taking her closer to the exit. When her legs came out again she made an effort to arrest her body's forward movement, grabbing at the coffee table to try and grip the edge. She only succeeded in upsetting the fruit bowl on top, spilling its contents onto the surface. As her bum began to move forward she made another desperate grab, but her naughty hand had other ideas and grasped something else instead. As her body was propelled away from the table she looked down and saw that she was clutching a banana.

She could not check her progress. Her free hand offered no resistance and the friction of the carpet rubbing her wet holes was too glorious to fight. It was all she could do to bite her lip to stop from screaming out what a filth-loving horny fat-arsed bitch she was. She could not imagine ever feeling as lost and as lusty as this. She was going at a pace towards the door now, shuffling across the floor while trying to bury the spine of the book into her quim, half gibbering with her need to make herself come while shouting obscenities. There seemed to be no way of overriding the irrational need to get out and show off her wantonness to the world, but one final effort saw her stretch her legs out and slam against the door to brace herself. Still, she was not sure whether she was doing this to stop her possessed body taking her outside, or because it was just a sensible safety measure to stop the Spinster coming in while she was there frigging upon the floor. What was indisputable was that she was lying helpless on her back, her legs against the door but apart, and the urge to put the banana inside her was becoming unstoppable.

Most of her wanted to thrust the fruit in as it was but she fought this, quickly bit the hard stem and broke the seal to allow the skin to be peeled away. She had the sour juice of the stem in her mouth, thickening her saliva. In another action that immediately had her squirming with shame, she leant forward and ejected the bitter spit to land on her bare belly, and then quickly wiped it off with her fingers to smear on her quim.

Somehow during her last resistance she had finally managed to throw the book aside. In this brief moment of lucidity she realised it might have been only that that saved her from going outside. However, the naughty spirit was still inside her and hadn't been shaken free.

All rational thoughts were sent packing by the feel of the fruit pushing between her labia. Now she was a slave to desire again. She moaned as she pressed on and forced the banana inside her molten puss. She was far too wet to stop its progress. On it went, the skin peeled back to allow more inside.

Her other arm stretched out at her side, the wicked hand by its own devices seeking the book and grasping it again. She was defeated now for sure. The book came open once more and she could feel the burst of energy coming from it and surging into her belly. The bliss from the fruit inside her was clouding her vision but the book would not let her close her eyes. It had opened on the last page of the chapter she had been told to read. She could just make out the heading of *Prēsteress Paculla Annia*. Below this was another fine outline drawing in black, this time of a beautiful woman sitting naked with her legs wide apart to show off a neat, delightful quim. Her hair was long, falling all the way to the floor and spreading out there. The face was pretty, with all features in proportion, and perhaps it could have been Morgana, although there was no striking similarity. Certainly the breasts were not the same. Morgana's were big, but these were at least twice the size, although no less firm and uplifted. Mimi couldn't know, but this wasn't Morgana. It was Paculla Annia as she looked when she first came to these shores, back in 1348, as the Black Death was also arriving.

Mimi gawped at the huge breasts and imagined the squirts of milk coming from them. She rammed the banana deep and plugged her pussy furiously, dropping the book with ease this time so that she could frig her pulsing clit with her other hand. Her head was full of images. She could see herself lying naked on a black platform in a large artificially lit room. Morgana was there, with breasts as large as the woman's in the drawing. The witch was rubbing her bare quim all over Mimi's body. Then Mimi was slurping at the pussy. She was dimly aware of her own voice, sounding husky and guttural, loosing a stream of dirty talk, the words surely too filthy to be coming from her mouth, although they clearly were.

The girls from the class were there in her head now, all dressed like medieval milkmaids, their frilly tops pulled down to reveal their chests, their long dresses pulled up so that they could slap their fingers in and out of themselves. She was sucking at the witch's huge breasts and her mouth was being flooded. She had breasts squashed to her own, to her back and bottom and thighs. Hard nipples pushed at her puss. Tongues were all over her and up her. The Priestess was spanking her hard, the open hand sending fire through her bottom. The trainee girls were slavering all over her body, pinching and tugging at her erect nipples.

Then there were pricks all over her too, being smacked against her face and breasts and bum. She had them jostling to get inside her from the rear, three or four unfeasibly together trying to breach her. Morgana then replaced the pricks with a huge tapering dildo made out of horn, like a two-foot elephant tusk. Mimi could feel the horn going inside her, the point as wide as the tip of the banana had been, but widening rapidly as it sank deeper. Pricks and breasts were being alternately forced into her mouth to suck and all the while the tusk was slowly driven in, impossibly deep, spreading her open wider and wider as the witch's hips closed up to meet Mimi's bum.

She could feel the stretch at her lips and the spearing point right at the centre of her body. She was picturing herself from the side, with Morgana pressed to her from the rear.

The males were all faceless except for Dominic and his load was the biggest of them all, ten times harder than he had ever managed in real life, blasting her as the witch drew her dildo fully out and then drove it in one hard thrust all the way back into Mimi's body. She could feel her heart being pierced, and that's what took her over the edge.

The spasms hit her and were enormous. She shrieked and bucked, slamming the soles of her feet against the door as the orgasm ripped through her and threatened to blow her apart. Her hands mercilessly kept on going at her crotch until the banana broke inside her and the heat of her insides turned it to mush. Her body felt as if it had been caught in a high-speed collision, but the over-riding feeling was of unparalleled satisfaction, almost like she had been purged. She could hear someone sneering that she was a dirty bitch and always would be – the dirtiest of them all. She managed to put her hand up to her mouth to pinch her lips and stop the words, but they still rang in her ears.

Just as the orgasm began to wane she remembered she had felt something long and solid writhing from her, like a serpent being dragged from her belly and out of her quim. She knew that the malicious spirit had slithered from her, but its wicked seed had been left inside. She had been tricked and possessed but she didn't care. All she wanted to do was celebrate rudeness.

She lay there for some time. Her breath was fitful and her body twitched and jerked as the climax slowly ebbed away. The clouds in her brain started to clear and although she was fatigued she began to see more clearly. Her body was immediately warm again. There was no trace of the chill she was sure she had felt. Her limbs moved freely. The sense of them not being under her control had disappeared. She felt as if she was coming out of a vivid dream, where what seems like reality is slowly blown away as you blink and find your bearings and grasp the true situation. She couldn't even remember the feeling of the mania that had gripped her, the desire to bare her fanny to the world on her way to giving herself to the witch.

Recall of the incident was skittering away, so that every second it seemed less and less believable that it had happened at all, except for the fact that she was lying bare-bummed, and there was a discarded banana skin lying next to Morgana's Book of Magick. The book, mercifully, was closed. She couldn't remember the words she had read in it but she knew they resonated inside her and she would have to fight like hell to keep at bay the instinct to run to the witch. Her head was clear now and strength was returning. She cursed herself for falling into this trap. Time was pressing and the longer she sat around in the presence of *that* book, the more chance there was of falling under its spell again.

She hurried upstairs to dress. It was late afternoon but the light would hold for a few more hours yet. She had no camouflage so she opted for black: a tight stretch top, leggings, and trainers, all brought in the optimistic belief that she would once in a while go to the gym. She packed a little satchel with a torch and an aerial photo of the estate courtesy of Google Earth, plus a bottle of water and a bar of chocolate for sustenance. She didn't dare touch the book again with her bare hands, but bizarrely donned a pair of oven mitts to stow it within her bag. She planned to dispose of it en route, regardless of the fury this might cause. At the last moment she realised that taking the car was no good, since she would be unable to conceal it. Instead she got her bike from the shed and, after a pause for a few deep breaths, set off on her brave mission to save the day. The trouble was she had no idea of the wickedness lying in wait for her.

9

Mimi held her breath and tried to stop her heart banging loudly enough to be heard in the corridor. There were more voices out there, female ones this time, a clamour coming her way. She could feel their growing energy, like mounting pressure that threatened to burst her door open and expose her. They were right outside now. The strip of light at the bottom of the door was blocked by their passing. Her nerves shook as the door was brushed by shoulders and elbows. It was like feral kids on a school trip, all talking excitedly over each other – except that this excitement was far more adult and sinister, and far, far wilder. She gripped the dildo tighter in her hand and pictured the girls with their own in place, sniffing the air for her scent, coming for her; these *bacchantes*, these female savages.

The stiffness in her legs was starting to hurt. She adjusted her position as silently as she could within the dark confines of the mop cupboard, asking herself, not for the first time, how the hell she had got herself into this mess. It had to be the book. Why else, if one discounted her habitual journalist's urge to snoop, would she have acted with such reckless disregard for good sense and self-preservation? Getting rid of the book should have been the easy bit. Just toss it into the bushes on the way to the estate. But she could not bring herself to do it, maybe through fear of holding it again and being instantly put under its spell.

She had kept well away from the witch's cottage, fearing the magnetic pull of the book, which might see her impelled slap-bang into Morgana's front door. This compromised her search for Dominic, restricting it to the land on the west side of the Big House, which turned up nothing of interest. Having spent over an hour sneaking around empty barns and smelly outbuildings, she gave up and found herself gravitating towards the Big House itself. She knew it would be empty and it had certainly appeared to be, the gates chained shut and the house showing no signs of life.

She had decided to give up and rethink her strategy when events unfolded in a flurry of activity. She had performed a high-speed, ungainly dismount of her bike into some bushes, having had to veer off the road at the sound of an approaching car engine. To her dismay she had belatedly recognised the driver as the estate manager, perhaps her only ally at this particular moment.

He could have helped her in her search. He could have rung his boss and the good Mr Pieter Bakkers would have instantly dropped everything, flown the trifling few thousand miles to get there and arrived just in time to once more save the day.

Having extracted herself from the hedge she had heard voices nearby. She crept through trees and saw two lads carrying boxes from a van to a small, windowless stone hut. She thought she recognised the two males from pictures she had often studied, published after they were reported missing. If these two were here, then Dominic must surely also be close by. When they left she had gone to inspect the unloaded contraband but found the hut empty, a trick even Morgana would have been proud of. They had to have gone under the floor, in this case beneath the rectangle of grubby carpet that had been laid there. However, the carpet was stuck down and only by accident did she stand on the little button that released the trapdoor and allowed her to lift it and peer down into the gloom.

She had seen a small flight of steps and the start of a darkened passage, heading east, back in the direction of the Big House. This had been the critical part. Don't go down, her head had told her. Remember all those scary films where you yell the same advice at the screen, where you pull your hair out with exasperation when they go against all good sense. But then the book must have been exerting its wicked influence because down she was going, closing the trapdoor above her to cover her tracks. The initial passageway had been dingy and dank. She had used torchlight to find her way the forty or fifty yards to the metal door at the end. Beyond that, though, things could not have been more different.

She found herself in what could be mistaken for a swanky subterranean London nightclub, or maybe *fetish club* would be more accurate. The corridors were all lit and the walls smartly painted. There was a modern kitchen that wouldn't have been out of place in a posh restaurant, plus a cloakroom that would have served a horde of club-goers, all swanky chrome and black marble. There were a couple of doors covered in buttoned black leather. Both were locked, which saved her racing heart the test of having to keep going through the suspense of finding out what lay on the other side. The place was deathly quiet but she sensed danger behind every door, round every blind turn.

The final corner presented her with double swing doors in metal. When she finally plucked up the courage to peek inside she discovered a room to make her gasp. Her eyes swept around, although the full information would not be fully processed until after, when she had fled to the mop cupboard. There was a central dancefloor, with a glitter ball and swivel lights above. Around it were various tables and couches, all apparently covered in black padding and cushions. There was a long wooden banqueting table with what seemed like a couple of thrones behind. There was a bar area, backlit so she could see all the optics in place. There was a row of high stools in plastic and chrome, their backs to the bar, each one with a veined rubber prick suckered to the seat.

These were not the only dildos around. They abounded, lying on ledges, on tables, on wall racks. Most had straps to secure them to the waist. The one she had been unconsciously grasping when she fled she later found to have a little ridged rubber pad on the inside, positioned to titillate the wearer whilst it was put to use. There were other things too, various machines, but these didn't get much scrutiny because her attention was mostly taken by a large cage towards the back, which just happened to contain a blindfolded and naked female. The captive hung there stationary, her arms secured above her by cuffs to a dangling iron chain. Her head was slumped forward and for a few spine-chilling moments Mimi had feared the worst.

The captive had then sensed some movement and lifted her head, tilting it towards the sound. The floor of the cage was dotted with thick candles in purple, black or red, all alight. The girl tried to manoeuvre herself around on her tiptoes to face the direction where noise might come from, careful not to upset any of the candles and burn herself. Mimi could see that a pentagram had been daubed upon her belly in red, she hoped not in blood. Across her breasts were red letters, which needed closer scrutiny but proved to spell out *sparagmos*, the rite of sacrifice that the book had told Mimi of. The girl was clearly wary and perhaps she had some knowledge of what was coming to her. Mimi wanted to help her, but had no idea what to do with her if she did. It had proved immaterial because there was a sound of a door closing somewhere and she rushed back to the swing doors to listen.

The sound of chattering male voices had driven Mimi back down the corridor, where she suddenly realised she had nowhere to go. The noise was coming her way and in a blind panic she secreted herself inside the tiny mop cupboard and held her breath as the males outside passed by. She tried to make an escape behind them but there were more voices, from the kitchen this time, and so she hid back in the cupboard and prayed that no one needed to mop the floor that night. In the last hour the voices had passed back and forth repeatedly and she realised she was well and truly stuck where she was. Even when the music came on and started to *thud, thud, thud* and rattle the door, she still knew that there was no way to run and evade capture.

Resigned to her fate she dropped her leggings and panties and squatted to make use of the bucket. As ridiculous as it was given her situation, she had already considered using the dildo on herself, to help ease the tension. It was that damn book at work again, blinding her to anything but the chance of pleasure. The noise of the approaching girls soon snapped her mind back into focus. Soon after she had thought she could *sense* Morgana passing by, maybe even thought she heard the sound of the witch's nails scratching across the door above the constant throbbing bass of the dance music.

She could only speculate at what was going on in the main room. Time and time again she had to prevent herself from going out to sneak a peek. The footsteps continued to pass back and forth at regular intervals, throwing shadows across the strip of light at the bottom of the door. She had grown almost impervious to it when stupidly she shifted her weight just as someone was walking by and the bucket scraped across the floor. In the cupboard it seemed loud, but surely outside it would be inaudible. However, the shadow stopped and a section of her light was blocked. Someone was outside. Seconds ticked by as she held her breath but the door stayed shut. The shadow started to move and she exhaled her relief. It was still gushing from her lungs when the door snapped open and she was blinking with the light and trying to focus on the figure facing her.

She was so surprised to see the familiar face she almost shouted his name. Dominic was so surprised he immediately shut the door on her again. He gave himself a few moments, presumably to gather his thoughts, before opening it again and demanding to know in hushed tones what the hell she was doing there. She was shocked by his terseness, but she put it down to shock.

'I've come for you!' she said. 'To save you!'

He looked stumped and flustered, possibly even annoyed. It probably didn't help his confused state that she was still clutching the dildo, nor perhaps that for some reason he was dressed in a toga. She could see he was thinking, weighing up how best for them to make their escape. In the end, fearing more unwelcome passers-by, he told her to hang on and wait for him. She stood back in the darkness but there was a sense of joy now. She knew he would have to save her as much as she him, but together they would get out and the story would be told. Shady would be done for at last. She waited five minutes, then ten. It would need precise timing, she knew that. After fifteen minutes she was starting to think something was wrong. Perhaps he had been seen, or been caught trying to make another exit from the room. At least he wouldn't tell on her. That was one thing she could be sure of: her ex-boyfriend, no matter what the circumstances, would never, ever betray her, because, well, he just *wouldn't*.

He would. The door sprang open again and there he was, looking stern. Behind him was a giant of a man dressed in a purple toga, the colour worn by the Emperors of Rome. He had jet-black hair to his shoulders and the coldest, scariest blue eyes she had ever seen on anyone outside the movies. The eyes told her all she needed to know and she felt her knees shaking and beginning to buckle. Before she could collapse the man's hand shot out and grabbed her by the neck. She was pulled clear of the cupboard and propelled towards the noise of the main room.

Shady did not speak to her. He dragged her through the mêlée and shouted instructions to a couple of lads also dressed in togas, who immediately went to the cage, released the captive and carried her clear so that Mimi could take her place. She couldn't fight. Candles were kicked aside as she was bundled in but essentially she had already given up. Her hands were easily secured in the cuffs above her head and she waited to have her clothes ripped off her, to be left as nude as the last captive. It didn't happen. She felt a pang in her belly and she couldn't quite tell if it was relief or disappointment.

Her arrival had caused a ruckus. Most of the girls were still on the dancefloor, but they were now static. All eyes were on Mimi, and those eyes were fiery-bright, glaring at her through strips of thick makeup. The dancers had wild rock-chick hair, damp at the sides and temples. They all had scarlet painted lips, a couple with red spill marks at the edges, like vampires who had been drinking blood, although perhaps it was from wine or maybe just makeup to look like blood. Those girls who were not yet topless wore cropped plain T-shirts, cut jagged below their breasts, all dampened by heavy perspiration that told of their exertions. All were barefoot and barelegged. They had thick, firm calves and thighs, all looking identically smooth and pale. The legs went up to very short, tight miniskirts in some kind of dark brown hide, which were barely long enough to cover their decency. Four or five of the girls had false cocks secured by harnesses at their crotch; a couple long and smooth, a couple thick and venous. All were pointing towards the new captive.

The sensory overload had stopped Mimi from taking it all in during the first flurry of being brought amongst them. Now in these few quiet seconds her brain was able to process more and give her glimpses of memory. There was danger here, that was for sure. She had felt it even as she was propelled past them, before they knew she was in their midst. Their dancing had been frantic, a weird high-energy fusion of club and tribal. She had seen their eyes wide and flashing, their snarls and bared teeth. She had witnessed some contact between them which, although they all looked like sisters, had not seemed particularly tender. It was grasping contact, gripping nails into bare flesh, pulling at tops, all somehow desperate. It felt like she had gone in just as things were building to a crescendo, where something huge was about to give. The air was full of it.

Those who had not been dancing had been feasting from the tables. From the corner of her eye she now remembered seeing them filling their mouths with meat, ripping it from drumsticks so that the grease glistened on their pale cheeks. Even the eating was done with animated fervour, like they just couldn't wait to stuff the food in. She could see now that none of the girls were skinny, all had meat on their thighs and bottoms. Some had little belly paunches though none were *fat*, none had a bum to match Mimi's. Yet they ate like fat people, like greedy bitches, like time was running out on them. She could see smears around mouths, the remnants of flesh and tendon hanging off bones still being clutched. Mimi had a sudden shiver-inducing image of ending up like one of those drumsticks at the hands of these savages.

The cage door could barely be swung shut before the girls were at her. Mimi could hear their shrieks and war cries above the thudding music. They smacked into the iron bars and reached through to try and grab her. Fortunately she was only just in fingertip reach from all sides, but she felt contact on her hair as they tried to snatch a handful, and their long black-painted nails snagged at her clothes. Mimi had to wriggle to ensure no grip was maintained. One girl was pinching her own bare nipples in exasperation at being unable to get to Mimi, stretching them towards the captive as if hoping they could grow long enough to stab her. Two had jammed their thighs hard to the cage to thrust their dildos into gaps between the bars, and were humping empty air, showing Mimi exactly what she would get when she came into reach. One or two spat at her; all of them cursed or bared their white teeth. Above her wide-eyed panic Mimi saw Morgana beyond them, relaxed and smiling upon a throne as she went through the contents of Mimi's snatched satchel. She had a feeling that only the witch could save her now, but she wasn't even looking her way.

More spittle landed on her cheek and Mimi's looked again at her would-be assailants in time to see them peeling themselves from the bars, their attention drawn to easier prey. The original captive had been thrown still blindfold and naked beside a low padded dais, where she simply sat and made no attempt to escape. The bacchantes leapt at her, dragged her by her hair up onto the platform, clutching her breasts as they did so, slapping her naked flesh with their open palms. She was laid on her back and those savages already wearing dildos were grabbing small pewter jugs off side tables and hurriedly pouring thick oil from them over their false pricks.

The girl's fate seemed terrible. Eight seething bitches were gathered around her, pinching and slapping and squeezing her, some readying their dildos with oil to give them some ease of entry when they slammed inside her. Her arms were held; she couldn't fight. How would Mimi stop them when it was her turn? What would this girl do to thwart them now? The answer sent a jolt of excitement through Mimi's body, since it proved to be so simple. As one savage fought her way into position, clutching her thick false prick, a smile of glee spread across the captive's face and she bent her knees up and spread them apart, raising her hips from the platform so that she was wide open and ready. She gave herself up completely, exalting in her ordeal rather than shrinking from it. The savage brought the plastic tip to the wet and willing sex, then jammed her hips forward and thrust it in, causing the captive to scream her pleasure.

Mimi could feel the tingle at her own groin, the contraction of the muscles inside as they begged to have the same. Shady was there again, his face also set in a snarl; their Master. He had both arms raised, his fists were clenched and he was bellowing into the noise.

'Fuck!' he was shouting at everyone. 'Fuck! *FUCK!*'

It was not an angry expletive. It was an order.

The bacchante girls began shrieking even louder than before, the sound cacophonous along with the music. They suddenly scattered, most of them leaving the one still slapping hard into the body of the blindfold captive, who was now crying with bliss and gripping her fucker's bottom to make sure the thrusts retained their weight and tempo. Tops and skirts were coming off and targets were being sought. An orgy was to erupt, like the one in the book.

One savage had run down and flattened another, and, taking advantage of the already fastened dildo, had sunk upon it and was riding it cowgirl-style. Mimi briefly watched the pale, gorgeous rump juddering as it was slapped down hard and fast, then her attention was wrenched elsewhere. Another had caught her ally and pushed her over a raised table. The skirt was up over her ample rump and fingers were going into her from behind whilst the other hand covered the squeals from her open mouth. One of the feasting girls was just wailing, standing where she had been before but now with her legs open and her skirt held up to reveal a pristine, shaved quim. She had shoved a meaty drumstick up into it, and was busily using it on herself.

The male slaves stood no chance. They were instantly targeted, some girls leaping over couches and fuck machines to get to them. Togas were immediately off to reveal already oiled athletic bodies and bare erections. Two of the lads had paired off and were kissing and grasping each other's pricks. They were granted no privacy. Three girls were soon at them, prising hands away to replace them with their own, sinking mouths down onto the hot cocks, engulfing ball sacks. The treacherous Dominic was having his prick swallowed almost to the hilt whilst another girl slapped his bare arse. Mimi was silently glad that he was being treated so roughly, until it dawned on her that her ex seemed actually to be enjoying it immensely.

209

Everywhere flesh was on flesh. It was a raging explosion of passion. There was no subtlety and little tenderness, but there was an understanding of each other's need, and that need was for huge, instant pleasure. Mimi could feel it. She knew that despite her perilous position her body was responding only to the rudeness of all she witnessed. She was so hot and ready that if she could only be penetrated now she would yell her glee, just like so many of the savages were doing. Orgies were obviously not meant for tenderness. The word that kept coming to mind was *abandonment*. It was like being set free, and not being afraid of that freedom. It was an exhilarating expression of your sexual being, with no limits and no judgements. One bacchante, for instance, was now hunched over a machine, her crotch squashed against a rubber pad that was vibrating with blurring speed. Behind her another savage crouched, thrusting a *very* long slim dildo in and out of her body, possibly in her bottom. The girl had her eyes screwed shut and was completely lost to lust, her noise audible beyond the music as she *screamed*, 'Fuck me!'

Imagine being her, right now, Mimi thought, and another shiver swept her body. Then Morgana was suddenly in front of her, blocking the view. She was stripped and sporting a beautiful shining chrome dildo at her waist. Her breasts looked ripe and beautiful, so firm. Mimi felt herself instinctively pulling at her chains. She wanted so much to be naked too, to be seen and heard screaming by all these people, to be used and abused before their eyes as the Priestess took her. She was ready to fuck with the same abandon. She was dying for it.

'Thank you for the return of my book,' the witch was saying, her voice magically audible over the booming bass even though she did not seem to be speaking any louder than usual. 'I hope you are ready to come to me now because I am your last remaining hope.'

Mimi was going to say that she was, even though she knew it was only lust making her decisions, not logic. She had no chance to answer. Morgana turned away again, pulled one bacchante off another by her hair, bent her over a table and pierced her from behind with the chrome dildo. Mimi almost cried with longing as she watched the Priestess's beautiful bottom thrusting back and forth against the girl. Anything – her life, her soul, anything at all – Mimi would have given at that moment to take the place of that girl, or be behind her Priestess giving her the same treatment, reaching round to squeeze those breasts, taking turns to indiscriminately fuck and be fucked as was allowed at such brilliant gatherings.

Mimi's vision was beginning to cloud because of the desire raging through her. She heard herself crying out to be untied, so she could at the very least masturbate. But what was her voice amongst all the rest? The orgy just kept on going, ever dynamic as bodies slithered from one to another. It became an almost surreal collage of pricks and dildos and tongues and fingers in succulent, ever-willing holes. Nothing was too rude, everything left her breathless and yearning to be a part of it. The smell of it was intoxicating too, the heady waves of citrus and spice and sex. The sound of slapping flesh was everywhere, some in time with the music, so that each new song brought a new tempo to the fucking. It was hypnotising. The bodies were glowing with sweat and oil, the tanned light brown of the males and the snow white of the females. She realised suddenly how *perfect* everyone was, how perfect all bodies were when fucking.

Drinks of various kinds were being consumed even while the bodies were in motion, poured from jugs into each other's mouths to prevent their passion and endurance from waning. The tearing, scratching assaults of the initial stages had calmed somewhat, but there was still urgency and roughness, and plain, shocking debauchery. It became like a dream, like a sequence of abstract filthy scenes. Mimi scanned around, wanting to absorb it all, unable to spend too long on one thing for fear of missing another. 'Please help me – my pussy is so wet!' she was shouting, but no one heard her.

Everything was a montage of rudeness that she was desperate to commit to memory in individual episodes that she could later recall. She saw all these things: a girl bent over the feasting table shoving handfuls of creamy cake into her mouth whilst a slave rammed her hard from the rear; a slave standing, being sucked by a girl, whilst another girl was up with her legs hooked over his shoulders, riding his face. She was pulling his hair as she ground into him and he was doing his utmost to keep her held up to be lapped at like she wished. A bacchante passionately kissing another and having her bottom squeezed and held apart by her, whilst a third very lovingly licked her bottom; this was perhaps the only properly tender episode Mimi witnessed. The same bacchante, now sandwiched between the other two, being fucked by both at once with strapped-on dildos.

The original slave was given no quarter, perhaps because her body was notably not as pure and beautiful as all the rest. It was hard to tell with the blindfold but Mimi suspected this was the same girl who had been given the *Purging* that night in the classroom. This evening she was ravaged by the fattest dildos, and covered by various girls with hot wax, mainly on her breasts and belly but also in her mouth and quim. Her behind was beaten red with hands and paddles.

Double-crossing Dominic was having his fair share of fun too. The first girl at him looked like she might bite his conniving cock clean off, but she had relented when he sent a huge spurt of hot seed into her mouth. Mimi had watched with bitterness as he grew hard again almost immediately. She had been shocked to see him later with his own mouth around another prick, a proud example belonging to the lad she recognised as being the first to disappear. Dominic seemed to be slurping on the prick with great attention and fondness.

Later still he had been over a table, the prick that had been in his mouth now deep in his behind. Again, this was apparently nothing but pleasurable for him. Beneath the table his own prick was rock hard and a bacchante sucked it for him and squeezed his balls. Just before his face screwed up with the hit of his orgasm he had looked across at Mimi in her cage. His eyes had been burning and defiant. This is why I'm not with you, they had said, and Mimi had to concede she could see his point. The load spurting into his backside triggered his own ejaculation. It was animalistic, but Mimi couldn't help being turned on by the dirty synchronicity of it, by the beauty of their timing.

Mimi had never considered the potential subtleties of an orgy. For her the main turn-on was always to be done in front of others, to be publicly used, though not necessarily by all and sundry. However, she could now see how wonderful it might be to fellate a cock whilst being done from the rear. It was the little things as well as the eye-popping amount of rudeness on view. To kiss one pretty girl whilst being licked by another; to be so near to a prick sliding in and out of a beautiful pussy; to watch two girls kissing up close, snuggling into one of them from behind ... No wonder these girls craved the orgies enough to give their souls in exchange. Once you had taken part in one, little would fire you up as much again.

The music kept on pumping out. The drink and food kept being guzzled down or smeared over bodies. The energy did not dissipate, the excitement could not diminish. Mimi watched bodily fluids spurting around, hitting faces, breasts, bums, bellies, the floor. Releases were only temporary halts to ever building pleasure. Wetness was everywhere. The bacchantes seemed to come almost incessantly and the slaves did their best to keep up. She thought she saw Dominic come four times, the last such a wrenching effort she thought he was going to collapse. Clearly some kind of magic was behind these physical feats but selling one's soul still seemed a good price to pay for such matchless ecstasies.

The witch herself seemed content to stay mainly in her seat, watching over it all with a wide smile of satisfaction. The girls came to her in turn through the night, primarily to suckle, to get the elixir that heated their desire. The jealousy and desperation to be out having her turn ripped at Mimi's heart. Some would be made to take a turn between the Priestess's thighs, licking her deeply and with love. It had never before struck Mimi just how beautiful it was to watch a girl using her tongue on a delicious bare pussy. It seemed so rude yet pure, the two sets of soft lips kissing, the glistening. Every once in a while Morgana would feel the need to bury her dildo inside one of her girls, and Mimi recalled the pad inside the harness that could give the wearer pleasure while it was used. Why hadn't the Priestess come to her? After all she had said, wasn't she even remotely tempted to force the issue?

Despite the fevered ravishings, Mimi was surprised that proceedings hadn't yet boiled over. Yes, there was flesh marked by nails and slaps, there were holes that had been stretched or plundered by seemingly impossible lengths, there had been plain nastiness. However, no blood was spilling, no throats had been cut, no one was being split apart or dismembered. For his part their Master seemed content to sit in his throne and take it all in, or occasionally walk among them for a better view. Mimi had not felt threatened by him since she had been locked into the cage. He was awesome but not the raving sadist she might have expected the leader of a demonic sect to be. He issued few commands, generally allowing the orgy to evolve in its own way.

Mimi realised she was desperate to see him strip and unveil his prick. The longer he didn't do it, the more her pussy itched and tormented her. She already had visions of a member of monstrous proportions and she wanted to see it used on these insatiable girls, maybe even on the boys – maybe on backstabbing Dominic, or was that being too cruel? The strangest part about the Master's apparent reluctance to free his prick and join in seemed to have something to do with an urge to *fill* the girls. Mimi watched him a few times using his fingers in a vacant hole when the other was being used, or forcing a girl's mouth onto a slave's erection whilst she was being filled at the other end. Two bacchantes had been wantonly riding the dildos suckered to the seats of the bar stools. They had been side by side, drinking shots between passionate kisses. He had come up and filled one's bum with his long, thick middle finger – a digit in itself as long as some men's erections.

His fingers were used on other girls, sometimes two at a time, or in combination with the thumb. At one point he delighted in having four girls riding simultaneously on his toes and fingers, then having them sucked clean. At another point he grabbed a girl and put her over his knee, then drew wine up a tube by some kind of mechanical pump which could then eject the liquid under pressure through a nozzle inside her. He gave maybe two or three such enemas, forcing the girls to hold on to the wine for ages, having other girls fuck them before granting a massive, messy, blissful release. Still no prick though. It wasn't like he had problems in that department. She could see the erection tenting the front of his garment, sticking out further than even the longest of the dildos around the girls' waists. And it was thick too. A couple of the girls had grabbed at it in their lust and tried to suck him through his clothes. They had not been able to close their hands around it. They had barely been able to get their mouths on it.

It was almost impossible to keep measure of time but surely more than an hour had passed before the Master finally allowed the girls to pull his clothes free and leave him standing naked in their midst. His skin was gleaming from its thin covering of oil. The muscles were clearly defined and he helped by striking a pose: raised up slightly on his toes to tense the calf muscles, twisted at the hip to clench his prime buttocks, belly in, chest out, arms by his side, hands in a loose downward point, like those statues of Greek and Roman gods. As he turned slowly, showing off his body to all, Mimi saw the prick in all its magnificence and felt her cheeks burning from the rush of blood. It wasn't just the impressive size, it was the *stiffness* of it, like it was hard as iron, like it could bear your weight if you stood upon it.

Once unleashed the prick was not to be ignored. The girls untangled themselves from whatever slippery grouping they were in and came to kneel at his feet, a dozen of them by Mimi's count, all bar the original captive and the Priestess. Their faces were radiant with awe and greed. The music seemed to magically drop so that all you could hear was their purring and lip-smacking, their heavy breaths and panting pleas to have

218

his cock. He seemed to pick them at random, grabbing their hair and pulling them forwards to receive his gift in their open mouths.

Mimi felt herself salivating. The savages sucked hungrily, gripping and tugging on his shaft, desperate to finish him before he pulled them away by the hair so that another could have her turn. It was like an adult version of Pass The Parcel. It seemed to Mimi that it was an impossible task, that the muscle of his prick was so hard that it wouldn't be feasible to stimulate the tube inside that carried the seed down the shaft.

He stopped the game and manhandled the girls like weightless dolls, pushing some aside, manoeuvring others into position. He ended with a stack of three on a padded platform a foot above the floor. Girl One lay flat on the platform surface, her crotch at the edge so that he could bury himself in her. Girl Two lay face-down upon the first girl, her head at the rump end, so that she could hold those fat bum cheeks apart for her Master, or take him into her mouth should he slip from the first girl's body. Girl Three lay upon the other two, face down once more but facing the same way as the first girl. Her hips were placed further along, so she was dangling over the back of the girl sandwiched in the middle. If the Master was buried inside the first girl he need only lean forward to get a face full of the third girl's bum and lust-swollen pussy. This he did.

Mimi held her breath as she watched it all unfold. Although other girls had been pushed aside they still knew what to do. Ewers and goat horns were produced from nowhere to fill the first girl with oil, then hands were holding her open and in place and guiding his prick to her. She screeched as she was entered but he slid on into her remorselessly. Thrusts were given as the Master continued to feast upon the third girl from behind. Then he pulled out and sank into the mouth of Girl Two, who sucked him as avidly as any porn star. Then he raised himself on to his haunches and with almost no hesitation drove his whole length into the pussy he had just been eating.

Up and down he went, plugging bottom then mouth then pussy in turn. Mimi felt the exaltation. To see such a fine prick being given such apt worship, three females giving him his dues one by one, each different and wonderful in their own right. The whole of him looked divine, the muscles tensed in his legs and buttocks and in his wrists as he gripped their flesh, the tendons in his neck straining as he gritted his teeth hard and pumped with speed and depth. He did indeed fuck like a god. It was basely carnal, probably even grotesque if looked upon dispassionately, but to be watching as a part of it, to see and hear and *smell* this supreme fucking, was simply thrilling. It was fabulous and fitting and beautiful to behold. He finished eventually in a bollock-wrenching gush.

Mimi could see his prick twitching as it began its very slow descent. She felt a massive sense of disappointment that it was all over, but she needn't have worried. For her it had only just begun. As the great prick went down, the volume of the music went with it, until it was barely audible. The Master had turned, his chest still puffed out, and now she realised that his cold, cold eyes were fixed directly upon her.

'It is time,' he said loudly, 'for a sacrifice to be made.'

10

Mimi stared open-mouthed, absorbing this sudden reminder of the danger she was in. His great prick might have been deflating but that just meant his mind would be able to turn to other things, namely his new captive. 'Sacrifice' was not a good word to hear. Morgana stepped from the shadows to stand alongside him. Her arrival should have brought comfort, but in this case, given what she was wearing, it didn't. It seemed ages since Mimi had seen her. It was surely inconceivable to take your eyes off her even for a minute, let alone long enough not to notice her unbuckling her silver dildo and replacing it with the deadly-looking two-foot horn she now had strapped to her waist. It was the one from Mimi's dream fantasy, when she had been under the power of the book. It was pure white, thick at the base and curving up into a fingertip-sized point. Mimi knew it would kill her.

'She will be hung up so that the Priestess can pierce her through her *cunnus*,' the Master announced to his hushed audience. 'She will be fucked to the heart and given up to Darkness. When the horn is removed her blood will be collected in a bucket so that I may bathe my cock.'

He was coming towards Mimi as he said these last words, his stare never leaving her. Right to the cage he came, then he unfastened the lock so that he could swing the door open and leave her at the mercy of the savages.

'Do it now,' he said.

Mimi would have screamed if she could have found her voice, but fear froze her. The girls were up and moving in a flurry of activity. He still stood at the entrance of the cage. It was so hard to drag her eyes off his but finally Mimi did, in time to see a few of the girls coming her way. They were clutching the original captive by her arms and dragging her along. Mimi could hear the captive's quiet pleas of 'No, no, no' as she was taken past the cage. Mimi felt a surge of relief but still fizzed from the threat of looming danger. He had stepped into the cage and was coming towards her, huge and foreboding, even in his nudity.

He reached above her and unhooked another cuff attached by a chain to the top of the cage. This one had a wider, thicker restraint, designed for the neck. He put it in place, forcing her chin up. She could feel the cold leather constricting her throat as he tightened it. Her panic was countered by the sounds of the original captive, fretting somewhere behind her as she was presumably tied to a rack against the back wall. The Master clicked his fingers and two bacchante girls were quickly beside him, knowing his instruction without it being spoken. In unison they knelt and pulled off Mimi's leggings, followed by her thong. He was close to her, looking down, his face just an inch from the top of her head. She knew he would be able to smell the scent of her desire as it rose from her exposed sex.

Her racing heart didn't even slow when she saw Morgana pass by in her periphery. It gave her some confirmation that the sacrifice was indeed not of her but of the original captive. She could see nothing of the activity. She would not see the piercing or the terrible plunge of the horn inside the girl. She could hear the wailing, the sounds of smacked flesh as the girl was restrained, the clicks and slurps of what might have been a rapidly wanked pussy, presumably to open her up. He just stood there, his body almost touching hers, shutting out the light, a wall of muscle. His hands went down to her thighs and, as more squeals and screams and squelching sounds emanated from behind, he very lightly stroked the smooth skin just to the side of her pussy, making her gasp and shiver. She looked up into his ice eyes and even found some comfort in their coldness, as if one's inevitable end was somehow more bearable if brought about by someone with such obvious mastery of it.

He clicked his fingers and another girl was instantly

there, handing him a small copper beaker. He put it to Mimi's lips and made her drink. She swallowed with difficulty due to the constriction of her neck. The thick, sweet liquid burned all the way down her throat and into her belly. As soon as it hit her stomach the burst of heat went through her. It was like fire sweeping her insides. She could feel her nipples engorging, the hot blood racing to fill them. They grew alarmingly, way more than ever before. She looked down and could see them poking out through her top, begging for his attention.

Then it was her clit, also filling and swelling with burning blood, expanding like it might burst. It felt huge, way beyond the physically possible. Normally such a little bud, it now felt fat and throbbing, thumb-sized, as big as a cock even, filling and growing and stretching out to him. If one had pricked it now to take a single drop of blood, it would have spurted a half-pint or more. She tried to look down past her chest to her groin but the neck cuff wouldn't allow it. The heat in her belly began to pass but the swelling burn in her tits and clitty just wouldn't go.

It was almost impossible to concentrate on what was going on behind her. However gruesome, it clearly wasn't fazing the group of girls watching it, judging from their noises. They were in awe of it, delighted by it. It sounded like they were masturbating to it. The captive's cries had faded away so maybe she had too. Mimi knew Morgana was a witch but surely such grotesque acts were beyond a woman of her beauty? A bucket was brought in by a girl and set on the floor at Mimi's feet. It was nearly full of dark-red liquid. It looked too pure to be blood, too perfect, more like fine claret, but then she had never seen a whole bucket of blood before. Morgana came into the cage and the horn was smeared red. The deed had been done and now it was to be Mimi's turn.

The witch was behind Mimi, while he was still so close at her front. Others were in the cage too, girls dropping to their knees at his feet. He stooped a little and grasped Mimi behind her thighs, then lifted her legs up and held her. Above her head the witch was undoing a wrist cuff, freeing one arm. Mimi felt the greater pressure at her throat and instinctively grasped around the back of his neck for support. Her other hand was freed and she grasped him with that too, locking her fingers behind his neck and gripping his waist with her thighs. If she let go she would be left hanging, only a couple of inches off the floor, but enough to finish her.

The girls at her feet knew what to do. She was transfixed by his cold stare but she could feel them at work below. They were employing the same mechanical pump as he had used to give the enemas, and the contents of the bucket were being sucked up the tube. She squealed into his face as her quim was invaded by the long nozzle and a jet of the liquid doused her insides. It was still warm. It filled her and then started to ooze out. It felt slippery, surely too much so for blood. It was not like the stickiness of the gore she had felt between her thighs in times gone by. There was not that same accompanying iron-like smell, just a faint fruity scent.

The sluicing liquid had bloated her insides but now most of it was dribbling down her inner thighs. She was clinging onto him and even though she had seen the frightening proportions of his hard prick she was willing it to grow again and fill her void. The girls below were obviously of the same mind. She could feel their hands at work on herself and him, her pussy lips being spread open and his prick manhandled to get it inside her. He was still soft, flaccid after his last ejaculation, but they were feeding his meat inside her anyway and she was so slippery from her sluicing that she was taking him.

She could sense the invasion but the lubrication inside her was so copious that she could barely feel his prick. It was definitely in there, and the girls were ensuring it didn't slip back out. In such a position, so open and unable to prevent any entry, it was something of a disappointment to have only this harmless soft sausage crammed up between her lips. His finger would have been bigger. He just smiled down on her as if savouring her desolation.

'Drink!' he said.

Mimi didn't know what he meant but the bacchantes did. A small beaker was offered up for him to drink from.

He gulped the contents, shuddering as it went down. It might well have been the same burning concoction Mimi had swallowed, the one that still had her nipples and clitty engorged and burning hot. He let out a throaty gasp. He snarled and then snaked his tongue out to lick her from chin to nose, an invasive animal act that set Mimi's nerves jangling. She had no time to dwell on it. As his snarls continued she could feel him growing slowly inside her, the prick filling and lengthening. He held her tight to him, his huge hands gripping her squashy bum, his forehead resting upon her crown so that she could feel his heavy breaths. On the cock went, growing larger, pushing at her walls and squeezing out the liquid to bring his flesh into contact with her delicate insides.

She knew she was already smiling but the prick wasn't finished. It expanded more, surging up towards her womb, stretching her open. It was both scary and supreme. She had never been this full and now she could gauge every millimetre of expansion within. It was glorious. She tried to grip him tighter with her thighs, hooking her ankles together behind his back to bring her into full contact with his groin, hoping to open herself ever wider and prevent him from splitting her in two. Her clit was pressed at last to his groin, a pleasure so great it made her wail. On the prick went until she thought it must be in her belly. It was stretching her too wide to allow any more liquid out and she could feel the heat of it inside.

She was spitted upon him. She clung to his neck and waist, trying to stop the pull at her throat that was draining the oxygen from her brain. He gripped her arse harder and started to lift her, sliding her up the length of his shaft and then easing her back down. She used her thigh muscles to help him so that between them they began to form a rhythm. She had her face pressed to his chest and she could hear the rapid beat of his heart. She felt safe. He might have had the eyes and the prick of the Devil but she wasn't scared. He wouldn't drop her to be strangled, and if he did then so be it.

As her muscles grew used to his proportions she began to move more freely, gripping his sides with her knees so that she could push herself up almost to the end of his length before sliding back down. Her head was spinning from the joy and the lack of air but her senses felt electric. She could see the red smears all over her legs and on his sides where it had rubbed off onto him. It was viscous like blood but this didn't daunt her. Her conscience might have bewailed the speed with which she had warmed to this beastly act but she couldn't stop herself now. She wanted to bathe his cock in it, more than anything. A sudden slap caught her unawares, the pain sharp in her left buttock. The thrill of it sent out another gush to soak his balls. He had spanked her. His hand was back on her bottom immediately, grasping the chastened flesh and helping to ease the sting. Then the other cheek got a taste of the same. His hand came off it then dealt a lightning-fast slap and gripped it again, to keep her weight held up.

On he went like this, with her riding him, hanging on for dear life as the rapture spilled through her body, the feel of his iron-stiff cock and the sting of his slaps giving almost equal pleasure. Then she felt something else at her behind. It took her a while to realise what it was but then the image was in her head. It was Morgana. Again she had forgotten the witch and she felt a terrible guilt. She had unconsciously been aware of her all the time behind her, that big horn at her waist. The sweet smell of the witch had brought comfort as she was being opened up by his growing prick. Now there was potential danger from the same source. The witch was positioning the horn at Mimi's undefended anus. The tip of it was pushing for entry. Surely Morgana wasn't tall enough to drive it far enough inside, but then the witch seemed capable of anything.

Mimi couldn't do anything other than accept her fate and carry on. The desire was far too powerful to stop. Instead of lifting herself up and down upon him she stopped and just held him tight, pressing her face to his chest to blank out all light. The witch's horn was maybe an inch inside her, just the fingertip point up her bum, but it was ready to be driven home to pierce her as it had surely pierced the first captive. Her end was seemingly inevitable, brought about by the same woman who claimed to want her as a lover. Soon the bucket would be topped up by Mimi's blood but still she wasn't scared. She just prayed for a few more minutes of this utter bliss before they despatched her. Imagine those final few seconds, where her virgin bum was opened up even wider than her puss, the horn plunging into her and sending an uncontainable climax blasting through her body.

She was already coming. Almost unconscious from the lack of oxygen and the ongoing joy of penetration, her orgasm didn't come as a massive jolt but as a wonderful warm tingling spread within. The prick was deep inside her, the horn still just an inch into her backside, which was still being spanked on alternate cheeks. She was almost crying out for the *coup de grâce*, the sensation was that great. How could anyone not give themselves over to this? She wanted to kiss him, for all his hardness and brutality, despite all his terrible misdeeds over the years. This was still the best moment of her life, even if it was to be her last.

She was vaguely aware of the neck cuff being untied and of the horn tip slipping from her bottom. She was almost sad not to have had it forced inside her. The Master was carrying her now, out of the cage. He placed her upon a platform, his prick still up inside her. She was spent, but of course he would need greater purchase to reach his own climax. He laid her like a rag doll upon her back and began immediately with his deep thrusts. Her eyes were screwed shut and the stars were flashing behind her lids. Her climax just couldn't subside. His plunging prick kept sending waves of joy through her, jellifying her limbs, melting every cell. The feel of his huge body almost crushing her was magnificent. It should have been frightening but all she felt was cosseted and safe. She could *love* this man, even with his cold eyes and cold heart. If he was always pressed to her like this she would never feel scared again.

He gripped her buttocks to keep her in position as his thrusts grew harder. Her bottom was sore from his spanking but she welcomed the pain. Now that her head was clearing slightly she could picture herself beneath his frame, his prick going in and out of *her*, of all the people in the room. He wanted to finish inside her and everyone was watching. Just the idea of that made her peak once more. Morgana, for all her sorcery, couldn't touch her under here. All those savage bitches who wanted to rip her apart just had to stand and gawp. Dominic, the double-crosser who wanted only pricks, would have to watch while she got the best of the lot.

'Give me the *Demon's Pleasure*,' he was whispering to her, his voice gentle in her ear, their little secret, if only she knew what he meant by it. At that moment she would have given him *any* pleasure he asked for, even if it cost her everything. She held him tighter so that he knew she wanted to do it, but he would have to explain.

'Tell me,' she whispered back, wondering what romantic joy this living god was after.

'Put your finger in me,' he hissed.

She reached down to find his hard buttocks. His tone might have scared her on another day but not now. Now she was full of him, in every sense. He even understood her psyche. He realised that her most thrilling fantasy was to be made to do the rudest things whilst being watched, the ruder the better. There could be little dirtier than this. He was deep inside her so that she could reach his muscular backside. Looking up she could only see his wide chest. His behind was greased, as all his body was. She located his anus, running her tip around its hardness and feeling the slippery smear of lubricant.

She pushed on gently, knowing how it would feel if she was too quick. He started to grunt and she slid her way in, her finger defeating the minimal resistance. She went knuckle deep, ashamed and yet gushing with her rudeness. He growled as she jammed it further up him and then stirred it around, knowing this would stimulate his sensitive internal gland. He started to pump harder, cursing her as a bitch as she waggled her finger inside him and gave him his demon's pleasure. It was pure filth, but she felt more connected with him than with any of her past lovers. Then his seed was suddenly shooting inside her, scorching its way to her centre, giving her one final sumptuous climax.

She lay basking in the warmth of her orgasms, glad that all present could see her slippery nakedness. She had survived. Morgana had lied. He wasn't the tyrant she claimed. She had felt safer clinging to him than at any time in her life. She would never forget the bliss of his prick growing huge inside her. Through her blurred vision she could see the original captive being untied from the straps on the wall and helped down. She wasn't dead either, far from it, judging by her smile of satisfaction. It had all been a performance to fool Mimi. Just the threat of having the horn driven into her bum had increased her orgasm tenfold. Maybe Shady wasn't the cold-blooded sadist all took him for. Maybe the warmth she had felt for him was not misplaced.

He was standing now, his robe back in place. She felt proud to have had him inside her, especially in front of all these witnesses. She wanted to gloat about the fact he had chosen her above the rest.

'As you all know, the day after tomorrow is the festival of *Rosalia*,' he was announcing, and Mimi swelled at his magnificence. How could she have been so wrong about him?

'We shall have another feast to celebrate,' he said, 'and to honour the occasion your Priestess will give herself to me, at last.'

There was a rising murmur among the crowd, all clearly surprised by this proclamation. Morgana herself looked stunned and stony-faced. Mimi couldn't wait, although already she was jealous that the witch would be receiving his prick, which lessened the chance of a repeat of her evening's rapture. Could she really fall for this man? Could she put aside her preconceptions now that she had felt him so close to her, felt his heart? His eyes were like ice but surely there could be no doubt that there was tenderness at his core? She would love him. He wanted her or he wouldn't have chosen her. She would give herself to him and hopefully become paramount, maybe even usurp Morgana in his affections. Perhaps, come the next time, Mimi would again be the one he fucked in front of them all, not the witch.

'Oh, and to help kick-start the celebrations,' he continued, pointing towards Mimi and making her heart race with the potential of what he was to say next, 'we shall gather on the hillside, and we shall put this fat-arsed, snooping journalist bitch to *The Hunt*. She will be torn apart, and all of you will get to share her blood.'

11

Dominic still couldn't contain his smug joy. Gavin had
been rougher in reality than in fantasy, but Dominic
had nonetheless loved every second of it. The person he
wanted above all had been inside him. His prick-end had
touched his inner pleasure centre. That same prick had
been in his mouth at last, and that had to *mean* something. It had to mean that things were all right after all,
despite any recent misgivings. OK, it was bad that Mimi
had popped up to almost spoil the party and yeah, it
was certainly not good that she had been held in a cage
all last night with God knows what fate awaiting her.
But, well, whatever. She'd have to take her own chances
now. He hadn't invited her here. The main thing was
that he *had* to be back in Gavin's good books, even if
the fucking he had been dealt by him was a little hard
and impersonal.

Dominic surveyed the mess of paperwork on the desk.
It was strange coming back down to earth after that

night of wildness, but he always got a secret thrill from receiving terse orders from the Master, even if it did mean another chore. It was nice to know he was trusted to be alone in the Master's office, but he was keenly aware that this was yet another thing that would normally only apply to Gavin, and he hoped the Head Slave didn't find out about it or it might set things back again. Christ, what a beautiful cock that guy had! No quarter had been given. Dominic had dreamed of a tender first coupling between them and the reality had been a searing entry followed by so many frantic, stabbing thrusts – but boy, was it fabulous!

He was never, *never* going to forget that heat inside him, the way his hair had been pulled by his lover in the throes of ecstasy, the flesh of his shoulder gripped so hard, even punched, as Gavin had cursed him and come inside him. It was possibly the very roughness that caused his own prick to shoot.

This desk really was a mess. Things just left everywhere, some obviously very private. He wasn't trying to look but the letter was partially open for him to glimpse. It was from Farsite Developments, a name he had overheard before. The Master had spoken to these people a few times over the last days.

Since Dominic's job was now to oversee the Master he found himself privy to such telephone conversations. The Master was the King of Phone Innuendo. Everything he said was carefully phrased to insinuate rather than to be plain, as if he was worried that his phone might be tapped. Dominic wasn't particularly listening but the conversation seemed to be about the sale of land, and the caller was seemingly worried that the sale could not go through.

'I will *make* it happen,' the Master had said, his teeth gritted, his eyes as cold as ever.

This letter seemed to confirm an offer in writing for the estate lands. Dominic didn't read the nitty-gritty, his attention grabbed by the size of the sum offered and specifically the number of noughts in it. He could see why the Master was in a rush to make the sale. It didn't bother Dominic that a move was apparently impending. It was a bit close to home here anyway, especially when snooping ex-girlfriends could just come along to ruin the fun. As far as he was concerned anywhere was fine, as long as Gavin was there too. Before last night things between them had taken a sudden backward turn and it had been burning Dominic up inside. It was not *his* fault the Master had been showering him with attention these last few days, but Gavin was treating him as if it was. Many times Dominic had wanted to shout that he loved *him*, not the Master, but he was worried that Gavin might throw it back in his face, or worse still betray him and repeat their conversation to the Master.

Dominic had tried to turn down his latest duties. Gavin

had turned as white as a ghost when they were both told. It looked like the Master had ripped out his innards. Dominic immediately said no. He started gabbling that he couldn't possibly be as good as Gavin, but the Master just held up his hand for silence. Gavin was soon to go on a well-earned holiday, the Master had said. Someone had to act as Head Slave in his absence. Dominic was told to begin immediately, even though Gavin was still there, so that the Head Slave could help teach his usurper. Once in private Gavin had hissed insults at the new charge, called him a backstabber, a sneak, a treacherous cunt. Dominic felt his own insides being pulled out. How to right this heartbreaking wrong?

He didn't hear the door open, so engrossed was he in that bitter memory. The first he knew was the thick arm closing around his neck and pulling him back against the massive torso. The arm began to slowly squeeze and he could feel the breath being forced out of him. He dropped the letter.

'I wasn't reading it, Master – I promise,' he gurgled.

'Good,' came the voice, soft and sinister in his ear, 'because people who pry into my life have theirs quickly finished.'

'I was tidying up like you told me, and it was just – open!'

'Do not worry,' said the voice, although the pressure at his neck was still being exerted with worrying force,

'I know that you would never tell anyone about things that you find in this office, about what you might hear, or see, or *do* whilst in my presence.'

'No, Master – never!'

The pressure eased just a little, just below the critical mark, but it was still great and Dominic felt tiny and fragile against the bigger frame.

'The letter is nothing,' the voice in his ear said. 'We might move from here, that's all. I have found us somewhere much better, more private, somewhere where we will have fewer *distractions*. But it is a secret, *our* little secret, so you must keep it to yourself for now, understand?'

The final words were spoken without the edge, to show there were no hard feelings, apart from the prick that Dominic could feel growing steadily against his behind. He nodded his assent, still trying to draw in enough air to stop his head turning blue. The light caress he felt on his chest did nothing to ease the panic. If anything it put him more on edge. He feared such moments, alone and trapped and his Master in an amorous mood. He thought he could cope with anything when Gavin was around but what about when he wasn't? The hand at his chest was dropping, slowly. It was gliding down over his belly and heading inexorably for his crotch. He felt his prick twitch. For fuck's sake! What was *wrong* with his prick? Even in these dark moments it was oblivious to danger, always looking for its next pleasure.

The hand stroked over his bulge and gave it a fleeting squeeze, just enough to check that it was indeed growing. Then the hand was undoing the belt and fly of his leggings, and down they came. His prick came free. It bobbed and twitched and then started to quickly lengthen, as if the cells were reacting with the oxygen in the air. Dominic had no control over it. It swelled and climbed and stood out, ready as ever. The hand slid off his belly, found his wrist and held it tight. He was made to grip his own hot erection and the larger hand closed over his fist and started to move it in a slow up-and-down motion. It hurt. His foreskin did not glide slickly, despite the seemingly ever-present tear of pre-come his prick had kindly produced. The hand came off his and there was an identifiable sound close to his ear of spit being deposited onto a thumb. Then the hand came back and the saliva was wiped onto his retracted foreskin. It was a filthy act, so starkly personal, but it made Dominic's legs weaken and that's when he knew he needed more.

He was still being held around his neck, so that only very little air was being allowed into his lungs. He felt light-headed and woozy, and this was not helped by the adrenalin still buzzing around his body after his initial fright at being discovered. The feel of the hand on his was good. It was exciting to be under someone else's control, in their power. The pace of his masturbation was being controlled and he liked it. The trepidation remained. His neck could be snapped at any moment, perhaps even while he was starting to ejaculate. However, his nervousness just heightened the pleasure in his prick.

The hand slipped off his and he continued alone, stroking with the same tempo as he had been shown. The hand was behind him now, working away. The panic rose. The Master's prick was being unleashed and there it was, as huge and hard as always, pressing into the crack of his bare arse, as warm as it was unnerving. Dominic began to fret audibly, seeing visions in his head of the Master bending him forward over the desk. He had never seen that huge cock being forced up another man's arse, and to his knowledge it never had, but he alone had witnessed the Master's tenderness to him recently.

He felt the hand going down behind him and then it was pushing at his crack, going into it. He tensed and yelped as he felt the thumb at his anus, barely stopping to let him relax as it pushed its way past the resistance and slipped inside. He whimpered but it felt good, even with the bruising of last night's invasion. He couldn't help but rub faster on his pulsing cock. The fingers of the same hand were not idle. The thumb just stayed inside him but the fingers snuck down and found his ball sack and gripped it. He could feel the thumb moving inside as the hand instinctively tried to close in a fist around his balls. The grip might have hurt but it only gave more pleasure.

The squeeze came and then relented, came and then relented again, a measured pace, almost like he was being milked. He was whimpering constantly now, sounding like a girl, not that he could stop himself. Every squeeze of his balls seemed to send another load of seed into his cock, ready for the final launch. It gathered at the base and his fist sped up to force it down the shaft. He hoped his Master wouldn't stop him because there was no going back now. His eyes closed, his head pounding from his exertions and from the lack of oxygen getting to his brain. The faster he wanked the closer he felt to passing out, but just in time the dam broke, the spunk jumped and with a squeal he was ejaculating all over the desk while his bollocks were squeezed empty.

He had to lie face-down upon the desk, such was the weakening of his body. He could have been taken like this but he would have done nothing to stop it. Instead the Master had gone around to his chair and was sitting, erection in hand, ready and waiting. Dominic dragged himself off the desk. The cock looked awesome; too huge to be inviting but spellbinding nonethe ess. He was being beckoned over. He was going to have to put his mouth on it for the first time. He had seen Gavin do it and had stared transfixed, shivering with jealousy as he watched the expert at work and imagined how it would feel. He opened wide and felt it stretch his jaw. He let his tongue go to work and heard the Master exhale in a little growl.

'You tell no one, you understand?' the Master was snarling. 'No one.'

Dominic got into a rhythm that he knew was being enjoyed, trying to mimic the technique he had seen Gavin use. The sense of danger was still there, like he was sucking on a gun barrel. He knew he had to make it go off in his mouth, or other openings might be utilised. He sensed he was doing well, building slowly but surely, showing the prick the reverence it deserved but not slackening the impetus. He was bringing the Master to the final stages when the mobile phone on the desk went off.

The Master swore but put his hand on Dominic's head as a sign that they needn't both be interrupted by the ringing.

'Yes?' he shouted impatiently into the phone. 'Oh, yeah, Grigor – how are you, my old friend? Listen, I need next month's goods a day early because I've other business to attend to. Is that going to be a problem? Good. One more thing, I am sending you someone, a boy. He is going on a holiday and I want you to take care of him. Yes, that *is* what I mean: permanently. The cocky cunt has got to go. Oh, and I might send you a girl too. She is some journalist bitch who has been snooping around. We have some games to play with her first that I doubt she will get through, but if by some miracle she does, I will send her your way. Don't get too excited, Grigor. She's too old for your tastes, but she is pretty and she's got a fat arse and some of your clients could use her. OK, talk later. Goodbye.'

The blood was freezing in Dominic's veins but he knew better than to show any sign of it. As soon as the phone was back on the desk he quickly returned to his former pace, as if nothing had happened, as if his body were not fizzing with alarm. There could be no mistaking what the Master had meant, but there was nothing Dominic could do about it. He was on his knees and he had to stay there and keep quiet and get on with his business, doing his level best to give the Master his pleasure. And that he did.

12

'I told you I was your only hope,' Morgana said, making Mimi jump. 'He is a killer. You will be hunted by the girls and you won't live to tell the tale. It took all my powers to keep his mind off sacrificing you last night. I have bought you a little more time but that is all.'

Funny how the witch always seemed to imbue one with a feeling of comfort without actually providing any. She had snuck up quietly, even dismissing the guard without Mimi knowing. She was carrying a long, narrow box in wood so dark and aged it looked almost waxy. In the hands of someone else, Mimi might have guessed it was perhaps a case for a precious musical instrument, a flute or clarinet perhaps. However, here the image that came to mind was from some anonymous horror movie in which the vampire hunter had opened just such a box to reveal a sumptuously lined interior housing a sharp, two-foot wooden stake designed for despatching the undead. It was a fair bet that the witch's thoughts were inclining her more to plunging things into Mimi's body than to playing her a bit of Mozart.

The Priestess looked as alluring as ever, in figure-hugging black velvet this time, the dress front split upwards nearly all the way to her crotch, revealing flashes of perfect white leg as she approached. Although she felt wretched from her caged confinement overnight and half of this day, Mimi still couldn't stop the tingle between her legs on seeing her visitor. It was like a seed of passion planted malevolently inside her, triggered to germinate and blossom whenever Morgana appeared. Others might have just called it infatuation or even love, but Mimi was convinced that in this case it was not a natural instinct but one that had been put inside her by nefarious means. The witch always promised a fantasy life of bliss and security, but despite her words Mimi was still locked up and, as far as she could tell, still certain to meet a gruesome end. So what did the witch want this time?

'I've come to convince you to love me,' Morgana said. 'I need you more than ever now, after the Master's announcement last night. I cannot let him have me. Believe me, I won't live much longer through the day than you, unless you agree to be mine. Being hunted might sound like good fun, all those sexy girls chasing after you with their big false pricks, but you saw what they can be like last night – and that was when they were acting with restraint. He means for them to fuck you to death, and they most certainly will.'

Mimi knew all this. The lad who had been guarding her had delighted in telling her exactly how much danger she was in. He had described the hunts in great detail, so she knew what fate awaited her. He was the one who had been the first to be reported missing, the one who had sunk his prick into Dominic's backside the previous night. He was every bit as smug and evil as his bastard boss. Mimi wondered if her ex-boyfriend would end up like them. Perhaps he already had. She reflected with bitterness on her stupidity at being drawn into all this, chasing after an ex who was happily living out some perverted dream of playing Roman slave and taking men up his backside.

One thing was for sure, there was no kidnapping involved here. These guys were all *very* content to be held as slaves. She had gone after a story that never was, and had run headlong into a peril she had frivolously under-estimated. Fancy thinking she could take on someone as heartless as Haydn Shady. He might not be a kidnapper as such, but whatever else he was – manipulator, sex monster, tyrant, killer – all this was immaterial since she could never let the outside world know because she was never going to see it again. Suddenly journalism seemed like the silliest, most pointless occupation imaginable. It was going to be the death of her.

'I need to make you fall in love with me,' Morgana said. 'We only have an hour. I managed to get that shit of a slave to agree to disappear for a while but he has never liked me, so he won't cut me any slack.'

The witch said it all so matter-of-factly that it didn't sound like the wonderful opportunity Mimi had been praying for.

'If you want me to love you, why not just *magic* it?' she asked, coldly.

'I've told you. It has to come from you. Magic is a natural entity, one that can be harnessed but never controlled. I can make myself beautiful for you and I can truly swear to give you all you will ever need, but only you can give me your heart.'

'And all I have to do is give up everything and start worshipping Satan?' said Mimi, dismissively.

The witch laughed, the first time Mimi had ever heard her do so.

'I don't worship Satan! He wasn't even *invented* when my soul was first born. The Master – that fool – he might do so, but that's because he stupidly thinks he is some demon incarnate. Some of the girls do too. He instils the belief and they like the idea because it makes them feel decadent and degenerate. It's an easy way to draw them in and keep them here. They have so much more purpose when they think they are acting against all decency. Fucking in the name of the Devil makes them come so much harder.

'The Gods I worship are *real* ones. They are spirits of

the ether, of nature. I don't worship evil. I believe in lust, in freedom and abandon, in taking pleasure all of the time and giving it to others, of sharing the wonders of our bodies. I don't believe in hurt. I believe in anything that brings you physical or mental rapture. It's not my fault society has come to think that what I believe is immoral. Sexual morality was only dreamt up by men too old and ugly and impotent to get their kicks without paying for it. They hated that others could get joy where they could not, so they sought to control it. Remember, I was alive to see them do it.'

Mimi's head was spinning. Surely the witch was over-playing her goodness? She tried to think of examples she had witnessed of Morgana's evil, but none came to mind. Spanking her, perhaps? But then Mimi had loved it, even though it was painful and done in front of others – in fact *because* of those things. Even being put under the power of the book had led to nothing more sinister than a massive, mind-blowing orgasm. Last night had seen an orgy of the most eye-popping proportions, with things going on that would freeze the blood of someone like the Spinster. It had felt dangerous and subversive. However, if one stripped it right down, was it really base and immoral? No one was hurt, unless they wanted to be. Everyone appeared to be having the time of their lives, so if it *seemed* immoral that was only because of the drummed-in religious concept that anything beyond the missionary position was depraved. Sure, it had felt like a cauldron of wanton corruption, with all those savages doing such dirty acts, but essentially everyone there had a whale of a time and seemingly couldn't wait for another opportunity. Even she, a total outsider, had felt the same – up to the point where she had been sentenced to death.

Haydn Shady clearly was an evil man, and one who planned to bring about Mimi's end. Association with him should have made one evil also. Even if she was now trying to distance herself from him, Morgana surely couldn't deny having something of a kindred spirit? You just couldn't *be* that beautiful without being ruled by darkness.

'So what will you gain from having my love?' Mimi asked.

'Everything. My power will increase exponentially. Without you I won't be able to stop him. He can defeat me in two ways, either by taking *me* or taking me away from this place. I am at the limits of my resistance already. A sustained effort will see me defeated. He doesn't know it yet but he will soon work it out. He controls the girls more than I do now. With their help he could finish me tomorrow. The only thing that might weaken him is the excitement of seeing your death. However, your end will inevitably condemn me to my own, one way or another.'

This was all beyond Mimi's comprehension and she felt no particular compulsion to delve deeper. She was trying to work out why she should feel any allegiance to the witch. Oddly, the answer that might have swung it when she had asked, 'What will you gain from having my love?' was not the rather indifferent one Morgana had actually given but something more personal and passionate, like 'You'.

'And how do you propose to make me fall in love with you?' she asked. It sounded like a business deal.

'By *making* love to you,' the witch replied, unbolting the cage door so that she could enter. 'There are many ways to lose a heart, but the simplest is through lust. It might sound empty and soulless, but only if you believe lust to be somehow immoral and not the prime motivator of our spirit that it actually is. Lust is our most intrinsic quality, the one that drives us to perform our only real function in this physical world. It is also the one that makes us best understand our potential in the spiritual world. That is why I count it so dear. Anyway, men have been falling in love like this since the dawn of time, so I don't see why women shouldn't.'

There wasn't going to be any escape. The witch had locked the cage door behind her but the key was still in it. However, Mimi knew she wouldn't be able to escape her clutches. The instinct had just gone from her. Her body wouldn't have let her run even if her mind told her this might be her last chance. With the witch, confusion and contradiction were never far away. Morgana was immeasurably alluring and Mimi couldn't remember wanting anyone more in her life. Yet she couldn't be sure this infatuation hadn't been artificially placed there. The witch spoke of falling in love yet was somehow detached from the emotion, as if it was something you could just do, some kind of pact agreed upon by the two parties for their mutual advantage. It was as if falling in love was something you did *at* someone, not *with* them.

The irony was, if the witch had ever chosen to go in all guns blazing, rather than to tease and hold back, Mimi didn't see how she could have possibly defended her heart. It seemed inevitable that she would have to fall in love because the witch was just so exciting and perfect that all else would have faded into irrelevance. It was the fact that Mimi had been made to *think* about it, about consequences. The witch could have just taken her heart, but, in being asked to give it, Mimi had to consider all the logical aspects – leaving one's family and job behind, being with a woman at all, let alone one who might be somewhat unhinged. Mimi was *dying* for this woman, but to sensibly consider falling for her and being with her for all time was impossible, because the reality was just all too strange.

However, Mimi had already pushed all this to the back of her mind because she was too excited about the prospect of being taken. The witch was down on her knees on top of the padded layers that had been provided as a mattress. Already Mimi could hardly breathe. The wooden case had been carefully set down, as if it might soon have its grand opening. Morgana was righting some of the candles that had been moved to the perimeter of the cage, out of the way of the padding, and was lighting them one by one to illuminate the area where they were to make love. The glow from the little flames made the already dim background fade to near darkness. It was like a screen had been thrown up, sealing the two of them off within these close confines. The anticipation was wrenching. Just knowing that it was about to happen was bliss.

Then she was there, without any further ado, taking Mimi in her arms. Both were up on their knees, pressed together. There was no teasing brushing of the lips this time. The kiss was full-on and immediate, the tongue right there from the start. The witch's mouth felt silky and hot – not warm but actually hot, like a turned-on puss, like she had just had a mouthful of steaming tea the instant before their mouths met. She tasted sweet too, slightly honeyed, a little like her scent. The embrace was strong, squashing their breasts together. Mimi could feel one hand gliding down her back to grasp her bottom and pull her in so that their crotches were tight against each other. The witch broke the kiss briefly to whisper in Mimi's ear.

'I like three fingers up inside me, when the time comes,'

she said. 'I know you prefer just the one, to have it sliding in deep and stirred slowly around, but I need the girls I love to fill me. This is the only way in which we are not the same. Everything else about us is completely compatible, so what you love, I will love too. I know you better than you know yourself. I see all your delicious dirty little secrets – the spanking, the dirty talk – and I want them all just as much as you do. Nothing between us will ever be wrong, however rude it seems. I will always know precisely what you need, and when. Anything you do to me will be exactly what I have been wanting. There will never be a time when we make love that it isn't entirely perfect, even the things that are new to you.'

Mimi could well believe it. Just hearing the naughty words spoken out loud was enough to melt her. The witch seemed to know her every dirty thought. She had always been too shy to share such intimacies, with friends or with lovers, but here the witch seemed to have read her mind perfectly. It was unnerving to find yourself so transparent, yet thrilling to know that someone knew *exactly* what it was you wanted to do and have done to you, and had a mind to make it all happen. She felt totally at ease, even though her kinky secrets had been so easily exposed.

She was being kissed again and Mimi found the confidence to return it with equal passion. She was not yet bold enough to strip the Priestess, however desperate she was to do so. However, her own clothes were coming off. Her leggings were down around her thighs and her tight top was being peeled upwards, interrupting their kiss as it was dragged over her head and off, sending out enough static to raise every hair on her lifted arms. Her nipples still felt sensitive from the potion she had drunk the night before and she was glad when her bra was unceremoniously pinged open and cast aside.

Her little pink teats swelled as they were freed. They were aching to be sucked and the witch complied, drawing them in turn into her hot mouth. This alone was nearly enough to make Mimi come. The witch was sucking hard at the stiff points, her forefinger and thumb pinching slightly at the soft tissue of the areola. She gave intermittent little light nips with her teeth, causing an exquisite tingle. It felt like she was drawing the nerve endings ever further out.

'You know I will teach you to give milk when we are together,' she said, en route from one erect teat to the other.

The thought made Mimi's belly flutter. Imagine the intimacy! Imagine this sublime sensitivity doubled by the rush of squirting milk! Although Mimi was now crying out to be taken, the witch was surprisingly patient, given that the slave might come back at any moment. Mimi found herself being slowly licked all over, every tingling part of her receiving attention, the witch seemingly able to slow time itself to draw out each new sensation for what seemed like an age.

Mimi's leggings and knickers came fully off and she was nude. At one point she found herself briefly on top, her legs open against the clothed thigh of her lover. She had shaved herself the morning after that first class, having seen all those bare pussies. Now the velvet of the dress felt so luscious against her smoothness, the pleasure exacerbated by the feel of the witch's fingernail at her little virgin anus, ever so gently grazing the surface of her tight hole.

Mimi had forgotten how wonderful kissing alone could be. It was even better with another female. That soft mouth was so entrancing that Mimi could barely wait to go down and kiss those other lips. Yet to leave these would be too much to lose. Strange how she could be so turned on but so content to keep it slow. Yesterday with the Master had all been about penetration. With men it was mostly about that – about a build-up, a fucking and a finish. This just seemed boundless and free, like it could go on for ever and never lose momentum. Never had her skin felt so alive. Her puss felt hot enough to melt the dildos of the bacchante girls, yet still she was able to hold back and gently rub it against the velvet of the dress. If the slave came back now and called a halt she would not have felt robbed. She would still think it one of the best times she had ever had.

When the penetration did eventually come it made her whole body jerk. She was on her back again with her legs open and the witch between them, on her knees. Her eyes were closed. There were fingernails tracing lines down her inner thighs, all the way down the inside of her leg. Her ankle had been grasped and lifted. Then her big toe had been engulfed by that hot, soft mouth. It had been enough to make her gasp. She had felt a warm gush escape from her puss and had had to fight the urge to slide her finger up into it. As ever, the witch read her mind. With the toe still being gently sucked, suddenly one finger was sliding deep up inside her and she was crying out and arching up off the floor to meet it.

The finger swirled around inside her, just as she liked it. It curved up to feel for the sweet spot and Mimi found herself quickly on the verge of orgasm. Before she could take it the finger had slid free again and Mimi opened her eyes to see the witch sucking upon it, a wide smile spread across her face. She had pulled her dress up and open at the front to expose her own pristine pussy. God, for a taste of it! She was sitting herself down now, putting one leg over Mimi's and sliding her hips forward so that their bare pussies could meet and kiss. Hers was as hot as a furnace, even hotter than Mimi's own. It was so wet too, the slide of quim on quim electric. Briefly they were glued together. Mimi thought she could actually feel her lips being sucked in by the witch's. Then their quims slid apart and Morgana was climbing on top again, so that they could each find a bare thigh to squash and grind their swollen clits against. It seemed to Mimi impossible to have such an intense feeling yet have nothing inside her.

She had the chance at last to hold and squeeze the witch's perfect bottom. The skin was so smooth, the flesh so soft, it almost made her cry. She wanted to touch the beautiful little bum. She had seen the briefest flashes of it at the orgy, when Morgana had been fucking the girl so hard from behind that the sumptuous cheeks had come apart to give a glimpse of what lay between. It had been so tantalising that she had spent maybe an hour of her sleepless night just thinking about being *near* it, about being so close to this bottom to sense its pristine beauty in infinite detail. Even in her imagination she had barely been able to part the cheeks, the thought of what lay between them, of burying yourself in that soft, glorious gorge, being too much to bear. She wanted to give her Priestess the *demon's pleasure* that she had given the Master last night, to see if she could thrill her as much as him. But this was no demon. This was a goddess.

Before she had a chance to gather her courage the witch was moving again. Mimi just lay with her eyes closed, feeling the wetness on her thigh left by her new lover, buzzing with the delight. The press came upon her body again but this time it was different. Breasts were squashed against her belly, arms were on her thighs, breath was on her wet puss. She opened her eyes and saw what she had already pieced together in her head. The rump came back and opened as it did so to reveal its hidden treasures and the witch's gorgeous bare pussy was now right above Mimi's face. The skin was like creamy flawless porcelain, thin and subtle, the lips pale pink and glistening moist.

Mimi pushed out her tongue tentatively, thinking that this puss needed to be treated with delicate reverence. She planned to give it the lightest of licks where the lips met. But her clit was suddenly sucked hard and in her shocked pleasure she jerked upwards and buried her tongue deep in the goddess, plunging into the pooled juice gathered there so that it flowed into her mouth and trickled down her chin. She wanted to continue gorging upon it, God knows she did, but the sensations in her own puss made it impossible.

Her legs had been raised so that she was completely open, her knees up either side of the witch's body. Her clit had been engulfed and it felt every bit as swollen and sensitive as it had after she had drunk the potion the previous night. She thought the witch must be carrying traces of the same tonic in her mouth. It was the most intense sensation she could remember: the sucking and the tongue-tip flicks, whilst one finger stirred inside her. She wanted to respond in kind but got no respite to do so. All she could manage was to remember Morgana's words and scrunch her three longest fingers together into a point and drive them up inside that peachy quim.

The witch moaned aloud but didn't let up on her sucking one bit. Mimi was already coming again, another long-drawn-out climax that spread through her body, so much more enjoyable than one of those jerking, almost aching wracks that she had teased desperately from herself whenever she thought of this woman. Her fingers looked so rude and yet brilliant inside Morgana. And there was that tiny tantalising bum above it, waiting for its due attention.

The chance eluded her before she could act. The witch was off her and Mimi was being brought to her knees again to be kissed. She could taste her own juice on the witch's tongue, magically sweeter than she knew it had ever been before. They broke off and the witch stared at her intently.

'It is time,' she said.

Time for what, to profess one's love? Mimi still didn't know if she could do it, not *honestly*. How does one even know? Physically she couldn't now bear to be without this woman. If that was all that was being asked of her then she would close her eyes right now and let the blood be taken from her tingling clit. But if more was required, if she was made to look deeper, then her head would surely say: What about all the witchy nonsense, the worship of wines and potions, the bizarre dancing and ridiculous spells? And what about the desertion of everything she knew to immerse herself in a world that she had thought plainly odd and wrong every time she had considered it?

The witch had reached for the box and was flipping its two little clasps so that it could be opened. Mimi was going to have to die; that was it. To become one of them she would have to have the stake Morgana was about to reveal driven through her heart. The witch had talked of immortality and this was how it was to be gained, just like in the films. The box came open and there was the silver silk lining just as envisaged. But it was neither a sharp-pointed stake nor even a prized musical instrument. It was a beautiful smooth dildo in clear ruby glass, half the size again of a real prick, the shaft curving gracefully up to a prominent head that belled out and then tapered to a tip.

'I'm going to have you in your bottom,' Morgana whispered.

It was the single most exciting thing that Mimi had ever heard.

There was still no rushing. Everything was done with measured deliberation. The witch took out the dildo and the attached leather harness unfurled. When it was on and secured the witch stood with it close to Mimi's face, so she could see it in all its glory, see the witch's thighs through the clear glass because it was so flawless. She was given ample time to imagine it sliding up her virgin bum. The witch took out a small vial from its compartment within the box. She eased Mimi down onto all fours and spread oil from the vial over her back. The slick liquid was smoothed into her skin, still unhurriedly, even with the threat of the guard's return. The whole of her back was covered, then her outer thighs and calves, although it was surely impossible for a vial so small to give out so much oil.

Finally her bottom was slowly covered, the lubrication massaged into her flesh with firmer motions, her slippery cheeks prised apart so that one single last drop could splash onto her anus to be gently smoothed in. The fingertip attention on her shy opening broke down some of her resistance and she could feel her muscles relenting. The oil had a very slight heat to it, just enough to add a tingle. Her hips were held and she could feel the slight pressure of the glass tip as it very gently began to open her up.

It was impossible to tell how long it took to take it all; maybe an hour, maybe only ten minutes. All Mimi knew was that she felt every rapturous tiny fraction of the penetration and it didn't hurt at all, except only briefly, and that bit she adored as much as the rest. So slowly it went up her even though it was a glide, the smooth surface bringing alive every single neurone, seemingly one by one, so the pleasure just built and built. Despite this gradual opening, the last four or five inches were still driven home in one long quick slide, causing her to yell her uncontainable ecstasy. The final push saw her collapse forward and the witch went with her, keeping it buried all the way inside. Mimi lay on her front, her face in the mattress as the witch lay on top of her and used her hips to slide the glass cock in and out.

Mimi felt every bit as full, the penetration at least as deep as with the Master's prick the night before, maybe even deeper. Perhaps it was because her bottom was so much the tighter passage, or possibly it was because being taken there was just so wonderfully rude and unique. She had felt the witch's hand go underneath her from the start, moving down to cup her quim. Now she was being pinched, her clit trapped between its own protective folds as the pressure was applied and maintained. It felt like her little bud was pouring electric current.

She came from the outset and it just wouldn't stop, the sensation carrying on and on along with the slow slide of the dildo in and out of her bum. All the while Mimi could feel the fizz on the skin of her ears and neck as the witch kissed and licked and nipped at it with her teeth. She was covered in goose bumps, all over her back and down her legs. Even the bottom of her feet felt like they had raised hairs upon them. Then the witch was whispering into her ear, telling her how pretty she was and the dirty things she wanted to do with her.

'Say my name out loud and tell me what you want,' Mimi heard her say, unless it was in her mind, just part of this beautiful surreal dream.

'Mistress Morgana, I love you and want to be yours,' Mimi gasped.

'Next time you say that you have to mean it. I will come back later tonight and you will tell me again. Then you will prick your clitty and give me my drop of blood, and that will bind us together for all time.'

Mimi wanted to declare her love now, to find anything to pierce her throbbing clit so that she could bleed for her Mistress. The bliss was too much though. It was growing unstoppably inside, filling her up and threatening to burst her. Finally, mercifully, it came down behind her eyes like red velvet and she slipped off into unconsciousness.

When she came to she was dressed. The door was locked fast and the key removed. The candle flames had been doused and she could see back out into the dimness of the huge room. The same guard was there in his chair as before, reading his paper, looking up to sneer at her and remark, 'Not long to go now.'

There was nothing to suggest the witch had ever been there, except the glow Mimi could feel in her crotch and bottom. She could remember her penetration exactly, way too accurately for it to have been a dream. Her behind didn't feel sore or bruised, just hot and tingly; wonderfully fucked, in fact. She knew the witch would come again and this time she had to give herself. She tried to imagine ever having a better lover. She tried to think of any situation that could ever match this one with anyone else other than Morgana. She said the witch's name over and over in her head, trying to convince herself that being with her was not ridiculous after all. She tried to tell herself that pleasure and hedonism were all you should seek in life and that nothing else mattered, not family or friends or working for a living. But her mind and body were exhausted and her eyes just wouldn't stay open.

She awoke again with a start, blinking to make out the figure pressed to the cage. This time it was someone less welcome: Dominic. He was turning the key and opening the door. He was telling her she had to get out and go, quickly, that the guard would be back any second. Mimi was fuzzy-headed and not convinced she wanted to go anywhere. Morgana would be back soon to keep her safe and Dominic, the double-crossing bastard, was the one who had got her locked up in the first place, and therefore clearly not to be trusted.

'He's going to have you killed. I heard him say it! Even if you live through the hunt he will sell you for a whore. He is going to kill Gavin! You have to leave now and get the police!'

She could see in his eyes that this was no joke. He was pulling her up and dragging her out of the cage, hustling her on her sluggish legs towards the door. He led her down the corridors still babbling his apologies for having her discovered, re-asserting the need for her to get away so she could save Gavin – and herself, of course. Out past the kitchen they went, out to the secret entrance, before she felt herself belatedly trying to resist.

'Morgana will stop him,' she said, not knowing what evidence she had to back this.

'No one can stop him, only you!' he almost shouted, exasperated. 'He is going to get rid of you and then Gavin. Then he is going to either get rid of the Priestess too, or leave her behind to pay for your murder. Either way, he is selling up and going, and you will be dead and I will never stand a chance of getting away from him again!'

Dominic was opening the trapdoor in the hut and dragging her up. It was like coming out of a cinema: the sudden daylight seemed incongruous. She had no idea what time it was, but thought it might be early evening. He was waving his arms, encouraging her to run, but her mind was ticking over, trying to work out what she had just heard, whether she was being tricked again. Finally her head was clearing.

'What do you mean, he is selling up?' she asked.

Dominic was trying to push her away but she stood firm, determined to get an answer.

'He is selling the whole estate so that they can build a road through it. I've heard his phone conversations and seen the letters. The deal is already done. He's going to get millions! He's taking us all away and no doubt your body will be buried somewhere under the tarmac. If you don't go now he's going to find out I let you go and then he's going to kill me too. Is that what you fucking well want?'

He almost screamed the last bit and she could see the sheer panic draining him of colour. She turned and ran. Her mind was working properly for the first time in a few days. She was calculating her route, retracing it mentally to where she had left her bike. Then she was working out the quickest, safest route off the estate. She couldn't go home. She would have to go straight to the police, in town. That meant calling a cab from a pay phone and hiding until it arrived. She had no idea how long she had but at least her lungs were so far holding out.

Then the wind came. It picked up suddenly and she knew they were after her. It was nothing more than a noise in the treetops but it was inexorably chasing her down. It was Morgana and her girls. She had betrayed the witch and nothing and nobody escaped that woman. She could hear the shrieks of the bacchante girls as an undercurrent to the rustling leaves. The panic swelled inside, sending her heart crazy, muffling her ears. She dared not look back, not for a second, even when she found her bike on its side in the bush just as she had left it.

She pedalled off but only slowly, her thigh muscles

almost bursting with the pain of her exertions. She was up off the saddle, her bottom out, as she tried to put some power into her efforts. The wind was gathering behind her, the noise increasing. The girls would have their sticks, like in the drawings she had seen of them. She would be run down and run through, the long points of the toys driven up into her stuck-out bottom as she tried to get away. Would she live long enough to have the dildos at their waists driven two, maybe three at a time inside her? How long before they spanked and bit and ripped her to death?

They were right behind her now and she was sobbing out loud, her muscles spent. Their whispers were in her ears. She could feel the fingernail swipes at her bottom, the lunges in the air behind her as they tried to grasp her hair, their breath hot at her neck. She was at her limits and had nothing left to give. Her head was telling her legs to move but they could not. She slowed, the tears falling down her cheeks as she capitulated, and came to a standstill. Awaiting the inevitable crash her eyes closed, only to spring open again immediately at the sound of an engine. The car was coming straight towards her and the life rushed back into her limbs. It was the same Land Rover as before. It was the estate manager, her only saviour!

She flagged him down and jumped in, gabbling at him to drive and get the police. She unloaded all the facts without a pause, about how Hadyn Shady was hiding out beneath the Big House, how he kept slaves and was going to kill one of them, how he had kidnapped her and was going to murder her too. It sounded ridiculous but the estate manager was listening intently, noting it all, ready to drive her to safety. He must have felt an idiot that all this was going on under his nose, but Mimi was in no mood to berate him. She was too overjoyed at being out of danger.

It was obvious from her relief that she wasn't making it up. Her saviour put his foot down and sped away. The girls wouldn't catch them now, but still she couldn't bring herself to look back, just in case. Her adrenalin was still raging but the cold fear was starting to be replaced by the warmth of huge relief. Strange, now that she was away from Morgana's influence the thought of becoming her lover seemed utterly ridiculous again. The woman was pure danger, nothing more. She was no doubt every bit as ruthless and scheming as Shady and needed to be locked up for just as long. To think she had just been so close to giving herself up to that mad cult!

She concentrated on planning how to present her evidence to the police, how to ensure they acted immediately and sent a squad there without hesitation. Her own recent incarceration and impending death might not be enough to sway them. She might have to embellish a little and say a murder had already been committed.

Maybe it had. Maybe Dominic had been found out and revenge already taken upon him. At the back of her mind the same nagging question kept trying to break through: how could Shady sell the land when it was no longer his?

The estate manager was reaching for his phone. Good thinking – he was going to ring ahead, to make sure the police were already gathering when they got there. He would help unearth the villain. There would no doubt be more damning evidence to find once the hidden bunker was searched, as long as Shady wasn't disposing of it at that very moment. Speed was going to be essential and the driver beside her was doing her proud in that respect. She wasn't really watching where they were going, concentrating so hard on what she was to say. She didn't see that they had turned back onto the drive that led past the Big House.

'You'd better meet me out front,' the estate manager was saying into his phone. 'I think I've got something that belongs to you.'

Mimi realised way too late to react. The car skidded to a halt and the group was already gathered, Shady at the centre and his slaves around him, including an ashen-faced Dominic. She was pulled out by her hair and dragged off. She could hear the car engine disappearing into the distance as she was taken back towards the stone hut with its secret door. She knew as she was steered down the same dark passage that there would be no escape this time. As Shady threw her back into her cage he said, 'I only want to know one thing. Which fucking bitch let you free?'

Mimi looked up at him, shivering at the sight of his cold eyes. She glanced around at the assembled slaves. All of them had smug grins on their faces, none wider than that of her former guard the Head Slave. All except Dominic, who was white as a sheet, silently imploring her to keep quiet. He had betrayed her and got her into this mess, although in fairness he had apparently tried to make amends, and she had no idea whether he had betrayed her again. Mimi didn't care for any of them. They were going to revel in her punishment and death.

'Him,' she said finally, her arm outstretched, her eyes firmly on Gavin.

'You lying *cunt*!' the Head Slave spat, but the Master had turned and cut him dead.

'I will deal with you later,' he hissed at her.

She was left for the night, having been reminded it was the last she would ever see. She hated them all and almost wished for her end to come soon, to release her from this madness. How could he sell the land when it was no longer his? How could he sell the land he had already openly sold to Pieter Bakkers? It hit her in an instant and she couldn't believe she had been so stupid: *Bakkers* stood for *Bacchus*, the god the Master now claimed to be. It was nothing but a thinly veiled alias.

No one ever saw the new hero because he didn't exist. Shady was able to masquerade as this apparent South African saint merely by growing his hair and removing his sunglasses. His eyes were so distinctive that you would know instantly if you had seen them before. But Shady never *showed* his eyes. No one had ever seen them, so no one put two and two together. It was the reverse of a disguise – simply revealing his true features transformed him.

There was still plenty she didn't understand, like why the facade of Bakkers was needed in the first place, but a fat lot of good it would do her to find out anyway. She was hidden beneath a private house within the grounds of a private, guarded estate. She would be taken out into those grounds in the morning and chased to her death. No one would hear it, no one would come to her aid. Nobody would ever know she had even been there. As an untraceable murder it would be about perfect. She sat on the mattress, pulling the one scant blanket provided around her, and wondered why the thought of the bacchante girls running after her with their deadly dildos strapped to their waists was still causing her pussy to clench and tingle.

Some time that evening Morgana ghosted from the darkness. Mimi was bleary-eyed and numbed from exhaustion, although sleep refused to come. She hadn't noticed her guard leaving. The witch was there for a while, masked by the dimness of the room. One last look at the condemned, perhaps? She clearly was not there to set Mimi free. She finally came forward and held out a small metal cup and told Mimi to drink from it. She hoped it was a poison to spare her her morning's fate. As Mimi drank she felt the fear draining away and sleep thankfully starting to overcome her. Her eyes closed and she could hear the witch retreating. She heard the woman's words, but was too tired to dwell upon them, let alone respond.

'If you hadn't betrayed me I might have saved us both,' Morgana said. 'Why do you have to keep running from me? Can't you see we are supposed to be together? Well, my darling, tomorrow you will have to run again, and this time, I'm afraid, it will be for the last time. There is nothing I can do for you now.'

13

The shadows were long from the early-morning sun spreading down the valley. It was already warm. Only the clump of bushes and trees in the dip at the bottom was still in shade. There was dew still on the lush grass but it would soon be gone. The noise from the car that had brought her here had died away and left only the clear chatter of birdsong echoing through the woods to the rear, and the occasional snort from the impatient horses. It was a beautiful day, certainly one too beautiful to die on. And yet ...

Mimi had been dragged here without ceremony, though she had at least been allowed to shower. She had even been granted a piece of toast: not the grandest of final meals. She stood on the top of the rise, facing him, already having to squint against the sunlight. He was mounted and flanked by two of his slaves, also on horseback. He was dressed entirely in black, including a wide-brimmed hat that he must have stolen from Zorro. She thought it ridiculous, but perhaps it was just bitterness from knowing she was to die at the hands of this brute.

Behind him were a couple of slaves on foot, including Dominic, who had always been too much of a wet blanket to learn to ride. He couldn't even look at her. He was hovering around the slave who had previously guarded her, the one she had lied to the Master about. She was pleased to see him standing against a big oak tree, his hands behind his back and a thick rope around his neck securing him to the trunk. It was some consolation that this particular smug bastard wasn't going to get away scot free.

The poor slave was looking pretty sick, as well he might. Unbeknown to Mimi he had just been informed in front of the others that later he was to have his erect prick cut off. It was to be stuffed with couscous, chopped dried fruit and chilli, plus his own lightly sautéed balls, then roasted and served as the centrepiece for the evening's feast. If he hadn't bled to death he was to be bent over the feasting table with his prick under his nose. Each bacchante would fuck him in turn, then the Master himself would have a go – the first time he had ever entered another male in front of the Order, and a prequel to the Grand Event where he plundered the Priestess's *cunnus* for the first time. The slave wouldn't get to see this. Once the Master had used him a bacchante would be chosen to replace the dildo at her waist with her *thyrsus* stick, and she would drive it into him, using just her hips and body strength to force the point ever deeper inside him, until finally it came out of his mouth. Then his carcase could be carried like a spitted pig to be disposed of elsewhere. It wasn't the kind of news you ever wanted to hear.

Away some thirty yards to Mimi's left was Morgana, astride a large white charger. She was adorned in a foxskin coat and tight hide leggings. She looked as sexy as ever, even at this distance. How was Mimi not able to just hate her? It would have made everything so much simpler. The bacchante girls were in a line to her front. Most wore tight leggings like their Priestess, and similar loose white smocks. Three or four of them appeared to be naked from the waist down, although it was hard to be sure because all of them already had a false prick in a harness strapped tightly to their groin. Some of these dildos looked frighteningly big. Each girl carried a long stick with some kind of bulbous point at one end, their *thyrsus*, although Mimi didn't know it. She dared not think what they would be used for.

Fright had shrunk her stomach and she was in danger of retching up her toast. She felt light-headed and numb-jawed. She was freezing, despite the warmth of the day. Her neck was aching from the strap around it, which was joined at her nape by a metal rod going down to a set of cuffs securing her hands behind her back. Because of this apparatus she had been forced to travel there lying across the back seat of the car, which meant she couldn't see out and had no idea where on the estate she now was. Not that it mattered. As far as she could tell there was nowhere to run.

'If you can reach the trees way up on the far side you might have a chance,' the Master announced, showing that Morgana was not the only one adept at reading minds. 'The cover there is much thicker and you will be harder to follow.'

Mimi glanced around to see where he meant but her heart wasn't really in it. The wood in question was a good mile away, up a long slope. The thought of reaching it, even with panic driving her on, was laughable.

'I'm going to fuck that fat arse of yours today,' the Master sneered, leaning forward on his horse towards her. 'Every single one of us here is going to go up you today, and more than one at a time. I've seen a girl on the web take three at once so I know it's possible – and that was just in the one hole. Even my horse here is going to get a proper ride this morning. We are going to sluice your bowels with a whole gallon of spunk and oil and before you die we will get to watch you spray it all back out. It will be a wonderful memory to take with you, don't you think?'

'I know that you are Pieter Bakkers.'

Mimi didn't know why she had said it. Perhaps just

in an effort to wipe the smile off his face, to show him he wasn't quite as clever as he thought.

'Well, bully for you for guessing the easy bit,' he said dismissively. 'I'm sure the Pulitzer is already on its way. Pity you won't be around to receive it.'

'And I know you are secretly selling the land.'

'Yes, but I bet you haven't connected the two things,' he said, and then laughed at her blank expression. 'Christ! You are going to die for your snooping yet you haven't even worked anything out! Well, let me put you out of your agony, as it's really quite simple. The planning permission for building a road has in theory been granted, pending agreement to sell a large parcel of these estate lands. Haydn Shady was never going to be allowed to buy those lands from the Baron, so I needed him to disappear. What you village idiots don't know is that as good old Pieter Bakkers, the saviour of the estate, I have been able to negotiate first refusal of the lands still owned by the Baron when he dies. Just by pretending to be nice for a while I've got that old fool to agree to sign it all over, easy as pie. This includes crucial parcels of land I need to sell to get the road built. It will make me twice what I paid for the whole estate. So, before the Baron gets wind of the planning consent and smells a very stinky rat, it would be convenient if he would just die. I therefore plan to, shall we say, *expedite* his death.'

'You mean you are going to murder him.'

'Almost immediately. You might consider a joint funeral?'

'What about the butterflies, the Site of Special Scientific Interest?'

'There is no S.S.S.I., you stupid bitch. I forged it all – the inspection, the certificate and documentation. When people are so trusting and so foolish, is it any wonder that I walk all over them?'

He spat on the ground in contempt for her apparent stupidity and turned to one of the mounted slaves.

'Take this whore over to the Priestess and have her use the pump,' he commanded.

The slave trotted forward and took Mimi by her hair so that she had to jog beside him over to the group of females. The bacchantes were all done out in their warpaint and were bristling with rage and lust. They still looked gorgeous, even though they were so deadly. The Priestess could barely bring herself to look at her, so there would be no clemency on her part. Mimi felt the anger swell. What right had this witch to expect anything from her? Who else would have given up everything, gone against all common sense, sworn herself into a life spent hidden from society, just on the vague promise that decadence and fucking with another woman was all your soul need ever crave? It was fanciful and utterly absurd, as was everything about Morgana.

'The Master wants you to use the pump on her,' the slave said, looking in the Priestess's direction.

'She won't be able to run,' Morgana replied, still not looking at Mimi.

The slave just shrugged and turned his horse away to return to his Master. The Priestess snorted and dismounted. She took Mimi by the shoulder and guided her back up to the treeline, where an open oak coffer was situated, displaying an array of dildos and other sexual apparatus. She took out the pump, a black rubber bulb connected by a tube to what looked like a clear plastic oxygen mask. Without speaking she knelt and pulled off Mimi's leggings to reveal her naked puss. Her face was level with it and oddly, for all Mimi's fear and anger and incredulity, still she wished the witch would lean forward and kiss her clitty as she had the day before.

'Those bitches are going to put their fists in you, you do know that, don't you?'

Morgana was speaking like an imploring mother, not like someone gloating at Mimi's misfortune. She had returned to the box for a plastic bottle that she squeezed to deposit a few spurts of clear oil onto Mimi's pussy mound. Lubrication was the key, to get a good seal. She smoothed the lubricant in with her fingertips and Mimi felt her knees weaken.

'They won't be anywhere near as gentle as I was,' the witch continued. 'They will go in two at a time. They will spank you and whip your arse with twigs. They will shove their fuck-sticks up you. Have you seen the nettles on the end of them? Have you any idea what it feels like to have nettle stings inside you? It's not as pleasant as you might think. They will tie you to trees and try to pull you apart while they ravish you.'

Mimi could have pissed on the witch right then, straight in her face, if only she had had the courage. The oiling had been done and now Morgana was busy pressing the face-mask part of the pump apparatus to Mimi's puss. The captive pulled at her restraints and tried to move away, but got a hard chiding slap to her bottom as a warning to stay still. Happy with the seal, the witch started to squeeze the bulb. Mimi could feel the gentle suction at her quim, a pleasant sensation amongst all the impending danger. Still she wasn't sure what was to be achieved with this pump, but she soon found out.

As the air was sucked from the mask encircling her quim, her flesh began to swell to fill the vacuum. As it was so tight around her cunt it was only the delicate flesh there that was affected. Her outer lips began to balloon, growing fat as if they had been injected with saline, like oral plastic surgery gone wrong. Mimi could see them expanding within the pump. The flesh grew taut, like two fat sausages of labia that were threatening to break their skin, with a grotesquely plump clit pushing out between them, the hood three or four times its normal size and the bud itself poking out, large as a thumb. It was horribly fascinating, a trick she could never have imagined possible.

The witch paused for a second, presumably to allow the flesh time to stretch without bursting. Apart from the fright it induced, there were no adverse effects, no pain – quite the opposite, in fact. Mimi could already feel the hugely heightened sensitivity there, especially now her flesh had swollen enough to meet the plastic casing. It was like a rawness, a tenderness so intense that even the slightest touch of a tongue or finger might have brought her to a quaking climax. The witch didn't stop but pumped the bulb again, drawing the flesh even further out, making the whole pussy ever more sensitive.

'Try not to let them sting you while it's still so swollen,' Morgana said. 'The orgasm might kill you. Why did you have to run from me? You are the only one who ever has. Together we might have been safe and I would have loved you like no other. You realise I would have taken you away from here if I could, away from him and all this? But I can't. I cannot leave this place and keep my power for long.'

Mimi didn't care about Morgana's power. She didn't realise that by 'power' the witch really meant 'life'. There were many intricacies that were beyond her, like the threat Morgana faced from the Master's promise to fuck her, or the threat of being forced from the cottage. She didn't know the Master was tired of being tormented by the witch and wanted an end to it, one way or another. She didn't know that Morgana was tied to the Master because without him her home would be lost. She didn't know that by spurning Morgana she had left her high and dry, reluctantly resigned to taking her chances on her own, hoping vainly to stave off the Master's advances. All Mimi thought was that this witch could save her if she chose to, but she wasn't going to. She was all empty words. She would enjoy Mimi's demise as much as the rest of them. She wasn't easy to love but she was certainly easy to hate and Mimi wanted to hurt her.

'He is going to sell the land whether you like it or not,' she said, with as much spite as she could muster. 'He already has. They are going to build a road right through it, so it looks like you can kiss goodbye to this place and your no-good powers!'

The witch eased the plastic cup away and Mimi gasped just from the breeze on her exposed swollen puss. It was true. Just gentle contact here might be enough to make her heart burst. Morgana was looking up at her, her eyes serious.

'How do you know this?' she asked.

'I know everything about him and Pieter Bakkers, and the clause to buy the rest of the land. He just admitted it to me! The sale has already been agreed!'

Mimi's surge of righteous glee died when she saw the

witch's face fall. She wanted to apologise for her smug-
ness but Morgana had stood again and turned and was
taking Mimi by the arm to drag her towards the girls.
All other thoughts were blown aside as Mimi was forced
to walk, the sensitivity in her quim making her wail as
her thighs brushed it. She was stood in front of the line
of girls, quaking from the electric tenderness between her
legs, close to collapse. As the witch removed the restraints
from her wrists and neck, Mimi saw that some of the
bacchantes were indeed naked below the waist, and a
couple of these were loosening their dildo harnesses and
fighting over the pump so that they could give their own
cunts the same nasty treatment. At least these would
struggle to chase her.

The Priestess was back on her horse, looking crestfallen
and even close to tears. Mimi couldn't fathom why her
words had caused such apparent distress. All she knew
was that this minor victory was likely to bring down
a storm of revenge once the witch caught up with her.
There would be no gentle fuckings this time. Why hadn't
she just given this woman her heart? How could a life
of unmatched pleasure not be preferable to all this? It
was all too late now. Cold rationality had defeated pure
emotion and left her with this senseless outcome. This was
the problem when you let your head do the thinking – it
silenced your heart. Never listen to logic. It will never
have anything over magic.

Morgana blinked back the tears and sniffed.

'You have as long as it takes that next girl to pump up her pussy to run,' she said. 'Then they are coming after you. Try to make it to the trees, that's the best I can tell you. I have little control of them once they are let loose so you will have to trust to luck. When they catch you, don't fight – it only makes it worse. You can try to defend yourself but that only makes them wilder and it wastes time. You have about ten minutes for them to do their worst before the men will come down. It will be a little easier from them but your end will be no less pleasant and if you succumb to the girls at least you won't have to drink so much filthy ball-juice. The men have all taken tonics so their spurts will be huge. When the time comes, if you can manage to picture me and say my name out loud, I promise it will give you an orgasm just as you pass away. That is the only comfort I have for you now. I am sorry it has come to this, but now, my lovely, you must run for your life.'

It seemed pointless to run but the survival instinct kicked in anyway and Mimi found herself taking off down the hill. The feeling between her legs was immediately too much, the over-sensitive nerves in her distended pussy set alight by her thighs moving back and forth. She yelled with each hopping, limping stride, but she was going steeply down now and her forward momentum kept her going despite the almost overwhelming sensations in her puss. She could hear the whoops and wails of derision from behind and knew the hunters would be following the target of her big white bottom all the way down, zoning in on it, ready to seek and destroy.

Her eyes were blurred with tears and the ground was uneven, nearly making her fall countless times. It was a miracle she had got down as far as she had. It helped that the extreme sensation in her groin had calmed slightly, making every step a little more bearable, a pleasure she could just about cope with. She was maybe fifty yards from the valley bottom when another whoop went up behind her, suggesting the girls were on their way. Her heart was racing but her initial panic had subsided almost completely. Even though they were coming for her she didn't feel the dread she should have. The reason was obvious and she knew it. She was mortified by it, but this didn't make her legs go any faster. As she came to the bushes and looked left and right for some cover she knew she was slowing on purpose. Her treacherous pussy was taking over. The need within it to be plundered was so great that it was outweighing all logic. Some greedy, licentious part of her wanted them to catch her. She was dying for those plastic cocks to drive into her and deliver her puss from its swollen torment.

She ran left, instinctively putting distance between her and where the Master had stationed himself. Was it possible to be fucked to death? The throbbing, yearning desperation of her cunt told her it just might be. She thought of the clash, the explosion upon and in her body, and couldn't feel any fear. She could sense them behind her now but it wasn't just on the wind like those other times. Now it was more palpable, as if the air itself was swelling and resonating with their arrival. Her bum would be their first target and it felt hot, damp and completely vulnerable. She realised that the witch had surreptitiously spread just enough oil into her crack to allow some ease of entry. She almost laughed aloud at the woman's subtle kindness.

Any moment now. She had a chance to break from the treeline and head up the slope at the other side but she declined, moving on aimlessly, barely covered by the undergrowth, barely jogging now. They were there and she could feel the pressure in her ears, fizzing in her blood, jolting in her quim. The touch, when it came, was only slight but down she went, bundled onto the grass so that she skidded along on her front. She could see the hide-covered backside of the first girl, who had overshot and was stumbling to her knees. Mimi's reaction was not to get up and run, but to roll onto her back and raise her knees up, to get her thighs wide enough apart so that when the first penetration came it would be deep and accurate, a plunging drive all the way up her begging snatch.

A second girl slammed onto her, knocking the wind

from her lungs, screaming into her face with her teeth showing white. Mimi thought for an instant that her throat would be torn out. The sharp nails were digging into her shoulders but despite the pain she was still able to realise that the savage smelt lovely and sweet. Then the dildo was rammed inside her and it was Mimi's turn to scream. The rapid slide almost made her pass out, the thrill of it like all her previous orgasms rolled into one. The thrust was so hard the dildo was driven all the way in, and Mimi was way too wet to stop it. The girl's crotch slapped against her swollen clit and sent the stars shooting behind her eyes. She felt a gush of wetness spraying her thighs and thought for a moment that her engorged lips must have burst, but a snatched glance showed that it was only the undammed juices of her desire.

The girl managed only three or four thrusts but each was dealt with a ferocity that suggested she wanted to split poor Mimi in two. Fortunately her quim was too wet and ready to allow this. Then the girl who had knocked her down was trying to get at her too. She was ripping at Mimi's top, trying to get to her breasts, pulling her hair and the hair of the other girl. She was screaming and spitting and trying to drag Mimi clear. The one on top of her responded by rolling, taking Mimi with her so that they were first on their sides facing each other, and then Mimi was on top. The dildo was still deep inside her and she was aware she had instinctively forced herself hard down upon it. She felt her arse cheeks being gripped and splayed. She knew what was coming and took a deep breath, trying to ready herself for it. The other girl was at her rear end, thrusting blindly, trying to gain access. For a moment Mimi thought her pussy would be stretched further by this new dildo but it pulled back and took new aim, and then her bottom was being spread open by the plastic head.

Mimi was barely conscious from the joy of her plumped-up quim, so this new penetration ripped the last ounce of strength from her. It was brutal and delicious, a merciless drive that took no heed of the tightened muscles in Mimi's back passage. It sent a sublime shudder through her, the searing shock mixed with total ecstasy. It was so beautiful that she kissed the savage still snarling beneath her and got her bottom lip bitten for her trouble, a sharp pain that only made her clit prickle even more. The girl behind humped her bottom, slapping against it and trying to drive in as deep as possible. She was yelling all the while, digging her nails into Mimi's back and shoulders, and eventually succeeding in ripping her tight cotton top apart. Mimi's bare skin was raked by both girls and her hair pulled by the one behind, but that only made her feel even more ecstatic.

All this happened in mere moments, an explosive attack that already had her on the brink of unconsciousness and possibly even oblivion. She knew the others had found her now and were massing. She could feel their slaps on her back and legs, the hands tearing away the scraps of her top so that her breasts could be got at. They were also pulling at the girl behind and eventually prised her free. The dildo was replaced almost immediately by another that opened her bum up just as it was closing tight, giving her another harsh penetration that sent jolting currents of sensation directly into her bursting sex. Her hands were grasped. The girls above and below were trying to hold onto their quarry but others had bound ropes around her wrists and were attempting to pull her free. She was going to be torn apart as they took her, as Morgana had predicted.

The one behind tried one deep plunge too many and fell out, no doubt aided by a pull at her hair from behind. Mimi felt herself being dragged forward. Although the girl below was grasping on for dear life, Mimi was hauled off, the dildo sliding out of her with a loud slurp. She was on her knees being propelled forward, smacks raining down on her bum. Someone was trying to fill her with her hand from behind but the forward motion was preventing it. She was heading towards a tree, two girls tugging on the ropes looped around her wrists. They got her to the trunk and were pulling her hair to make her rise off her knees, but her legs were buckling from the explosion of pain across her buttocks, caused, it seemed, by blows from thin cane-like branches or switches of thorn stems. Thank God her bum was fat enough to protect her bulging cunt from these cutting strikes.

Her arms were pulled around the trunk and secured so that she was hugging it, her tits squashed against the rough bark, the contact harsh on her erect nipples. Then her legs were pulled from under her too, so that she had to grip the trunk with her thighs. Ropes were fastened around her ankles, pulled tight and secured. She was now tied to the tree, completely off the ground. The switches on her bottom were being joined by lashes from nettles and her skin was fizzling from the rashes raising and spreading across it. That made her panic again, and this in turn exacerbated the sweep of fire over her skin. It was frightful and frightening, but at the same time almost unbearably scintillating.

Her grip on the trunk would never be strong enough and despite the ropes she felt herself slowly beginning to slide down, scratching her tortured nipples further. A body slammed into her back to hold her in place and began jabbing away before finding her open puss with the dildo and sinking it in. She was ravished thus, the dildo being slammed in and out. The false prick mostly slid in and out of her sex, but twice it found her arse instead and drove up it with no less gusto. Mimi had a distant, detached notion that those orgasms were the hardest and the best. Eventually gravity took over and she continued to slide down until her fucker could not bend her knees enough to keep up the penetration. Mimi got a few precious seconds of respite, sitting in a heap at the base of the trunk, but only while they untied her.

She felt the noose go round her neck and she had the notion that they were going to haul her off the ground and try to fuck her as she dangled, the rope cutting off her air supply. Even this did not alarm her. There was too much else going on and everything was surreal. How can you worry about being hanged when you had at least six fingers slapping in and out of your inflamed pussy, two thirds of a plastic cock in your arse and your nipples being stretched to three times their normal size? The noose idea didn't come to anything, because the girl up her bum won the day, pulling Mimi back so that they were both facing the sky, Mimi on top. The girl reached down, grasped Mimi's thighs and pulled and pinched at the skin until she had drawn Mimi's knees up and could take a grip behind them.

Mimi thought she might have had a smile on her face, even though tears were streaming from her eyes. Her endorphin rush had long since kicked in, so now everything was plain glorious, just layer upon layer of pleasure that had her delirious. She felt suddenly clear-minded and detached from her fate, able to calmly consider each element of this terrible, wonderful fuck-explosion that would eventually end her. She was able to analyse each sensation in isolation. She decided she rather liked having her cunt spanked, and the feeling of nettles being dragged over her sensitive lips. She loved the rudeness of fingers that had been in her bum and the hunters' bums being wiped on her face and pushed into her mouth. She liked having her belly fat bitten, her nipples forced by scraping fingernails up into a tight bottom.

With her knees up and apart she was ripe for the taking and the invitation was not refused. A fat dildo sank into her open sex. She might have screamed. She had no idea if she was even awake any more. She seemed to be watching it all from above, able to see the beauty of their perfect white bodies and pretty, makeup-strewn faces. They looked wild and rabid but totally alluring. She wanted them all over her, all at once. How would a single penetration ever be enough for her again? It was perhaps just as well she would never have to worry about such things.

With her bum full and her quim being rammed in and out, there was still more to come.

If she thought about Morgana and called her name she would climax, that's what the witch had said. She couldn't call out. Her brain was shutting down and her mouth was full. In her head the witch was coming to her, floating beside her somewhere in the treetops so that they could look down upon the sight together. Mimi said Morgana's name. She said that she did love her after all, and the two of them kissed. Mimi's pussy felt fabulous, slick and full and ultra-sensitive. This had to be what heaven was like. As they kissed, the sun came out from behind a cloud and shone bright upon her face. Then she was gasping for oxygen. Morgana still had her by the hair, reaching down from her horse to clasp it.

'Get her up here so I can whip her!' she cried.

Mimi was shattered to have been saved from such a comforting, blissful demise, only to have further torture visited upon her. Any more was almost pointless. She could barely feel it. She was dragged up by the ropes at her wrists. She was forced into the flank of the witch's mount and the ropes taken over its back. Then she was hauled up by four of the girls, her feet lifting clear of the ground. The witch had her by the hair and was pulling too and Mimi found herself bundled over Morgana's knees, one hip jammed hard against the front of the saddle.

The whip came down hard across her prone behind, the force jamming her poor puss into the witch's knee. The girls gave out more banshee screams and danced around with the joy of seeing their Priestess in action. Mimi felt the strokes land, her bum still not so abused that it couldn't feel more pain and send the shock straight to her clit. It was too much though. She could take no more and come no more. It was an immeasurable cruelty of the witch to drag her from her calm passing and inflict more torture. She wouldn't get the chance to slip away so contentedly again. The endorphins would wear off and the men would come to ravage her. She didn't know how many of their cocks she could take. Nasty, sadistic Morgana – why did the witch hate her so?

Then the Priestess yelled and the horse jerked beneath them, scattering the gathered girls. Mimi felt the hand press hard upon her back and the slapping, hurtful impact of her face against the horse's side. Then she realised – they were moving, fast. The horse was galloping and Morgana was urging it on. The wails of the girls behind were turning to screams of rage. A *thyrsus* went gliding past, a foot in front of her face, thrown in anger. They were out of the trees and going up the hill towards the safety of the wood. Although she thought she might bounce off at any moment, Mimi managed to look back and watch the savages rush out of the wood, screeching and jumping and stamping their feet, gnashing their teeth because their quarry had been taken from them.

She watched them as the horse galloped her away. The girls did not follow. They just stood pulling each other's hair and trying to gang-fuck the ones already bare down below. Just as the fleeing pair reached the summit and the cover of the trees, the Master emerged from the wood on horseback, flanked by his escort. He looked like he might spur on his mount and give chase, but in the end he stayed put. It was impossible at that distance, but Mimi was convinced she could make out his piercing eyes glaring at her. Then they were in the wood and the witch was steering them swiftly between grey trunks, never letting up. It still took a little while for it to dawn upon Mimi that she was being rescued.

Some time later Mimi was aware that they had stopped somewhere amongst the trees. The witch had spread her foxskin cloak on the ground and laid Mimi upon it. She was giving her comfort and telling her to wait, but Mimi wasn't going anywhere, because all she wanted to do was sleep. Then she had her head raised and was told to sip the tonic from the metal beaker. She was dimly aware that she was now dressed, in the combination of tracksuit bottoms and T-shirt worn by the trainee bacchantes at their class. Her body ached, but her quim still felt hot with pleasure. It seemed she was never going to escape that feeling when close to the witch.

'I'm sorry I had to whip you,' Morgana was saying, 'but I had to get you on the horse without making the girls suspicious. They wouldn't have let me take you from them without a fight. I've soothed your body with my juniper lotion so it should heal quicker. Does your bottom hurt much? I have a spell that can take the bruising away inside but it means taking a live adder up into it and I'm fresh out of them at the moment.'

It was still all too surreal but the tonic was having a calming effect. The bitterness had left Morgana's eyes, so she just looked young and beautiful again, even a little lost. Mimi dropped off and slept fitfully while the witch tended to her as best she could. Sirens woke her, and the sound of overworked car engines. She could see flashes of blue in her periphery.

'Are they coming for you?' she asked.

'Yes,' Morgana replied. 'For all of us. I think that shit of a slave must have brought them here. I did recite a little incantation to make his ropes undo, but I wasn't sure if it would work.'

'If they catch you, will you go to jail? Have you done much wrong?'

'I have been alive for over two thousand years. I have a different idea of morality from you. I've done a good many things that society says are wrong, some of which that slave knows about and will have told the police. And no, I cannot go to jail. I will die there within weeks. I have been condemned many times over the years, always by men. They hate that I might have some power over them, some control. Even if I promise to give them everything, they still cannot bear to defer to me, even in this day and age. They will always want to defeat me. Don't worry, though. My soul knows how to survive them, even if this body cannot.'

'I won't tell the police about you. If they ask I will say you only ever treated me with kindness, that you saved my life. I'm sorry I couldn't be your lover. The idea was all a bit … bizarre.'

'I know, sweetie,' the witch said with a smile. 'A hundred years ago you wouldn't have thought twice about it. You would never have had the slightest doubt that I am who I am. But not these days. These days the magic has all gone. And now you must go too, while it is safe to do so. If he has run, he will surely find you, and I can't protect you any more.'

'Why did you help me? If you had let them take me then no one would have ever found out. The police wouldn't be here now.'

'Because it was over for me one way or another. I might be able to crawl away and live for a year or more but I wouldn't know happiness and my spirit would be crushed. That is no way to exist. And because I love you. I know you don't believe it but I do. I can't help it, it just is. There is no spell I know that can take it away. Sometimes the life of someone you love is more important than your own.'

'I hope I see you again,' said Mimi.

The witch smiled. The poor girl still didn't understand. She had bumbled into the world of the coven without ever grasping its reality. It was amazing how few people these days were prepared to think and consider and believe. Everything was so superficial, yet offer them pure pleasure and guiltless sex and all they wanted was to raise moral objections to it.

'Maybe,' Morgana said.

Then Mimi was up and stumbling on shaky legs out of the trees and into the road, where she managed a few more paces before sinking to her knees, and a policeman was shouting and pointing at her and running to her aid.

Epilogue

It was actually Dominic who had freed Gavin, not the witch's magic. As soon as the Master had gone after the hunter girls, he had released his fellow slave and together they had run to the police. Gavin knew an awful lot about his Master's wrongdoings. He knew where the drugs were hidden, where the damning documentation and ledgers had been secreted, even where a body had been buried. Gavin was now in a witness protection programme. Shady was in jail pending trial, with no chance of bail. The bacchante girls had to be released, since there was nothing obvious to charge them with. They slipped back into society, to continue their wanton lifestyles in other ways. The slaves were sheepishly reunited with their families and given counselling. They were considered victims of a cult.

Dominic had his place at university reinstated, albeit a year late. His evidence was logged but he wouldn't be needed at the trial, not with Gavin as a star witness and the villain caught with over a million pounds' worth of cocaine in his possession. Shady had all his assets seized by the Crown, including the estate lands, which were deemed forfeit and put in trust. They were now overseen by a committee including the aged Baron and his heirs. The plans for the road seemed to have been scuppered, although while unscrupulous minds were at large there was always a chance that the scheme would come back to haunt the village.

The villain's accomplice, Miss Morgana Innamorato, remained at large, there having been no sign of her in the nine months since the police first swooped. The hunt for her was still officially on, since only a couple of people realised that, once driven from her home, she would be unable to survive for long. Few missed her, but Mimi was among them. The young journalist had seen her exclusives grace the front page for a week immediately after the event, and there were related articles at regular intervals during the following months. Her standing at the paper improved immeasurably. She was often given the prime jobs, such as the one she was on her way to at the moment, a meeting with a certain Dr Paulina Calan of the British Lepidoptera Society. It seemed the notion of rare butterflies on the estate lands was not so far-fetched after all. If their existence could be proved, perhaps protection could be granted to keep the land safe at last.

Mimi was very much looking forward to the meeting. She had been studying a picture of the scientist earlier that day, and felt an all too familiar twinge between her legs. The photo had showed a very attractive blonde, with a wide forehead and high Slavic cheekbones, beautiful cobalt-blue eyes and a sexy dimple in her chin. Who would have thought that Mimi could have been turned on to women so easily? It now seemed the most natural thing in the world for her to admire them, lust after them and fantasise over them as much as she would a man, if not more. She seemed to have taken no adverse effects whatsoever from the dramatic events that had so recently threatened her life. She could view it as some kind of frivolous sexual adventure, almost as if it were all an intricate, tantalising fantasy rather than a dangerous reality. The witch's spells had at least protected her from the mental torments of her ordeal.

She closed her front door and set off, since she could walk very easily to her meeting. She could even wear the high heels and fishnet stockings she thought might look most alluring on her, without worrying about her feet hurting. She was considered something of a heroine in the village now, having brought to light the underhand dealings of the road developers. Many thought it a fitting reward when the Estate Trustees offered her possession of the empty cottage once leased by the fugitive witch – at a reduced rent, of course. So her job was going from strength to strength and she now had a coveted place of her own in the village. It didn't even feel strange living in Morgana's old house. She felt it was meant to be. Also, whenever she was there, she only needed to shut her eyes to remember with absolute clarity her first time within those walls, the time the witch first seduced her. It still made her come without fail. Memories of Morgana were to be cherished, whatever society thought of the woman.

Over on another part of the estate, in a glade within a small wood, Dr Paulina Calan stooped to view the chrysalis more closely. She closed her hand around it and eased it from the twig where it was hanging. The warmth of her hand soon brought movement. She could feel the gentle scratch of the shell as it started to break open. Only when she felt the light brush of wings on her palm did she open her fingers to view her creation.

It was a white butterfly, technically from the genus *Pieris*, but unlike any other found on these isles, since its wings were pure white, with no marks or coloration. It was as white as the skin of the girls who used to hunt in these woods, indeed as white and perfect as her own. She would christen this new species the *Priestess* butterfly, in memory of the reputed witch who once lived close by. This discovery would ensure the land could never be sold for development.

It was very early in the year for butterflies but not

impossibly so. Anyway, people would accept it because they accepted anything if they thought science was behind it. It was when magic was mentioned that the scepticism started. She had been living among these trees for nine months now, using that magic, along with nature and her wits, to get her through. If Shady could do it then so could she. She had bided her time and waited for things to settle. She had thought long and hard about her new appearance but this time she thought she had it right, a look that Mimi would not be able to resist. Her chosen name wasn't great – a quickly devised anagram of *Paculla Annia* – but it would do. It would be enough to fool Mimi; she was never one to look too deeply into things.

The bogus scientist heard the call and turned to see the smiling girl approach. Her heart leaped. This time she would make sure the girl knew her true feelings. She wouldn't blind her with magic or confuse her with things mystical. She would try to act like a normal human being until Mimi was ready to know the whole truth. The plan was very simple: seduce the girl, become her lover, move in with her. Once back within the seat of her power her magic would blossom again. She would be supreme once more and this time she would have a lover by her side to safeguard her power. The witching could begin all over again. My, what she wouldn't give right now for a dirty, drunken all-girl orgy!

'You had better ring the guys at Natural England,' she said with a big smile to the approaching Mimi. 'I think we might have made a rather important discovery!'

Mimi loved her afternoon with the woman. She was so clever and disarmingly gorgeous, so flawless and elegant. She had the slightest hint of a foreign accent that made her seem even more exotic. She made Mimi laugh. She also made Mimi wet down below. She tried to keep things serious but she couldn't stop her eyes wandering to that sumptuous bust with its peek-a-boo cleavage, and to the impossibly round rump stuck out at her a few times as the woman bent to inspect the undergrowth. She was the most attractive female Mimi had ever set eyes on, and she had a body to match that of a certain somebody she still very much missed. It would be way too much to hope that the feelings of attraction were mutual, especially as the woman was attentively going about her business. But then, just when they were about to part and the opportunity would be lost, the woman stepped forward and gave Mimi a very light peck on the cheek to bid her goodbye. Then she hesitated, her breath warm and sweet in Mimi's ear, and she whispered, 'I really want to spank your delicious fat arse.'

Mimi's heart nearly leaped from her chest. Her legs turned to jelly. Her breath wouldn't come and she thought she might be rendered mute and miss her golden chance. With the moment threatening to pass by, she managed to drag up the last vestiges of her composure and, her cheeks burning, her words barely audible as they came out, she said, 'Please spank me and then fuck me. Please do it right now.'

And so, as easy as that, it all began again.